Jeanne

"Are you plann water?" Con

She smiled and shook he room for me, and well you know it."

"You could sit upon my lap." Though he meant the words as nothing but flirtation, his imagination conjured up a sensual vision of Aileen...

She came closer and began unlacing his tunic.

The soft touch of her hands moving across his chest inflamed his lust. The knowledge that he could not touch her with his injured hands made it worse. It was torment, having a woman's hands upon him and not being able to act upon his own desires. He suppressed a groan, stopping her from lowering his trews. "If you wish, I can—"

"You can remove your own trews?" she asked mildly.

Though her words were not a taunt, it reminded him of his unwanted weakness.

"I want to kiss you," he said huskily. Her lips opened in a startled reaction. The invitation hung between them, but she did not move away....

* * *

The Warrior's Touch
Harlequin® Historical #866—September 2007

Author Note

Irish legends and Celtic mysticism inspired the story of Connor MacEgan and Aileen Ó Duinne. Upon reading about the ancient Bealtaine ritual, more commonly known as Beltane, I was fascinated by the idea of two strangers becoming intimate on a night filled with magic. I wanted to write a story about a woman in love with a man she couldn't have, and the stolen night between them. It's a story of healing, both physical and emotional, and I hope you enjoy it as much as I loved writing it.

Please feel free to visit my Web site at www.michellewillingham.com to read excerpts from other books in THE MacEGAN BROTHERS series, subscribe to my newsletter, and view behind-the-scenes photographs from the books. I love to hear from readers, and you may contact me at michelle@michellewillingham.com.

Available from Harlequin® Historical and
MICHELLE WILLINGHAM

Her Irish Warrior #850
The Warrior's Touch #866

THE
WARRIOR'S TOUCH

MICHELLE WILLINGHAM

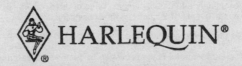

HARLEQUIN®

TORONTO • NEW YORK • LONDON
AMSTERDAM • PARIS • SYDNEY • HAMBURG
STOCKHOLM • ATHENS • TOKYO • MILAN • MADRID
PRAGUE • WARSAW • BUDAPEST • AUCKLAND

ISBN-13: 978-0-373-29466-4
ISBN-10:   0-373-29466-2

THE WARRIOR'S TOUCH

Glossary of Irish Terms

a chroí—my heart

a dalta—an affectionate term toward a foster-son, literally *my student*

a ghrá—my love

a iníon—my daughter

a stór—my treasure, my darling

aenach—local fair

aite—foster father

bean-sidhe—(banshee), a female of the fairies

brat—a woolen shawl worn around the shoulders by both men and women

brehons—judges who listened to court cases

cailín—girl

corp-dire—body price, usually a fine paid for bodily injuries

craibechan—a savory dish made of chopped meat and vegetables

dia dhúit—Hello, literally *God be with you*

ech—war horse

eraic—compensation fine, literally *blood money*

flaiths—noblemen

léine—a long gown worn by women or a long shirt worn by men

méirge—a colorful banner

níl—no

rath—fortress

sibh—fairies

sibh dubh—dark spirits

tú—yes

tuatha—town or village belonging to a clan, literally *the people*

Thank you so much to Dr. Emily Doherty and to Elise Lestz for their invaluable advice regarding broken-bone injuries and physical therapy. To my husband, thanks for allowing the house cleaning to wait another day and for always supporting me in this dream. And to my children, who bring me the greatest joy a mother could have.

Chapter 1

Ireland, 1175

'Aileen! There's a dead man in the fields!' Lorcan dashed inside the stone hut, shifting his weight from one foot to the other with excitement.

A dead man? Aileen Ó Duinne dropped the garlic bulbs she had picked that morning and stood. 'Are you sure he is dead?' Anticipation rippled through her with the faint hope that the man was still alive.

Lorcan shrugged. 'He wasn't moving. And there's blood everywhere.'

Likely the boy was correct. Aileen tried not to get her hopes up. But if he wasn't dead, she might be able to save him.

'Where did you find him?'

'I'll show you.' Lorcan thought for a moment, his brown eyes growing worried. 'Will I get into trouble for telling you? He's already dead.'

Aileen shook her head. 'Do not worry. You did right to come to me.'

It is forbidden, her mind warned her. If her chieftain Seamus Ó Duinne found out, he would punish her. She was not allowed to heal any of the tribe members.

But there was no time to worry about that now. *Belisama, please let him be alive.*

Lorcan followed her inside the hut while she piled her basket with fresh linen bandages, comfrey and yarrow. Turning, she regarded Lorcan. 'Take me to him.'

The boy scampered off in the direction of the north pasture. Aileen ran behind him, past several of the neighbouring stone huts. One of the men stopped his work in the fields, staring at her with distaste. Aileen tore her gaze away from him.

Don't worry about what he thinks, she told herself. *You did nothing wrong.* Even still, her cheeks burned with humiliation. The villagers hadn't forgotten the bad luck that followed her.

The morning dew dampened the hem of her gown as she followed Lorcan. The boy raced on ahead, pointing toward the lee side of the hill.

Ragged summer grasses swayed in the wind. A small patch lay crumpled by the man's body lying face down. The awkward position of his limbs suggested a fall from a horse. His blood stained the grass, and Aileen's hands shook as she reached out to touch him.

A low moan escaped the body. Sweet saints. He was alive.

Thank the gods. They had granted her a second chance to prove herself, and she intended to make the most of it.

'Go and fetch Riordan,' Aileen ordered Lorcan. 'I'll need help moving the man. Tell him to bring one of his horses.'

She would not let this man die. No matter what anyone else thought of her skills, she *would* heal him.

After Lorcan had gone, she turned the man over. His swollen face stopped her heart. Despite his injuries, she would recognise him anywhere. Connor MacEgan. She had never thought to see him again.

Fear and reckless longing pulled at her, shredding her composure. Of all the men for Fate to leave in her hands, why did it have to be him?

His face, the face of one of God's angels, had haunted her dreams ever since she was a young girl. With firm lips, a straight nose and a strong jaw, the traces of Viking ancestry on his grandfather's side were evident. Blood matted his dark golden hair and seeped from a gash at his temple.

She had loved him once. Pain arced through her at the memory, but she forced it away. Her hands trembled as she unlaced his tunic. With her dagger, she sliced the dun-coloured wool to reveal a warrior's hardened chest. He had been stabbed several times, but the cuts were shallow. Almost like torture…

She shook the terrible thought away. How long had he been here? From his grey pallor, she wondered how much blood he had lost. It might be too late to heal him.

Do not think of it. She swabbed his chest, and then turned her attention to his head. She held pressure upon his temple to stanch the bleeding. It was then that she noticed the dark swelling upon his hands and wrists. The broken bones would need to be splinted.

He must not die. She needed to bring him back to the sick

hut to treat his hands and to stitch the deeper wounds, but she couldn't do it without help. Where was Riordan?

The horizon stretched into emptiness with not a sign of either of them. She couldn't rely on anyone else to come to her aid. Most of the villagers believed she was cursed.

She withdrew several garlic cloves from her basket, pressing them gently against Connor's chest. She bound the wound tightly and prayed that the garlic would ward off the demons of fever.

At last, she heard the sound of a horse approaching. It made her breathe a little easier. She waved to Riordan and he dismounted. A sturdy man, accustomed to working in the fields, Riordan stood a head taller than most men. His cheeks were ruddy, and he was easily recognisable with his bright red hair.

From the obvious look of pleasure upon his face, he was glad she'd summoned him. He found excuses to be near her, now that she was widowed. And he was the one man whom she could trust to help her.

'Is the man alive?' he called.

'Barely. I'll need your help bringing him back to the sick hut.' She supported Connor's body, raising him into a seated position. Throughout the awkward motions he did not stir.

When Riordan saw Connor's face, his sympathy transformed into anger and jealousy. 'Connor MacEgan.' Bitterness lined his tone. 'You should leave him where he lies, the bastard.'

'I am a healer,' Aileen argued. 'If the Devil himself needed my care, I would give it.'

Connor might as well be the Devil, she thought. With him, she could not detach herself into the calm world where nothing else existed, save her healing. His very presence unnerved her.

Riordan grumbled, but helped her lift Connor on to the horse. His body hung motionless against the horse's mane. As they guided the horse back towards her land, she found herself wanting to move faster.

'What has brought him back here?' Riordan asked. 'I thought he'd returned to his kinsmen.'

'If he lives, you may ask him that yourself.'

A dark look eclipsed his face. 'I am helping him only for you, Aileen. I've no wish to speak to him at all.'

She hid her exasperation even as she urged the horse onward. 'We must make haste. He has to live.'

'Why? Because you've feelings for him?'

'Because if he dies, it only proves that I am cursed. I cannot lose another person. If he lives, Seamus might let me heal again.'

'No one knows you found him,' Riordan pointed out.

'Lorcan found him first. Everyone will know of it by nightfall.' She had no doubt of that. 'Did you send him home again?'

'I did, yes.'

'Good.' Fear sank deep within, freezing her with worry that Connor would not wake. He had not moved once during the journey back to her land.

'I still do not like it. We should bring him to Seamus instead.'

Aileen was not about to surrender this chance, not from one man's jealousy. She laid her hand upon his shoulder. 'Let your mind be at peace, Riordan. After he heals, he'll be gone.' Her touch sparked a flash of interest in his eyes, and she suddenly wished she had not made the impulsive gesture.

He gave her hand a squeeze, and yearning spread across his face once more. Aileen reminded herself that a steady, good husband such as Riordan was a sensible choice. She had long ago abandoned dreams of handsome warriors. Men like Connor MacEgan simply didn't notice her.

Within moments, they reached the small plot of land she called her own. As she passed the rows of plantings, Aileen considered iris root or marigold flowers, should Connor's wounds worsen. Silently, she said a prayer to both the Christian God and the gods of her ancestors for healing.

'Bring him inside the sick hut,' she ordered. The stone dwelling, erected a few paces from her own hut, was designed for treating the wounded and ill members of their tribe.

In the past two moons, not a single person had trusted her enough to make use of it. She had kept it meticulously clean, hoping that one day the villagers might call upon her. Inwardly she feared her chieftain would force her to go elsewhere when another healer took her place. Seamus had not forgiven her.

Bitterness welled up inside of her. Men had died because they were too proud, too superstitious to seek her help.

She opened the hide door and ducked beneath the bundle of dyed wool hanging to ward off evil spirits. Inside, the temperature was cool and it smelled of damp earth. Riordan set Connor's limp body upon one of the pallets filled with soft straw. Though his unresponsive state suggested worse injuries, she held fast to her hopes.

'Do you need a fire?' Riordan offered.

Aileen hesitated. Though she knew he wanted to help, she preferred to work alone. 'I will build one.'

'It is no trouble.'

He started to gather peat to bring inside the hut, but

Aileen blocked his path. She didn't want the cloying scent of smoke to interfere with her healing. 'Thank you, Riordan. I will be all right on my own now.'

'I don't want you alone with him. He is not to be trusted.'

She repressed a sigh. 'He is unconscious, Riordan. I doubt the man could lift his head if he wanted to.'

Her logic seemed to reassure him, and he lowered the stack of peat. 'Shall I come back this eve?' Hope lit up his expression.

'Another time, perhaps.'

His shoulders lowered. 'We should send a messenger to MacEgan's family. I would be glad to do so.'

She eyed him suspiciously. 'So eager to help him, are you?'

With a look toward the sick hut, Riordan crossed his arms. 'Anything that will send him far from here would give me pleasure.'

'You've nothing to fear from him.'

'I will come on the morrow, should you need my help again.'

She managed a smile. 'I will be fine, thank you.'

When he had gone, she breathed easier. Though he only wanted to offer his assistance, Riordan's presence interfered with her concentration.

She worked rapidly, dropping the stack of peat into the outdoor hearth. Within moments, she kindled a fire and moved heavy river stones into the flames to heat. She set a pot of water to boil over the fire.

Then she entered the sick hut and sat beside Connor. For a brief second, his eyes fluttered open. She froze, not knowing what he would think of his whereabouts, but, in the dim light, he showed no sign of recognition. It was as if he didn't see her at all.

Aileen tamped down the feeling of disappointment when his eyes closed once more. She adjusted his position to make him more comfortable. His hands had swollen up to nearly double their size, the skin tightening with blood. If it were winter time, she could bring the swelling down with snow. Instead, she poured cold water into wooden bowls and laid his hands inside to soak.

Darting outside, she returned to her own hut for splints. She gathered fresh linen and wood, but in her hurry she dropped the bundle. It was then that she noticed her shaking fingers. She needed to calm her racing heart and concentrate upon the medicines.

Stop behaving like a foolish maiden, her heart warned. *He probably won't remember you.*

She filled a fold of her woolen *brat* with the linen and splints, using the shawl to carry them.

Stopping by the fire, she filled a bowl with heated water from the pot. *The river stones.* She'd almost forgotten. She dropped the splints and bandages inside the threshold, then set the bowl of hot water near her herbs. Last, she returned to the fire and used an iron rod to roll the heated granite stones to warm the interior of the sick hut.

Connor had not regained consciousness. Aileen took a deep breath and gathered her composure. She knelt beside him and cut off the rest of the blood-soaked tunic with her knife. He hadn't moved even once. Voices of doubt began to undermine her confidence. What if he had slipped too far past the barrier between life and death?

Stop worrying about what you cannot do, and concentrate on what you can. She searched her memories for advice the elderly healer Kyna had given her. Lily roots or mallow leaves, should the swelling worsen. Would it be enough? Connor was the chieftain's foster son, well loved by the family. If she saved him, it might help mend the animosity.

Aileen removed the linen bandage and garlic bulbs. Then she cleansed the blood from his face, dipping the cloth into cool water. She voiced a quiet healing chant to keep her roiling emotions calm.

She washed his chest wounds again, noting which cuts would need to be sewn closed. As her fingers moved across his torso, unwanted memories sprang forth.

The forbidden taste of his kiss had once filled her dreams. Connor's powerful body had embraced her on a moonlit night, strong muscles pressing against her willing flesh. A shiver raced through her, and Aileen quelled the forgotten sensation of desire. She stood, wrenching her concentration back to his wounds.

As she moved away from Connor, she walked past bunches of drying herbs hanging from the ceiling. The spicy fragrance helped clear her thoughts. She stopped before a small table where she kept her medicines, selecting comfrey for his wounds. Using a mortar and pestle, she mashed the root until it became a moist pulp. Then she poured hot water over the root.

She sat beside Connor, placing the mortar within reach. Threading a bone needle, she began to stitch the deep gash upon his temple. From his waxen skin and the way he did not react to the piercing, she wondered if he might die after all.

A tendril of regret unfolded in the recesses of her heart. She had tried to hate him, tried to purge the feelings she'd once had. But a part of him would always remain, though she might wish to forget the past.

Aileen held the torn flesh of his chest together while stitching the wounds closed. Though she had sewn countless wounds, healing even the worst sorts of gashes, it was as if the needle pierced her own flesh.

Why couldn't she separate herself from this task? Why did it frighten her to see him struggle to live? She had thought those feelings were long gone.

She poured the warmed comfrey root upon his chest and bound it once more. Now it was time to turn her attention elsewhere—to the broken bones. The awkward angle of the bone and dark purple bruises upon his right hand revealed a broken wrist. His left hand had swollen fingers, the knuckles raw.

Strange. These wounds were not from battle. Someone had deliberately tried to crush the bones. The thought of torture rose up again. Her stomach twisted, and doubts invaded her mind.

Did she have the skill to heal such intricate wounds? Or worse, did she possess the courage to remove his hands, if it was needed to save his life? Should the skin turn green or blacken, she'd have no choice. Her heart faltered, nausea rising at the thought of causing such pain. She sent up another prayer against the demons of sickness.

'Mother, is everything all right?' Her daughter Rhiannon entered, and Aileen halted at the sight of her. With all that had happened, she hadn't thought of it. Her daughter, though fostered elsewhere, visited often to learn the trade of healing.

Aileen glanced toward Connor and saw that he had not regained consciousness. Putting an arm around Rhiannon, she led her daughter from the hut. 'Everything is fine.'

Rhiannon's face dimmed with confusion. 'Would you like my help? The man back there—'

'Not today.' Aileen struggled to keep her voice calm. 'But you may offer prayers for him.'

Rhiannon's expression turned critical. 'Will the prayers heal him?' She twisted her dark brown braid, a worried expression puckering her face.

'It can do no harm.'

'Let me help you,' her daughter begged.

'No.' The word came out sharper than she'd intended. Aileen forced herself to smile. 'He will be well soon enough. It is not as bad as it seems.' The lie added to her burden of guilt.

'You are a good healer, Mother. No matter what they say,' Rhiannon said. With shining eyes, she added, 'I want to be like you.'

Aileen's skin warmed with embarrassment. 'I hope that you become a better healer than I.' She was grateful she was to have such a bond with her daughter. Most children grew closer to their foster parents than to their own flesh and blood. Rhiannon's frequent visits meant that and with each passing year Aileen loved her daughter more.

'They are bringing a new healer,' Rhiannon admitted, a frown shadowing her face. 'I heard Tómas speak of it.'

'When?'

'Within a sennight.' Rhiannon took her mother's hand. 'But she can't be as good as you. What happened wasn't your fault. They—'

'It does not matter,' Aileen interrupted. 'Your foster parents will be waiting for you. You must go now.'

'Shall I see you on the morrow?'

'Not until this man is gone.'

'But why? I have helped with battle wounds before.'

'Do not argue with me. When he has returned to his people, then you may return.' Aileen drew her daughter into an embrace. She stroked Rhiannon's deep brown hair, murmuring, 'I shall see you after that.'

Rhiannon held her tightly. 'I'll come back to see you soon, Mother.'

'I love you, *a iníon*. Be good.' She touched her nose to Rhiannon's.

'I will.'

Aileen waited until her daughter reached the top of the hillside before she returned to Connor. Thank the gods Rhiannon had not questioned her further.

Inside the hut, Connor lay still. She picked up his right hand, and he flinched. It was the first physical reaction she'd seen from him. Good. He might live after all. It looked as though someone had smashed a mallet against the fingers. The same treatment had been applied to his right wrist.

Such unusual wounds. If his enemy had wanted him dead, a simple arrow or dagger through the heart would suffice. This was a punishment, it seemed. Connor had no weapons, which suggested he had been a prisoner. They had discarded him in the midst of a field, and, were it not for Lorcan's interference, Connor might be there still.

She needed to set the bones properly. As she looked through her supply of wooden splints for the right shape and size, her thoughts returned to Rhiannon. Love filled her at the thought of her sweet-faced girl. She could not imagine life without her.

No one would take Rhiannon from her. Especially not Connor MacEgan, the man who had fathered her.

* * *

His hands were on fire. Pain such as he'd never known coursed through him. Connor jerked, his muscles seizing at the vicious agony.

'Lie still. I have to set the bones.'

Connor could no more cease his movements than he could prevent the roar that escaped him. The woman moved another of his bones, and he prayed for the blessed darkness to consume him once more.

Her ministrations made that impossible. Instead, he focused his mind on what had happened, with fleeting images of Flynn Ó Banníon's men holding him down. He'd fought against them as knives sliced into his flesh. The pain was nothing compared to what came next. His former friends had held him down while the chieftain raised a stone mallet.

Blinding pain coursed through his hand and wrist from the crushing impact. A cry tore from his throat when they struck his other hand. Thanks be, he'd lost consciousness after that.

But the healer's torment far outweighed that of his enemy's. He didn't remember how he had escaped, but Ó Banníon's parting words burned in his mind. 'Now you'll never touch another woman again.'

The healer set another bone, and he gasped with pain. 'Have a care.'

'I am nearly finished.'

'Thank God.'

'Then I'll start on your other hand.'

The other hand? Sweet Jesu, the woman had been sent by the *sibh dubh* to plague him. Dark spirits held more mercy than her. Never had he known such torture, the excruciating anguish in his hands. He kept his eyes closed, trying to block out the pain.

'Where am I?' he asked, breathing slowly to avoid the searing ache in his ribs.

'Don't you remember? You were fostered here at Banslieve. With the Ó Duinne tribe.'

He had not visited the lands of his foster family since he was a lad of seventeen. He had fond memories of Banslieve.

Connor studied the woman who had tended his wounds. Her braided hair resembled the deep brown of a polished wood, her eyes a soft grey-green.

'Your name is Aileen?' he asked.

At her assent, he wondered if she was the same young girl who rarely spoke and hid in the shadows. 'I remember you.'

She stared at him, and for a moment he thought he saw accusation in her eyes. The flash of anger disappeared and grew calm. 'It was a very long time ago.'

'Where is Kyna?' At his mention of the ancient healer, he caught a look of sadness in Aileen's eyes.

'She died last winter. I am the healer now.'

'Is there another healer in the village?' He didn't trust Aileen; she was far too young to know Kyna's healing methods.

'No.' Her lips pursed with angry pride. 'I am the only one.'

He cared not if he offended her. If his bones were not set properly, he could lose the use of his hands. Being a warrior was his life. He closed his eyes as searing pain throbbed in his hands.

Flynn Ó Banníon had chosen Connor's punishment, believing false witnesses. And all for a crime he hadn't committed. Fury burned within him, along with the pain of betrayal. Flynn had once been a friend to him, as well as a sword master.

'How bad is it?' he asked.

'How bad is what?'

'My hands. Will I regain the use of them?' He needed to know whether he would lose his hands. His skin prickled, suddenly cold with fear.

'I do not know.'

He stilled. All his life, he'd been a warrior. He'd fought in battles against the Normans, against enemy tribes, until his sword was a natural extension of himself.

'What of my sword? Will I be able to fight again?'

He tried to sit up, but a gentle hand pushed him back. 'Again, I do not know. But you have your life, and for that you should be thankful.'

Even as she answered, the icy hand of Fate taunted him. There was no life he could imagine, save that of being a soldier.

'Sleep now,' Aileen whispered, lifting a potion to his lips. He drank the bitter liquid, feeling as though he were made of stone. For if he could not wield a sword again, he was as good as dead.

Chapter 2

The feast of Bealtaine
Seven years earlier, 1168

Aileen Ó Duinne brushed her long brown hair, plaiting it with the blue ribbons her da had given her. She wore her best overdress, a cheerful matching gown the colour of the sky with a cream-coloured *léine* beneath it. It made her feel more grown up than her years of sixteen. It was the feast of Bealtaine this night, an ancient ritual celebrating life and one necessary to preserving their good fortune. She smiled dreamily, her thoughts drifting upon the possibilities of finding love.

A hand jerked at her braid and she yelped. Her older brother Cillian grinned. With deep brown hair and laughing green eyes, Cillian was both her favourite brother and the bane of her life. 'Planning to find a man this eve, are you?'

'Of course not,' she lied, her face flaming. 'They hardly notice me anyway.'

Her brother shook his head knowingly. 'They notice you more than you think, Aileen.'

'You must be thinking of another sister.'

'You are my only sister,' he argued. 'And if they cannot see you for what you are, I'll be thrashing them soundly.'

His compliment tugged a smile from her. 'I washed my face in the dew three times this morn,' she admitted. 'I don't think it's working yet.' It was said that beauty would come to those who bathed in the dew on the morning of Bealtaine. She still held out hope that perhaps the effects might happen later that evening.

Bealtaine was a night when many a maiden might find love in the arms of a handsome suitor. Last Midsummer's Eve, she'd received her first kiss. It had not lived up to her expectations, being a tangle of wet tongue and lips. She shuddered at the memory, but didn't blame the boy for it. He hadn't had much experience either.

'I know where your thoughts lie, Aileen Ó Duinne. You're wanting Connor MacEgan to handfast with you.' Cillian started making kissing faces, and Aileen swatted at him.

'Stop your teasing,' she warned. 'Weren't you supposed to be gathering the wood for the Bel fires?' She knew her father and their other brother Bradan were busy assembling the cattle. After they drove the herd between the Bel fires, their good fortune would be assured.

'That was hours ago,' Cillian answered. A knowing smile creased his face. 'And I'll be finding a fair *cailín* to pick out the splinters for me.'

'You'll need luck for that.'

'As will you,' he answered. 'I've sad news to impart.' He let out a mocking sob, as though his heart were breaking. 'Connor has been chosen to play the part of Belenus. You won't be having him as your lover after all. Lianna will be Danu.'

It wasn't hard to imagine Connor as the sun god. But Aileen's good spirits wilted a little. It meant that Connor would become Lianna's consort this night. They would consecrate the Sacred Marriage and become lovers.

She shivered, just thinking of it. Why couldn't she have been chosen? Even as the thought flew into her mind, she cast it aside. Her plain face and untamed mass of brown curls made her nothing but a sparrow beside Lianna's swan beauty. More than once, a young man had looked past Aileen, his attentions fully upon Lianna.

'Chin up, sister,' Cillian said. 'I could hold Connor down for you, and you could steal a kiss. I don't think he'd struggle too much.'

She rested her fists on her hips. 'If you so much as breathe a word to him, I'll—'

He laughed and ducked outside. Aileen wanted to groan. Cillian knew that she secretly dreamed of Connor. But if he valued his life, he'd not tell a soul.

She raised her *brat*, wrapping the woollen shawl across her shoulders. At the threshold, a soft wind blew across the hills, soothing her wounded feelings. Tonight she wanted to shed her youth, to join hands and promise herself to one of the tribesmen.

On this night lovers slipped away together, celebrating the fires in their own way. Anything could happen, particularly magic. And it would take a bit of magic to get Connor MacEgan to notice her.

Aileen's mouth went dry at the thought of him. Though only a year older than herself, he had trained most of his life to be a warrior. He moved with stealth and power, a man on the brink of becoming a legend.

His hair was the colour of burnished gold, and he was so tall, she had to lean back to look at him. His grey eyes could stare into any woman's eyes and make her feel beautiful. In the fields she had seen him ride, his powerful thighs gripping the horse with consummate control. A flutter rose within her skin, just remembering him.

Was it so wrong to wish that she could lie in Connor's arms this evening, learning the ways between a man and a woman?

But then, such thoughts were foolish. She had best put them aside and hope to find someone else who would look upon her as a suitable bride.

'Aileen! Come and help me,' her mother called. 'I must prepare the baskets for the feast.'

Aileen wrapped loaves of bread inside linen, breaking off a piece to set upon the threshold for the faeries. They had been careful not to use any steel knives when preparing the bread, for steel was deadly to the faery folk. Tonight the veil between her world and the world of the Folk would lift. The offering would ensure luck.

'Are you ready?' her mother asked. Aileen nodded, picking up her basket once more. Outside, a small mountain of wood rested atop each of the two hills in readiness for the bonfires. All of their hearth fires had been extinguished the previous day, for the new fires would be lit from the Bel fires.

The evening light had begun to wane, the sun descending into an ocean of scarlet and purple hues. Soon, they would light the sacred wood.

Her father and brothers stood with their cattle among the rest of the tribe, waiting to drive them between the fires.

Aileen followed her mother into the crowd. As they passed the huts, she saw flowering hawthorn branches laid across some of the homes. Her heart clenched, for no sweetheart had brought flowers for her.

'Now remember,' her mother warned. 'If any young man tries to force you—' Her green eyes filled with concern, lines furrowing the edge of her mouth. She seemed torn by an invisible decision.

Aileen gave her mother a gentle hug. 'I shall tell him no.' She understood her mother's fears, though there was no reason for them.

''Tis your choice if you wish to take a lover and honour the Goddess Danu tonight, my daughter. But you needn't. You are still so very young.' Though her mother honoured the gods of their ancestors, she did not look at all willing to see her daughter become a woman in the truest sense.

'I will be fine, Mother.' And she would. She stiffened her spine and put on a bright smile.

All around her, the sound of cattle lowing blended with the crowd of voices. The air was fragrant with flowers, and ahead she saw Lianna and Connor. Both wore green, and a crown of hawthorn and primroses adorned Lianna's hair. Connor wore a matching garland of the same flowers.

Aileen drew closer, wishing with all her being that she could take Lianna's place. She turned to join the circle of girls and stumbled into a man. Eachan caught her before she could fall, steadying her balance. 'There, now. It's not every day that a pretty cailín falls at my feet.'

His lips curved in a smile, the lines at his eyes creasing with humour. Nearly the age of her father, Eachan had always been kind.

'I am sorry.' Aileen's face reddened, and she tried to escape his notice.

'Don't be. And may I say that ye look lovelier than the May Queen this evening?'

Aileen recognised the intent in his eyes and decided to let Eachan know her feelings. 'It's lying you are, if you say so.'

'I do not lie. Anyone can see that Lianna has naught but wool for brains. You far outshine her.'

Aileen decided that Eachan had drunk too much mead. 'I must go.' She excused herself and found a place where she could stand and watch Connor and Lianna. Lianna laughed as Connor's elbow brushed against her breast.

Aileen froze, as if Connor had touched her instead of Lianna. Her skin rose in response, her nipple growing tight against the wool of her gown.

'MacEgan bastard,' a male voice muttered from beside her. Aileen heard the jealousy in Tómas's voice. A full head shorter than Connor, he resented not being chosen as Lianna's consort.

'He should not be here. He belongs with his own tribe.'

Aileen did not argue that Connor had been fostered with the Ó Duinnes since he was a babe. Tómas wanted Lianna as his bride and made no secret of it.

'I'll kill him if he touches her,' Tómas threatened beneath his breath.

'And bring bad luck upon us all if you do such a foolish thing,' Aileen scolded. 'He was chosen. There is nothing to be done about it.'

'I won't let him have her.' The dark tone in his voice unnerved her.

'*Tá*, you will, and, if you stop behaving like a sulking boy, she may come to you later.'

'What would you know about it, Aileen? No man here wants a plain-faced girl like you for a bride.'

His words stung, but she raised her chin. 'I know enough to hear a boy speaking nonsense instead of a man.'

He pushed away from her, and Aileen blinked hard. Apparently the Bealtaine dew had not yet worked its magic upon her face.

She joined in the dancing, trying not to be hurt when the young men smiled eagerly at the other girls. She would make just as fine a wife as any of them. Hadn't the village healer Kyna taught her the skills of treating the sick?

Then she came face to face with Connor. His palm joined with hers in the dance, and it was a wonder lightning did not crackle from his touch. Nervous tension twined within her.

'Hello, Connor,' she squeaked. By the Blessed Danu, what had happened to her voice?

'Hello.' He turned her in a circle, smiling warmly. 'I've been wanting to thank you for tending my hound. Ulric seems to be back to his old ways again.'

'I am glad he is better.' She had done nothing more than mix a mint infusion for the dog after the beastie had eaten more than his share of table scraps.

Connor took her right hand and squeezed it. 'My thanks to you.'

At that, Aileen decided she would never wash her right hand again. They switched partners again, and she was saved from embarrassing herself when Eachan joined her.

'You've a fancy for him, have you?'

'I don't—he just—'

Eachan laughed and took her hands in his own. 'An old man like myself is no match for young Connor. Still, you're a sensible lass and one worth knowing. Shall I tell him and put in a good word for you?'

'No!' She was horrified at the idea of Eachan recommending her to Connor like a prized mare.

A teasing chuckle resounded from his throat as he passed her to the next partner. 'Think upon it, young Aileen.'

She blushed. Though a few visiting men came from nearby tribes, none gave her their attention. She watched as men and women paired off, joining hands in preparation for the fires.

Alone, she stood, feeling like an outsider again. Even Eachan, for all his teasing, had left her. She rubbed her arms, braving a smile she did not feel.

When the bonfires were lit, the crowds stood to watch while men drove the cattle between the two blazing fires. Against the black sky, the orange flames cast a stark, spellbinding glow. Connor and Lianna circled one of the fires three times, then took a running leap across the Bel fire.

Aileen's heart beat faster, as though she were the one to jump across the burning flames. Connor caught Lianna in his arms, dipping low to kiss her. Aileen turned away, pretending she had not seen it.

Mead flowed freely and, as the feasting continued, couples began to disappear into the undergrowth. Aileen heard the sounds of lovemaking and, at the muffled cries of satisfaction, something deep within her stirred. She moved to the edge of the clearing, standing near the forest. Darkness enfolded the trees, shadows guarding the lovers in secrecy.

Upon the dais, Connor held Lianna's hand in his, whispering to her. It was time for Lianna to honour the Goddess, to join with Connor in the hut set aside for that purpose. Lianna smiled, though her eyes rested upon Tómas. The man's face was rigid with hatred. Aileen feared suddenly that he would do something rash.

In the distance Aileen watched Connor raise Lianna's palm to his lips. Moments later, her friend walked toward the hut to prepare herself. While Connor endured the raucous jests from the other men, Tómas was moving toward the hut.

Aileen would not put it past him to destroy the ritual, regardless of the consequences. In desperation, she looked around until she found Lianna's older brother Riordan.

'I am worried about your sister,' she said. 'Tómas is jealous of Connor.'

The deep relaxation upon Riordan's face revealed the quantity of mead he had drunk. 'Lianna can take care of herself,' he said. His eyes grew deep, his expression relaxed. He reached out and patted her head. 'Go on, now.' Stumbling forward, he moved toward a group of women.

Aileen moved away from him, her blood pounding with embarrassment. She fled, pushing her way past men and women. Familiar sounds surrounded her, children whining in their mothers' arms, and the seductive sounds coming from the grove of trees ahead. Before she knew what had happened, she found herself standing before the ritual hut.

Anticipation coursed within her veins, her sensitised skin rising. What would Lianna be feeling right now? Were she in her friend's place, she'd not be able to breathe. The very thought of making love with Connor MacEgan, feeling the strength of his hardened body against her own, sent shivers through her.

The flickering blaze of the Bel fires drew her inside the hut, though she could not say why.

'What are you doing here?' Lianna whispered. 'He's coming soon.'

'I know. I—I wanted to wish you good fortune.'

'It isn't good fortune, not at all. Tómas may try to kill Connor. I don't know what to do. He warned me not to lie with him.'

'Tómas cannot interfere with the ritual. He wouldn't dare.'

'I pledged myself to him,' Lianna admitted. 'He thinks no man has the right to touch me. And—' her face flushed '—I am no longer a virgin.'

Aileen's eyes widened. 'But…what will you do?' If Lianna was no longer a virgin, then the act held no meaning.

'It's pagan nonsense,' Lianna scoffed. 'Merely an excuse for a man to join with a woman. Connor won't notice or care.'

'How can you say that? Haven't we been blessed with a fruitful harvest this past season?'

Lianna gave a bemused smile. 'You believe in it, don't you?'

'Of course I do. As should you.' Aileen was deeply shaken in the fear that Lianna's falsification would bring ill fortune upon them.

'Wait.' Lianna's eyes glittered. 'You're a virgin, aren't you?'

'I am.' Aileen suddenly grew afraid of her friend's interest.

'Good.' In one swift motion, Lianna extinguished the torch that lit the interior of the hut. In the darkness, Aileen could see nothing.

'Take my place,' Lianna urged. 'That way you'll ensure a good harvest. Connor won't know the difference, and I can appease Tómas.' Before Aileen could answer, Lianna crowned her with the hawthorn and flowers. She removed the ribbons, unbraiding Aileen's hair until it spilled across her shoulders.

'We should not do this,' Aileen argued. She could never deceive Connor in such a way. And it was wrong. She was not the May Queen. If anyone found out, she would be punished.

'You want him, don't you?'

'That does not matter. He'll know, Lianna, and he'll blame me for it.'

Ruthlessly, Lianna stripped away Aileen's clothes and removed her own léine. 'I'll wear your gown. We'll switch back later before anyone notices.'

Aileen did not protest because in her heart she feared the consequences of desecrating the ritual. The woman personifying the Goddess must be a virgin. And she understood that enacting a pure ceremony was far more important than who had been named May Queen.

But when she heard the sound of voices approaching, Aileen panicked. 'Lianna, I cannot do this!'

Her friend had already disappeared from the hut. Naked, Aileen moved beneath the coverlet, her heart beating a fierce rhythm against her chest. Connor would discover her ruse and shame her before the others. Fear and panic consumed her.

'Lianna?' Connor called out into the hut. 'Are you there?'

Now was the moment for her to admit the truth, to reveal herself. A virtuous woman would never rely on trickery.

But of all the men at Bealtaine, she wanted the embrace of only one: Connor MacEgan. She knew it would never happen, not if he knew her identity. But Fate had granted her a single chance.

Lianna had given her virginity to Tómas already. By taking Lianna's place, Aileen could assure a fruitful harvest. Was it so wrong to wish good fortune upon her people?

Before she could lose her courage, she whispered, 'I am here.'

She heard him enter, drawing the leather flap closed behind him until they were surrounded in darkness. The soft furs tantalised her bare skin, sensual and inviting.

She could not believe she had agreed to this deception. But it was far too late to turn back now. She heard the soft shush of Connor's clothes falling to the ground, then felt the weight of him as he sat upon the pallet.

'You know what is expected of us,' he said. His voice, a deep resonant sound, fell over her like a caress.

'I know it.'

His hand moved until it touched the wreath. He removed it, drawing his fingers through the length of her hair. She shivered and his hands moved over her bare shoulders.

'You are beautiful,' he said and, for a moment, she believed him. She reached out and her palm fit within his.

This is wrong, she thought. *But this night I will have no regrets.* If Lianna had no wish to play the role of the Goddess, Aileen could do so.

Connor leaned down, threading his hands through her hair. His mouth brushed against hers, teasing her. His tongue tasted her lips, and the light, gentle touch sent fires racing within her. Her breasts tightened as his mouth descended on hers, evoking a thousand sensations of pleasure.

With her palms, she touched the firm muscles, the warm

male skin. His kiss tasted of mead and girlhood dreams. He pushed the furs away, cupping her breasts in his palms.

Feeling bolder, Aileen kissed him back, letting her mouth move against his. His tongue entered her mouth and she moaned as he slid it inside, the way he would enter her body later. An aching heat surged between her thighs.

Every part of her body exhilarated under his touch, and she discarded the guilt. There would be time for that on the morrow.

For now, for this night of Bealtaine, Connor MacEgan belonged to her. And she intended to enjoy every moment of it.

Connor reached out to Lianna in sleep, but found her gone. Only the barest hint of warmth upon the fur pallet gave evidence to her presence. He rose and stretched, staring at the place where he had joined with her.

The ritual had become a sacrament, though he had not fully believed in the superstition. Lying in Lianna's arms fulfilled every adolescent dream he'd ever had. In his mind, he viewed it as a preliminary to their wedding night. He wanted Lianna as his wife.

Already he had offered a respectable bride price for her, but her father had turned him down. His pride stung at the memory. With nothing but a few head of cattle and sheep to call his own, it seemed his prospects were not strong enough.

He rose and donned his trews, his mind still filled with her. If Lianna would agree to handfast with him, they might overcome her father's misgivings. He needed to find her and ask.

For a moment, he stared at the empty furs, wishing she

hadn't left. He wanted to awaken with her soft skin against his, smelling the light fragrance of herbs in her hair. The thought made him yearn to have her beneath him once more.

Outside the rain fell, spattering mud against his trews as he walked. He didn't care. A lightness seemed to spread across his spirit, in spite of the storm.

A woman's moan caught his attention, the sound coming from a grove of trees. His steps grew hesitant, but he heard a familiar sound of laughter. Then he saw her, bare from the waist up, embracing Tómas.

The black fist of jealousy caught in his gut when he saw them together. Only hours ago, Lianna had given herself to him. And now Tómas.

Connor took a step back, his blood flowing like ice in his veins. How could she betray him that way? It made him sick to think of how she'd gone from his bed into the arms of another man. Had she truly been a virgin? Or was that a lie, too? He'd thought she was, but perhaps he had been too green to know any better.

He didn't stop to confront them, couldn't think clearly as his footing slipped in the mud. As he righted himself, he broke into a run. Without looking, he passed the small plots of land with the beehive-shaped cottages.

'Connor!' a girl's voice called out to him. He turned and saw Aileen.

Clad in a green *léine*, her hair hung down to her waist in a riot of dark curls. Her cheeks were flushed as she held out her hand in greeting. 'I need to speak with you.'

'Not now, Aileen.'

But she refused to listen to him, dogging his steps. Connor increased his pace, hoping to get away.

'This is important.' She reached out and touched his shoulder. 'I must tell you—'

He didn't want a woman clinging to him, especially after Lianna had deceived him into thinking she wanted him. 'Leave me. Whatever it is can wait.'

Hurt spread across her face, but he paid it no mind.

'Please,' she whispered, her eyes beseeching him.

'I said, leave me!' He wrenched away, and she lost her balance, stumbling into the mud. He hadn't meant to be so rough, but his wounded pride had suffered a blow.

Her hands dug into the mud, her dress sodden with the rain and dirt. Instantly, he regretted his actions. 'I am sorry.'

She said nothing, but he offered a hand to help her up. Aileen ignored it and rose to her feet.

'What did you wish to tell me?'

The disappointment in her face had transformed into a rigid shell of hurt. 'It was nothing.'

She turned away, and he wished he had not been so harsh. It would have taken but a moment to hear what she'd wanted to tell him. He knew Aileen favoured him, but he didn't hold the same affection toward her. If he granted her his attention, she might believe it was more than he intended.

Connor watched her return home, her shoulders slumped forward. He had made her cry and the realisation troubled him. He was accustomed to making women smile in flirtation. He could not take back his transgression, however.

He continued walking in the opposite direction until he reached the dense forest. Tall hazel trees and rowans interlaced, growing so near to one another that in places he had to turn sideways to pass the natural barriers. The heavy rain slowed against the leaves, and he sought shelter beneath one of the oak trees.

With his face in his hands, his heart ached, the steel bands of anger surrounding it. Foolish, he had been, to believe Lianna when she'd embraced him. Foolish to believe her soft whispers that she'd dreamed of being with him.

This was his last summer with his foster family. The Ó Duinne tribe meant as much to him as his own blood. Though he had intended to wait until Samhain, perhaps it was best to leave now. He had no desire to watch Lianna with Tómas, or to see the pitying looks upon his friends' faces.

He would gather his belongings and return home. And he'd not look back upon the past.

Two moons had come and gone since Connor's departure. Aileen had spoken nothing to her parents about the night of Bealtaine. Though her tears had soaked through her pallet each night, the terrible humiliation burdening her, she had another reason to weep.

Her menses had not come. She could no longer deny the fact that she carried Connor's child within her. Instead of bringing her joy, the knowledge made her weep harder.

Never should she have taken Lianna's place. Her friend had already wed Tómas, and Aileen remained alone.

That morning, the sun dawned clear and bright above the emerald horizon. She walked through the forest and into the clearing, her hand pressed against her abdomen. A part of Connor grew within her, yet she could not forget the way he had spurned her.

He believed he had lain with Lianna. And she hadn't told

him the truth. She couldn't bear to see the disgust upon his face, were he to realise it was she.

The sound of a horse walking behind her drew Aileen's attention. She saw Eachan dismount and tether the mare to a nearby shrub.

'May I walk with you, Aileen?' he asked.

She inclined her head, not knowing why he had sought her company.

'Do I seem an old man to you?' he asked, offering a friendly smile. His question startled her, but it forced her to regard his face.

Though the weathered planes of his cheeks bespoke his age, his hair had not yet grown white. His demeanour had ever been gentle, and she could not fault him for his persistent courtship.

'No,' she replied. 'You are not so old.' He fell into step beside her, and they walked among the wild orange crocosmia blossoms flowering upon the hillside.

'I know of your grief,' he said, his hand brushing against hers. 'You should have told him.'

Aileen grew rigid. 'What do you mean? Told whom?' Eachan could not know the truth of what she had done.

'Told Connor that you carry his child.'

Her hands moved to her scarlet cheeks. Was it that evident? Did everyone know her secret?

'Why—what makes you th-think—'

'I saw you that night. And it was right that you offered yourself to protect the harvest.' He gestured over the land, the fields swelling with stalks of grain and green corn. 'The gods have blessed us for it.'

He took her hand in his. 'I do not fault you for it. I know you care for him, and you do not care for me.'

His kindness eased her battered heart, and unbidden tears swelled. 'It isn't that. You have been good to me.'

'I would take care of you,' he offered, squeezing her hand. 'You and the babe. No one need know that it isn't mine.'

The tear spilled over. 'Eachan, you do not deserve a bride such as me.'

He raised her hand to his lips. 'I would like to think that we could be friends. And you need a father for your child.'

She knew there were herbs to end the life of the unborn babe, but she could never consider taking them. Eachan's offer brought a tear streaming down her face. He wiped it away with a knuckle. 'Will you accept me as your husband? Will you let me look after you?'

She did not consider refusing him. His kindness enfolded her like a warm woollen shawl. She put her hand in his, even knowing that it meant abandoning her dreams of wedding a warrior like Connor.

After the summer waned and the harvest grew ready for threshing, Aileen took Eachan as her husband. But even as she spoke the vows binding them together, he knew her heart belonged to another.

As the child grew within her, and Eachan continued to court her, Aileen made her own vow. She silently promised to be a good wife to Eachan. She would put Connor from her mind and learn to love her husband.

Chapter 3

Banslieve, Ireland
1175

His days and nights ran together in a faded tapestry of pain, helplessness, and anger. Connor had grown to despise the pungent aroma of garlic that Aileen used upon his wounds to prevent fever. But more than that, he hated his inability to control his healing.

The cuts and bruises joined a host of other scars. The Ó Banníon's primitive form of justice spurred his rage and bitterness. His friends had turned on him, men he'd trusted with his life. They'd obeyed their chieftain's commands blindly, and it was their betrayal that bothered him most of all. So be it. When he regained his strength, they would regret their actions.

If he regained his strength, he thought dully.

His hands had swollen up to three times their normal size, the pain only relieved when Aileen gave him a sleeping draught.

'Ó Banníon's men,' he asked Aileen one evening when she held out a wooden mug of bitter liquid. 'Have you seen any of their tribe?'

'No. Were they the ones who did this to you?' She tipped the drink into his mouth, offering him little choice but to drink it. He felt like a newborn babe, helpless to even hold a cup.

'They were. I wondered if they came back for me.'

'If they did, I heard nothing of it.' Aileen took the cup away. 'Why did they attack you?'

'I was punished for a crime I did not commit.'

'What happened?'

Connor kept silent. He had no wish to relive those moments, nor to share his shame with a woman he barely knew. 'I do not wish to speak of it. But when I find them, they will regret their actions.'

'You should let the Brehon courts settle the dispute,' Aileen argued.

'The courts would require a fine, nothing more. The Ó Banníon chieftain deserves to suffer as I have.'

Connor struggled to rise from his pallet, but Aileen forced him to lie back.

'And if you have your revenge, will that make you a better man than he is?'

Her calm words kindled more anger. Aileen knew nothing of what he'd endured. He held out his injured hands. 'An eye for an eye is all the justice I need. I care not about being a better man.'

'What will you do if you cannot fight again?' she asked.

'If you set the bones properly, I shall.'

She stared at him, her grey-green eyes filled with pity. Her chestnut hair, pulled tightly into a braid, allowed a few curls to escape. In her face, he could read the doubt. It pulled at his insides, fraying his hope. 'I did all I could do for you. The rest is up to God.'

'How long, Aileen?' Connor wanted to grasp her by the shoulders, to demand the answers he sought. But the useless hands could do nothing. His muscles grew heavy as the sleeping draught weakened his senses.

'Another moon cycle, at least. Perhaps two.'

The helpless rage at being unable to control his body's healing made him want to lash out at something. He was a soldier, a man accustomed to commanding others. To be a victim was not in his nature.

He managed to gather the threads of his anger and pull them back into submission. 'I have to regain my full strength. You must see to it.'

'I am not an enchantress.' She stared at him. 'I can only do my best.'

'And if your best is not good enough?'

She paled, her eyes damning him. 'Then your own healer can help you. She can remove the bandages and cast whatever spells she may.'

He'd touched a nerve. Beneath the complacent tone, he sensed hurt.

Connor took a breath. 'I did not mean that the way it sounded. You have done much for me, and I am grateful for it.'

She said nothing, but picked up a broom and began to sweep the interior of the hut. With even strokes she cleared out the dust and swept it outside. The coolness of the evening breezed inside the hut.

He fought against the sleep threatening to pull him under.

When he returned home, his brothers would share his desire for vengeance. But he didn't want his older brothers to shoulder this fight for him. War was not his intent. Only justice.

Wounds such as these rarely healed well. And his brothers might share the uneasy suspicion that he was no longer the same fighter as before. Connor did not wish to see the regret in his brothers' eyes.

From the time he was old enough to lift a wooden sword, he'd known he was meant to be a warrior. It was the only path for him. As one of the youngest sons in his family, he had virtually no property. His only chance of gaining a stronghold of his own was to fight for it.

It was the way of Ireland, men competing to become a chieftain or a king chosen by the people. Since he would not depose his own brother, his only path was to be a strong enough leader to command another tribe.

He didn't want anyone, particularly his brothers, to see him in such a state of helplessness. His pride bruised at the idea. But to avoid it, he would have to stay here with a healer whom he'd insulted.

With effort, he opened his eyes again. He didn't know how to mend the harsh words that were spoken, but he had to do something.

'I remember you,' he said at last. 'From when we were children.'

'We never talked,' she said, tying bundles of herbs and hanging them to dry. 'You couldn't remember me.'

A wave of pain spiralled through his hands, but he masked it. 'You used to have wild brown curls flying about your face.' With a forced smile, he added, 'You used to watch me, when you thought I wasn't looking.' He thought he detected a faint reddening of her cheeks, but it was difficult to tell.

'I never watched you.' Aileen gathered several stalks of dried herbs, crumbling them into a stone mortar. She smashed the herbs with the pestle, grinding the stone mortar until the helpless plants became dust.

Before other plants could fall victim to her ire he asked, 'What happened to your husband? I heard you married.'

She added melted fat to the herbs, mixing it into a thick paste. Her hands moved in a rhythmic motion before she answered at last, 'Eachan died a few moons ago.'

Connor had not known Eachan well, but none had ever spoken an unkind word about the man. Grief shadowed Aileen's face, and he regretted his earlier words. 'I am sorry to hear of it.'

When she made no reply, he added, 'I imagine you have your children to bring you comfort?' He kept a questioning note in the remark, for he did not know for certain.

'I have a daughter,' she said. After a moment of hesitation she added, 'She is being fostered with another family.'

Connor forced himself to concentrate on the conversation at hand. His vision swam and he struggled to stay awake. 'Did you have any sons?'

'I lost several babes,' she said, making him wish he hadn't brought it up. Aileen busied herself with putting the herbal ointment away, and then she set the pot upon the peat fire to boil water.

'When my husband Eachan was alive, we fostered many children,' she offered. 'Lorcan was among them.' Disappointment darkened her face. 'I was not allowed to keep him once Eachan died.' She sprinkled herbs into a wooden cup and filled it with boiling water to make a tea. 'I wish I could have. He was a comfort to me.'

He could understand that. His youngest brother Ewan had come home six years ago, after his foster-father was killed in battle.

'Do my brothers know I am here?' Connor asked.

'We sent for them, yes. But it will take days for the message to arrive and days more for them to come.' She cast him a look.

Connor had no desire to be paraded across the country-side in a litter. 'What if I wished to stay?'

'I thought you did not believe in my healing skills.'

He hesitated, for it was true. And yet he saw no alternative.

'I would prefer to remain in Banslieve until I regain my strength.'

Aileen turned her back, busying herself with her herbs again. She had wanted to heal him, to prove to the people that she could save Connor's life. But would it be enough? They would only see the terrible damage done to his hands.

She shook the errant thoughts away. Saving his life wasn't enough. To prove herself, she needed to bring him back to his former strength.

Doubts undermined her confidence. She had treated broken bones before, but nothing like this. Her heart warned her that she would almost certainly fail. How could a man with crushed bones grasp a sword again, much less use it?

'Aileen,' he murmured, 'I don't want the others to see me like this.' His eyes were glazed with exhaustion. He held up the splinted hands.

'You won't have a choice. Seamus will demand that you come and stay with them.' Were it not for a raid, the chieftain would have been here already. The Faelain tribe had stolen nearly a dozen cattle, and Seamus had gone with his men to steal them back again.

'And I'll refuse,' he said firmly. 'I'd rather my foster-father remember me as I was.'

'You speak as though you're dead.'

His face dimmed. 'Perhaps I am.' He closed his eyes, no longer resisting the heaviness of the sleeping draught. As his chest rose and fell, she drew nearer. She lifted a coverlet over his bare chest. The bandages remained dry; no blood seeped from the cuts.

His flesh was warm and firm, a body honed to fight the enemy. He needed her skills. She understood his desire to stay and rebuild what had been lost.

Softly, she murmured goodnight and rose to her feet. Outside the small hut, she leaned against the wicker framing. She covered her cheeks with her hands, filling her lungs with the crisp night air.

What was the matter with her? She was a healer, he was her patient. She could shield her feelings well enough. He'd never know about her secret.

But in his handsome face, she saw her daughter's smile.

'There are visitors, come to see you.' Aileen said. She suspected she wouldn't be able to hold the women off without donning a shield and spear. Nothing would deter the unwed maidens from seeing Connor.

'Visitors?'

'Seamus's daughters.' Aileen grimaced. Though the women were friendly enough to her face, she knew exactly why they were here—to coax Connor to the chieftain's home. This was Riona's doing. She wondered why Connor's foster-mother hadn't come herself. But then, Riona hated her and made no secret about it.

'What do they want?'

'To worship at your feet, I would guess. Their arms are filled with cakes, flowers and tokens.'

'Really?' A hint of interest darkened his eyes, and he suddenly stared at her with a look that made her knees go wobbly. He'd seen her reaction, and his voice grew deeper. 'And am I the object of your worship as well?'

'No,' she snapped. 'You most definitely are not.'

Humour creased his eyes. 'I suppose not. You might soil your gown should you get down upon your knees to worship at my feet.' Connor leaned back upon his pallet, adding wickedly, 'Now, if you removed your gown, it wouldn't be such a problem, would it?'

'The only thing I will remove is your head, should you continue speaking such nonsense.'

A pounding noise sounded upon the door, and the women's voices called out greetings. Connor propped himself up on the pallet, while Aileen went to answer the door.

In an instant, the door to the sick hut opened. A pair of women descended upon him like vultures.

'Oh, Connor, it's been years since we've seen you!'

'What happened to your hands? Do they hurt?'

'Your pillow needs adjusting. Here, let me fix it.'

Both were pretty, smelling of fresh spring flowers. He tensed, suddenly realising that Seamus's daughters were on a quest of their own. He had become their target, a potential husband.

Connor pretended to enjoy their attentions, but, in truth,

he watched Aileen slip into the background. She wasn't as fair as the other women, but her face held his interest.

One of the women offered him a succulent meat pasty. What was her name? He couldn't remember since she'd been fostered elsewhere. The fair-haired woman slid her fingertip into his lips while she fed it to him. The rich juicy mutton tasted far better than the bland pottage Aileen had served him this morn.

He kissed her fingertip, and she giggled. Aileen rolled her eyes with exasperation. Interesting.

She behaved like a jealous wife. Why should she care? Yet Aileen looked as if she'd rather chase the women from the room with a club than allow them to visit.

The day had suddenly grown more entertaining. Connor cared little for the flirtation of the women; not that he would have acted upon their interest even if he could engage in bed sport. But Aileen's reaction intrigued him.

The women wore colourful gowns of scarlet and green, while Aileen's overdress and léine were a serviceable brown. He'd noticed that she rarely wore an overdress that would draw attention to her. Faded wisps of memory made him recall Aileen's shyness as a young girl, waiting to be noticed by anyone. Browns, greys and the colours of the peasantry were all she donned. She had the right to wear richer colours, from her status as a healer.

In their hair, the women wore golden balls. Bracelets adorned their arms while long earrings hung from their earlobes. Aileen wore no jewellery that he could see, save a simple ring upon her finger.

The one feature that set her apart was her clear, beautiful skin. Not a blemish or wrinkle marred the delicate pale complexion. It made her eyes stand out. He couldn't quite tell what colour they were. Sometimes grey, sometimes green, depending upon the light. The rigid, intricate braid kept the dark brown curls at bay. He imagined the thick length of her hair surrounding her hips.

A startled smile crept across his face at the thought of Aileen sharing his bed. The earth would burn into ashes before such a thing would happen.

One of the women mistook his smile as an invitation. 'Have you taken a woman to wife yet, Connor?' she teased.

He thought her name might be Grainne or Glenna, but he didn't remember. 'Not yet, Glenna.'

'Grania,' she corrected, smiling broadly. 'Were there no women to your liking?'

'There were too many,' he bantered. 'I could not take all of them to wife.'

The women laughed, but he noticed the distaste upon Aileen's face.

Grania emitted a sigh. 'Oh, Aileen, I nearly forgot.' Her face became a mask of innocence. 'My father is on his way here. You are to bring Connor to our dwelling this night.'

'He is not well enough to walk yet,' she argued.

Connor frowned, for nothing was the matter with his legs. His chest and head ached still, but they were healing. 'Tell Seamus I don't wish to see him now. I'll come to the *rath* when I've healed. Not before.'

Grania's face furrowed. 'I will tell him. But he wants to speak with Aileen.'

'Now?' Aileen asked. Anxiety lined her face, and Connor wondered why. Seamus was a good chieftain, a well-respected leader. What reason would Aileen have to fear him?

'Yes, now.' An air of smugness surrounded Grania.

Aileen departed with haste to meet her chieftain, her gaze averted. The door closed, and Connor was left to wonder what she hadn't told him. He tried to bring his attention back to Seamus's daughters, but with little success. He wanted to know what Aileen had done.

'Why would Seamus wish to speak to Aileen?' Connor asked.

'She is forbidden to heal.' Grania's face shifted to anger. 'After what she did, none here will let her be the healer again. Cursed, she is. You'd do well to leave this place and let our new healer help you.'

'A new healer?' Conner grew still. Aileen had said nothing to him about another healer. A rigid suspicion fouled his mood. He'd thought Aileen was the only healer in the Banslieve. But she'd lied.

'You may come and live with us,' Sinead offered, lifting a dab of honey to his mouth. 'We would be happy to look after you.'

He ignored their invitation. 'Why is Aileen forbidden to heal?' he asked.

Grania exchanged a look with Sinead. 'Our father will tell you of it.'

A moment later, she changed the subject. The shrill chatter of the women made his head ache, and though Connor tried to keep a good humour, he wanted them gone.

'Do your hands hurt terribly?' Grania asked.

They did, but he refused to admit it. 'They are fine.'

He could hardly concentrate, for questions crested inside him. 'But I would like to rest again.'

They murmured their sympathy, and he was thankful

when they left at last. When they'd gone, he stared at his bandaged hands. The swelling had not improved, and the pain seemed magnified.

Worse was the dawning fear that Aileen had not fixed his hands properly.

'You were not to tend any of my people.' Seamus's tone was quiet, but it held the power of a chieftain. 'You disobeyed my orders.' A tall, heavily muscled fighter with long grey locks that fell to his shoulder, none dared to suggest that Seamus had grown too old to be a swordsman. He had not changed his clothing from the raid, and sweat lined the flanks of his mount.

'Connor needed help,' Aileen argued. 'He would have bled to death if I'd left him.'

'You should have brought one of us there.' The unyielding set to Seamus's face revealed his opinion of her healing.

Aileen gripped her shaking hands tightly. 'His wounds would have become poisoned.' She couldn't have stood by and watched him suffer. He had needed immediate help, his wounds sewn and his hands splinted. Enough men had died in the past few moons from lack of care.

Seamus did not respond to her remark, but directed his horse towards the sick hut. 'I am going to bring him back to our *rath*. The new healer will look at him.'

'And who is she?' Aileen stiffened at the mention of her replacement.

'Her name is Illona. She is the healer of the Ó Banníon tribe and has offered to share her skills with us, since our land borders are so close.'

'Do you not realise that the Ó Banníon men did this to

him?' Aileen exploded. 'How could you even think of letting that woman near him?'

Surprise transformed Seamus's face. 'Has Connor said this?'

'He has. And you should be wary before you let their healer near the tribesmen and women.'

'Do not presume to tell me what I should or should not do, Aileen. He will leave the sick hut this night.'

'He does not wish to see you. Not until he has healed.'

'Then I will hear that from his own lips. Not yours.' The chieftain's tone turned threatening. 'Have a care, Aileen. I did not bring your case before the *brehons* for judgment, though I could have. No one has forgotten what you did.'

Hot tears swelled, but she held them back. He couldn't forgive her, though, by Danu, she had done everything in her power. She had saved his only son's life, two years ago, but even that could not erase Seamus's grief. He was blind to everything but what he had lost.

'I will speak with him now.' Without waiting for a reply, Seamus spurred his mount forward.

Aileen's stomach churned, and she stood upon the hillside in view of the sick hut. Her limbs felt wooden, her steps weary.

'Aileen, wait!' a young voice called from behind her. She turned and saw Lorcan. His dark hair bobbed as he ran toward her, skidding to a halt.

'What is it, Lorcan?'

His small face held regret. 'I am sorry. I shouldn't have told him about the dead man.' He shifted, studying the grass. 'Well, I suppose he isn't really dead.'

'He would have been if you hadn't brought me to him in

the field that day.' She reached out and tangled her fingers in his hair. 'It's all right.'

'I didn't mean to make him angry.' He hugged her waist, looking up for forgiveness.

'I know you didn't.' She released him. 'Go on, then. You don't want to get into trouble for speaking to me.'

Lorcan scurried off, and at the sight of him, her heart warmed. Always she would think of him as her foster—son. It was easier to walk the journey home after his impulsive embrace.

The sun nudged the horizon, rimming the land with gold. She walked slowly to her land, trying not to think about Seamus's command. Her chance of redeeming herself as a healer was gone.

Connor's face burned with fever, his hands throbbing with pain. When the door to the sick hut opened again, he heard a familiar voice murmur, 'What has she done to you, young Connor?'

He raised his head and saw the face of his foster-father Seamus. Forcing a smile, he said, 'Your healer Aileen has tied me to the bed, she has. I haven't the strength to escape.'

His jest met with Seamus's bark of laughter. 'Then let me rescue you, my lad. Our healer can look at you.' His lined face drew downward with concern. 'How did this happen?'

'I was falsely accused of seducing the Ó Banníon's daughter. His men crushed my hands.'

Seamus cursed beneath his breath. 'You can be assured I'll be bringing this before the *brehons*.'

Connor made no reply. 'Later, perhaps.' He gritted his teeth against the pain. 'I understand you have a new healer.'

'We do.' He came closer and sat beside the pallet. 'Illona Ó Banníon is her name.'

Connor showed no emotion at the mention of the Ó Banníon name. It seemed a cruel trick of the gods, to send the enemy in the form of a healer. 'I won't be seeing her.'

'I can understand your anger, but I have forbidden Aileen to heal any more. She is too young and has not the skills.'

Connor glanced downward at his splinted hands, but he pushed back the feelings of doubt. He didn't entirely trust Aileen's healing either, but he wouldn't consider letting the Ó Banníon healer touch his hands.

'I'd rather she splint my hands than anyone bearing the Ó Banníon name.'

Seamus expelled a breath. 'I've come to take you back with me.'

Though he knew Seamus meant well, he'd rather take his chances with Aileen. 'I thank you for your offer, but I will be staying here.'

'I cannot allow it.'

'But you will. You know why I won't trust the Ó Banníon healer. And here I can remain in isolation until I've healed. I don't want to endure anyone's pity.'

Seamus leaned back on his heels. 'I do not like it, lad. Because of her…' His voice trailed off.

There was pain in the man's voice. Connor didn't ask, for he knew whatever had happened would only bring up harsh memories. Instead, he took a deep breath, pushing back his own pain. 'I make my own decisions. And here I will stay until I have my strength back.'

* * *

When Aileen reached the door to the sick hut, she found Connor lying upon the pallet, his face pale. Perspiration lined his brow, but he opened his eyes when she neared him.

'Why didn't you tell me?' he demanded.

'Tell you what?'

'That you are no longer the healer. My hands—' He broke off his own words, closing his eyes with the pain. Aileen stoked the fire, hanging a pot of water to boil.

'They're hurting you. I know. It's the swelling.'

He struggled to stand, his balance swaying.

'Sit down. You've a fever.' Aileen eased him back down.

She mixed herbs together that were good for fever, including willow bark. Adding the boiling water to a wooden cup, she steeped the mixture and allowed it to cool.

When it was ready, she raised it to his lips to drink. He winced at the bitter taste, never taking his eyes from her. There was weariness and pain in his eyes.

'Kyna taught me all she knew,' Aileen said. 'There is nothing wrong with my skills.'

'Isn't there?'

She heard the accusation in his voice, but refused to back down. 'Do you truly wish for Illona Ó Banníon to treat your hands?'

The frustration and fury in his eyes were damning. Aileen busied herself with the pot, suddenly realising that she had prepared nothing for the evening meal. For the past two moons, she had only herself to care for. More often than not, she simply ate a bit of bread or vegetables from her garden.

'Can I get you something to eat?' she asked, when he'd finished the tea.

'No. I require nothing.' He turned his gaze away. He had shut her out of his thoughts, and Aileen knew better than to force him to eat.

'Did you enjoy your visit with Sinead and Grania?' she asked, trying to end the awkwardness.

'I've no wish to be treated like a child, fed by hand, my pillows fluffed.'

'I don't recall fluffing your pillow,' she said.

His face relaxed a little, and she watched for signs of the pain receding.

'I suppose I have no choice but to stay here and let you tend me,' he said. He lifted his bandaged hands, his gaze boring into hers. 'What's done is done. You've already set the bones and it cannot be changed without creating more damage.'

'If you return home, your own healer can tend them.' She spoke as if it were of no matter to her. But it hurt, knowing that he held no confidence in her skills. She had done everything she could to save his hands.

'And as I've said, I am not returning home. I'll lose respect among my men if they see me like this. They won't believe I can ever wield a sword again.'

Aileen did not voice that it was a very real possibility.

He softened his tone to one of teasing. 'And with you, there's no worry about you trying to seduce me. You would not care, were I completely naked upon this pallet,' he said.

Her throat closed up and Aileen tried not to imagine his body, sleek and smooth with carved muscles and a taut belly. Worse, she had never forgotten what it was like to be held by him, loved by him.

'You are right,' she lied. 'Your body holds no interest for me.' She opened the door, needing to be far away from him. He might see the truth upon her face.

'Good. Then it's settled. I'll stay until I've healed, and then I'll return to Laochre.'

She didn't reply, but returned to her own hut, her cheeks burning. How could she have Connor so near each day while his wounds healed? It would be like having a husband again. While Eachan had brought her comfort and friendship, Connor intimidated her. His strong presence shadowed her, making her yearn for the things she couldn't have.

She had borne him a child, a secret she wanted to keep. Rhiannon was a precious, stolen moment. If he learned about his daughter, he would despise her for what she'd done. She couldn't bear to see the disgust upon his face. All she had left was her pride.

Even now, he doubted her healing skills. He wanted to stay, but only as a way of hiding himself from the world. The thought of sharing such intimate moments, living together with him for the next moon, brought back her childhood fantasies. He was everything she desired, and all that was wrong for her.

Could she be strong enough to resist him? Surely it had been so many years; it wouldn't matter if he stayed.

But inwardly, she knew the truth. Her heart wouldn't last a single day.

Chapter 4

Waves of heat closed upon him, smothering Connor in a web of misery. Visions and hallucinations tempted him to let go, to sink into the silken arms of oblivion. He tasted bitter herbs, and his hands grew numb.

In his dreams, he craved vengeance against his enemy. He hadn't laid a finger upon Deirdre, no matter what the enraged Flynn Ó Banníon had claimed. He didn't deserve the punishment, and he longed to see justice done.

But as he watched Aileen mix potions and replace his bandages, he cleared his mind of the rising hatred. For now, he had to regain his strength. And he would need Aileen's help, even after the bandages were removed.

Connor remembered a soldier who had nearly been buried alive when a wall collapsed upon him. The man had lived, but after the accident he could no longer care for himself. The soldier had become a burden upon others, relying on his family to feed and dress him.

He couldn't let that happen.

Connor didn't know what to believe about Aileen's skills.

The foul-tasting potions and poultices did alleviate his pain. But he grew uneasy about his hands. Why was she forbidden to heal any more? What had she done? He should have asked Seamus when he'd had the chance.

Though Aileen masked her feelings beneath a veil of calm, there was a desperation in her healing efforts. She stayed with him in the sick hut for many hours, changing the bandages, sponging at the cuts. It was as though she were trying to atone for a serious mistake.

A few strands of hair had escaped the tight brown braid, surrounding her face like a soft halo.

'Connor, look at me,' she commanded. Through the haze of fever, he stared back at her. 'You must drink this broth.'

'I am not hungry.'

'You've hardly eaten in the past two days,' she argued. 'And I'll not let you starve.'

The terrible-tasting fish broth made death seem inviting. Though her herbal teas and potions worked well, her cooking left much to be desired. 'I prefer starving to eating that,' he muttered.

'It will bring back your strength.'

'By making me retch? I think not.' He grimaced. 'Perhaps that is your plan. To be rid of me by serving me the most foul dinners you can conjure.'

'I can conjure up worse meals than this.'

Was that a glimmer of amusement he detected in her face? It surprised him. She rarely showed her feelings, and especially nothing to make him smile.

'I imagine your husband was very proud of such a skill.'

'He liked my cooking,' she admitted. He caught the flash of grief on her face.

Aileen lifted a spoonful of liquid to his mouth. He tasted fish soup mixed with the bitter herbs and winced. 'I fear I must disagree with Eachan. Your cooking is the worst I've tasted, Aileen.'

'It is the medicines,' she assured him, holding the bowl to his mouth. 'Drink. It will help you to heal faster.'

He did, half-choking it down. In a way, he was grateful that he could speak his mind around Aileen. With her, he need not smile or tease, feigning strength he did not feel.

In the amber glow of firelight, he could not see his broken hands. The swollen joints made it impossible to move them. After he finished the broth, he met her gaze evenly. 'I won't lose my hands. Even if it means my death.'

He expected her to disagree with him, but instead she said, 'If that is your wish.'

She leaned close, a defiant spirit in her eyes. 'But you should know that I am a better healer than that.'

He wanted to believe her, but between her lost status of a healer and the swelling upon his fingers, his doubts lingered.

'Besides,' she added, 'it is easier for me to get you out of my cottage if you walk out on your own feet. I've not the strength to drag you home.'

Connor could make no reply, for she lifted a cup of mead to his lips. The drink expunged the terrible taste of herbs.

'Aileen, may I ask a boon of you?'

'What is it?' She had turned her back to him, loosening the long *brat* she wore about her shoulders until only her thin *léine* remained. The swell of her breasts silhouetted against the soft firelight distracted him. 'Well?' she prompted. As her fingers worked to unbraid her hair, the chestnut length of it spilled across her shoulders and down to the rise of her hips.

'The women,' he began. 'I know they wish to visit me—'

'You mean they wish to offer themselves to you upon a platter.'

A smile twitched at the corner of his mouth, but he did not respond to her jibe. 'Could you keep them away, at least until my wounds have healed?'

'Do you not wish them to feed you sweetmeats with their lips? Or rub your shoulders?'

He didn't like her mockery. 'I do not require such. But should you wish to do so, I'd not complain.'

Aileen let out a huff and turned to leave. 'That will never happen, MacEgan.'

He hid his smile as the door closed behind her. It was no secret he liked women. He enjoyed their company, their softness. His brothers had oft times teased him that a woman could murder him and he'd thank her for it. He'd been blessed with the ability to charm most women into whatever he wanted.

He saw no harm in it, as most wanted to flirt. Sometimes he took advantage of a night in a willing *cailín*'s arms, but more often he slept alone. With little land to speak of, a marriage to him was not attractive to the noblewomen of his tribe. They wanted a bold Irish warrior in their beds, but not in their homes.

He refused to allow a woman to use him in such a way.

In his mind, he imagined a fortress of his own, a stone *rath* spanning a hillside across lands rich with grain. A son who would drag a wooden sword across the training field, struggling to follow in his footsteps. A wife, welcoming him into her bed when darkness fell.

Despite his damaged hands, he would not let the Ó Banníons destroy him.

* * *

The next morn, Connor awakened with less pain. He eased himself to a seated position and then stood up. Though his limbs were stiff, walking caused him no pain. With slow steps, he eased towards the sunlight. He squinted at the light and saw a smaller thatched hut. Aileen's dwelling, he realised.

Standing before the hide-covered door, he tapped it lightly with his foot. Silence. When he entered the dim hut, no one was inside. For a moment he stood at the threshold, studying the interior.

Though he could cross the length of the hut in four strides, Aileen had everything organised. Her herbs hung to dry on one end, while other vials contained potions and other healing salves. A small trunk held her personal belongings, and during the day her pallet was stored in another part of the room.

Upon the hearth he saw a cauldron of bubbling oat pottage. He winced, wishing for anything but the pasty gruel. Perhaps her cooking was his penance for previous sins.

The door opened slightly, interrupting his thoughts. He saw Riordan, and vaguely he recalled Aileen saying that the man had helped bring him back.

'MacEgan,' Riordan said in acknowledgement. Though his words offered a polite greeting, Connor knew Riordan held no friendship towards him. As lads growing up, Riordan had been overprotective of his sister Lianna. He had never approved of Connor and made no secret of his animosity. 'Where is Aileen?'

'She is not here,' Connor said, not wanting to prolong the visit. He kept his bandaged hands hidden behind his back, meeting Riordan's gaze evenly.

'I came to see you. Your brothers have been sighted and

should be here within an hour.' The fact pleased Riordan from the thin smile upon the man's face.

Connor showed no reaction to the news. Instead, he took a step forward, openly challenging Riordan. 'I do not intend to go back with them,' he said. 'I am remaining here until my hands have healed.'

'Aileen does not want you here.'

'We have an arrangement. It does not concern you.'

Riordan's fist balled up, and Connor kept his eyes trained upon the man, showing no fear. He didn't trust him. The invisible lines of confrontation were drawn.

'Always arrogant, you were, Connor. I have offered to wed her. As her future husband and provider, I demand that you leave.'

'Has she accepted your offer, then?'

'It is too soon.'

Connor hid his satisfaction. Aileen deserved better than a hot-headed man such as Riordan. 'So you say.'

The man's jealousy darkened. 'Stay away from Aileen.'

Wounded or not, Connor had no intention of letting the man intimidate him. He held his ground, meeting the open threat with an even expression. Riordan's temper held by the thinnest strands of self-control, his fists curling up.

The door swung open, and Aileen entered, carrying her basket. It brimmed over with handfuls of fresh clover and lavender.

She directed her attention to Riordan. 'What is amiss?'

'Nothing,' Riordan replied. 'I came to inform Connor that his brothers will arrive soon.' He appeared satisfied with himself.

Connor was less than pleased by the news. Convincing

his brothers to leave him behind would be difficult. He stared at Aileen. Her eyes did not quite meet his.

His brothers would have much to say about his injuries, and he doubted if they would understand his reasons for wanting to remain.

'I must begin preparations for our noon meal,' Aileen said. 'Thank you for letting me know about the MacEgans, Riordan.'

He reached out and took her hand, offering it a squeeze. 'It is always a pleasure to see you, Aileen.'

Connor did not miss the way Riordan's eyes coveted Aileen. He watched her like a man treasuring a possession. A thin needle of warning pricked him, even as the man left.

After he had gone, Aileen unwrapped the cloth package of mutton. He eyed it with wariness. 'Are you certain you know how to cook that?'

Her eyes narrowed. 'Of course.'

He shrugged, not entirely convinced. She had not prepared a true meal for him in the fortnight he'd been here. If he never saw another bowl of pottage, that would suit him.

'I look forward to tasting it,' he said softly. Her gaze snapped toward his, her face flaming. The colour in her cheeks suggested she was thinking about tasting something else. Though he hadn't meant the words in that way, he grew aware of her mouth. It was sweet with the palest hint of rose.

He shook his thoughts away. Why would he think of kissing Aileen?

'Why are you here?' she asked. She appeared uncomfortable having him inside her home. 'I thought you would remain in the sick hut. I was going to bring you a bowl of pottage.'

'I grew weary of lying down.' He gestured toward the

hanging herbs and the neatly organised medicinal plants. 'This is where you live?'

'It is. My husband Eachan built it when I became the tribe's healer. I wanted to be closer to the sick hut.'

Hastily she scooped out a ladle of pottage and handed him a wooden bowl. Her face flamed when she realised he could not hold it. 'Sit down and I'll feed you.'

He'd rather eat mud than endure another bowl of pottage. 'I am not hungry.'

She set the bowl down. 'Will your brothers wish to stay for the night?' she asked. Without waiting for an answer, she babbled, 'How many of them are there? Shall I pull out an extra pallet or two?' With a knife she began slicing the mutton. Her eyes brightened at the prospect of visitors.

'I will ask them and find out.' He needed to speak with his brothers before they arrived. He opened the door and stepped outside.

'You're not going to meet them,' Aileen protested. 'You cannot walk that distance. Be patient and await them here.'

'It is my hands that are injured, Aileen, not my legs.'

'You're weak. You lost too much blood with the knife wounds.'

'I will be fine.' The walls of her cottage had begun to suffocate him. He needed air and a moment to stretch his legs.

Outside, he walked past Aileen's garden. The summer grasses swayed in the light breeze, the rich green fields stretching across the land. While awaiting his brothers, he sat down. He smelled the fecund aroma of ripening harvest, enjoying the sun upon his skin.

In the distance, horses and two riders emerged. Shielding his eyes, he recognised his brothers Ewan and Trahern.

As the youngest, Ewan had endured more than his fair share of teasing. Though he would never possess the swordsmanship necessary to be a warrior, Ewan held a quiet courage that revealed the shadow of the man he would become.

His older brother Trahern was a stark contrast. Large in stature and able to best most men in battle, Trahern needed no man to guard his back. His true talent lay in storytelling, and Connor knew he would bring tales to Aileen this night in return for her hospitality.

His elder brothers Patrick and Bevan had not come, and Connor did not expect them to. Both had wives and children, along with other responsibilities.

They had brought a third horse tethered between them, a gelding for himself. Connor stood and walked closer, raising his hand in welcome.

Trahern dismounted, scrutinising Connor with concern. A moment later, he clapped him on the back, a thump that nearly sent Connor sprawling. 'I see the Ó Banníons did not kill you after all.'

Ewan had grown several inches since Connor had seen him last. Thin and tall at eighteen years, his brother was caught in the awkward stage between boyhood and manhood.

Ewan's attention centred on his hands. 'What did they do to you?'

Connor held up his bandaged hands, trying to make light of it. 'They're broken, but the rest of me is whole. A few nicks with a dagger, a bash upon the head. That is all.'

'Did they break your hands or crush them?' Trahern asked quietly. Connor sensed the edge in his question.

'Broken or crushed, what does it matter?' he asked, keeping his tone hopeful. But he met his brother's grave expression, acknowledging the possibility. They would not speak of it in front of Ewan.

'How long must you wear the bandages?' Ewan asked.

'Another moon, perhaps two.'

Ewan uncurled his own palms, white scars lining the edges. Four years ago, the boy had faced an enemy Norman knight who tortured him for information, carving his dagger into Ewan's palms. Only a miracle had saved the lad's hands, for though the cuts were deep, no tendons had been severed.

A pity there was no such miracle for himself, Connor thought.

'They've healed well,' Connor acknowledged, offering a friendly smile to Ewan. 'But I'd rather hear of your travels to England,' he said. 'You studied swordplay with Genevieve's father, didn't you?'

'I did.' At the mention of his travels, Ewan hurried into a story about his training. His sister-in-law Genevieve had offered Ewan the opportunity to study with a master swordsman. Ewan had eagerly accepted the invitation, but Connor had his doubts as to whether the boy had improved. His brother's fighting skills had never been strong. Now, he himself might face the same ridicule.

While Ewan chattered, Trahern caught Connor's glance. In a lowered voice he asked, 'What will you do?'

The question was one he had expected. Trahern was not asking about his immediate plans, but rather, what Connor would do if he could never fight again.

'I do not know.'

'There are other ways to fight,' Trahern suggested, 'ways where a man does not need a sword.'

'That may be.' But he had spent years training to gain the

skills he possessed. He refused to consider giving it up, not when there was a slight chance of recovery. 'But you need not have come. I'll return to Laochre when I have healed.' The familiar towers of his brother's fortress had been his home until he'd gone to serve the Ó Banníon chieftain.

'Is there another reason you wish to stay?' Trahern asked.

Connor flashed him an easy grin, letting his brother believe what he wanted. 'There might be. But I'll have to convince her.'

Ewan's mouth dropped open. '*You?* There's a woman in Éireann who has refused you?'

He began to laugh, and Connor wished he could box the boy's ear. Instead he growled, 'There is, yes.'

'You should return to Laochre, brother. It is where you belong,' Trahern advised.

Would that he could. He had spent a full year away from his family, and he longed to see the familiar *rath*. And yet, he didn't want to return as a broken man. 'Later, perhaps. But in the meantime, I'll be staying here.'

Before they reached Aileen's cottage, Connor turned serious. 'The Ó Banníons took my sword from me. I'll be needing another.'

Without question, Trahern unstrapped his sword and fastened the scabbard around Connor's waist. Then he offered a bag of silver pieces. 'You may need these as well. I'll put them among your things inside the hut.'

'I'll take care of the horses,' Ewan offered.

'The gelding will stay with you until you are ready to return,' Trahern said.

No one could fault the open generosity of his older brother. Whenever there was need, Trahern provided without question. Saint Trahern, his brother was. But Connor did not resent him. Trahern was a good man, and he had earned the respect of others.

Ewan opened the door, and Connor invited his brothers inside the hut. The sumptuous aroma of mutton stew filled the air. Aileen offered a warm smile. Her face glowed from the fire, her hair escaping its braid once more. The russet overdress and cream-coloured *léine* she wore accentuated her slight figure and the curve of her breast. At the sight of her, Connor realised that he did find Aileen pleasing to the eye, though her tongue was sharper than he'd have liked.

'It's welcome you are,' she greeted them. 'I am Aileen Ó Duinne.'

Connor introduced Trahern and Ewan. His younger brother blushed and grinned with appreciation when Aileen offered them a cup of mead. 'Please, sit and rest.'

They removed their shoes and Aileen offered basins of water for them to bathe their feet. Afterwards, they sat upon the floor, a small low table between them.

Aileen gave each man a round loaf of bread with the insides removed, filled with mutton stew. The spicy aroma made his mouth water, but Connor suddenly grew aware that he still could not feed himself.

Aileen behaved as if nothing were amiss when she lifted a spoon to his lips.

Connor tasted the rich stew seasoned with rowan berries and teased her for his brothers' benefit. ''Tis not every day a man is given his food by a lovely *cailín*.'

Aileen smiled and shoved another scorching bite of stew into his mouth, not waiting for it to cool. Her unspoken message was clear.

The next time she brought the spoon to his lips, Connor

turned his face aside, joining in conversation with his brothers. Ewan abandoned himself to the food, mumbling a few words.

'Ewan and I are grateful for your hospitality,' Trahern said, smiling broadly at Aileen. 'But I should like to hear your stories of my brother. I know he was fostered here, and I am certain you know a tale or two that would humble him before his brothers.'

'I do,' Aileen answered Trahern with a warm smile of her own.

Connor was startled to see the shyness gone. It transformed her, giving her the look of a seductress.

'I've my doubts of that,' he said. 'I was never anything but the most innocent of lads.'

Ewan choked upon his mead, Trahern laughing as he pounded his brother on the back.

Aileen offered Connor a sip of mead, and he drank slowly, meeting her gaze with his own. The drink tasted sweet upon his tongue, though there was no sweetness in Aileen's expression.

'It was many summers ago,' she began. 'Connor was fifteen, I believe. He was in love with Lianna, a girl from the village, but she'd not have him.'

'A woman who didn't want our brother's affections?' Trahern teased. 'I cannot believe such a thing. I am astonished to hear it.'

'It isn't so very difficult to imagine,' Aileen quipped, darting a glance at Connor.

He feigned a smile, but it disappeared when she began the tale of a time when the village girls had stolen his clothing while he bathed in a stream. He'd been forced to return home without even a loincloth. The memory still made his cheeks burn. Though he knew she intended merely to provide amusement to his brothers, he didn't like it.

Trahern began an amusing tale of a man who had gone to sleep and awakened in a maiden's hut without his clothes. Ewan and Aileen both laughed, and Connor grew more withdrawn. His hands ached, and he hoped to dull the pain with the mead.

Awkwardly, he leaned down and tried to grip the goblet with his forearms. He could not tip the cup of mead without spilling it down his chest. Aileen took it from him and held it to his mouth. Connor accepted her help, but found it difficult to look at her.

Trahern rose and stretched. 'Thank you for an exceptional meal, Aileen.'

She acknowledged his brother's praise with a nod. Then she asked, 'Have you decided to return to Laochre, Connor?'

'I'll stay here until I have my full strength again.'

Her eyes turned troubled. 'Until I remove the bandages,' she corrected.

A moment hung between them, and Connor saw her reluctance. Why? She was not allowed to heal anyone else. It was not as if she had others to tend.

Her hesitancy must have been evident to Trahern, for he said, 'Would you care to walk with me? After such a fine meal, I'd like to enjoy the afternoon sun.'

Aileen glanced at Connor. 'I don't know—'

'Go with him.' Connor lifted his hand in agreement.

She didn't want to, especially when she noted the pale lines of pain upon his face. Inwardly she berated herself for not adding a mild sleeping draught to his mead. She reached for her medicines, choosing the herbs she needed. Chamomile and mint would be mild, perhaps with a little willow bark to ease his discomfort.

'Go and enjoy your walk,' she suggested to Trahern while she added hot water to steep the herbs.

'He wants to talk to you alone,' Ewan interrupted.

Trahern glared at his brother. 'Could you be a bit more subtle, lad?'

Ewan shrugged and pointed toward the door. Aileen didn't want to leave, but at last relented. She set the tea in front of Connor, realising too late that he could not drink it without help.

But then, whatever Trahern wished to say would not take long. Outside she followed him, walking along the edge of her field. High above them, the sun burned brightly.

'You've known our Connor for many years, haven't you?' Trahern began.

'I have, yes.'

'And does he seem to you a man who wishes to take advantage of others?'

'No, of course not.'

'Has he harmed you in any way?'

Aileen levelled a hard stare at Trahern. 'What is it you want?'

Trahern's green eyes softened with kindness. 'I think he would heal and grow stronger, were he to stay under your care. You are more skilled than he knows.'

The flattery did not have its intended effect. Aileen bristled, wishing they would all leave the matter be. It was true, he might heal and help her prove her skills to the tribe. But what if he didn't heal? What if he was right, and she lacked the ability to restore his strength?

Being around Connor brought back all her feelings of awkwardness. She felt herself slipping back into the shadow of the girl she had been, the girl who felt unworthy of being around him.

'If Connor wishes to stay in Banslieve with the Ó Duinne tribe, then stay he will,' Trahern asserted. 'A grown man, he is, with a mind of his own. A man who does not want to face his tribe until he is whole again.'

'His hands, you mean.'

'*Cinnite*. Can you not understand why he would rather remain here than face his men? He'll not want to return until he is healed.'

'And if he does not heal?' Aileen asked.

Trahern's face turned grim. 'Then he may never return home.'

'You speak of him as though he intends to die.'

'A warrior who cannot use his hands is as good as dead. We all know it.' Trahern circled their path back towards Aileen's hut. 'The question is, will you help him?'

'I have helped him to the best of my ability.'

'No.' Trahern stopped to regard her. His long beard brushed his chest, his dark hair spilling over his shoulders. She had to tilt her head up to look at him. 'There is more you can do for my brother. It is this that I ask you. In return, I will grant you anything within my power.'

'What more can I possibly do?'

'Help him to become the fighter he once was.'

Aileen lowered her gaze, shaking her head. 'You ask too much of me. I cannot change his injuries. I know nothing of a soldier's training.'

Trahern's expression softened. 'You have lost much, just

as he has.' He reached out and joined her hand with his. 'Think upon my words.'

She knew it. Connor's stubbornness rivalled her own. But the longer he stayed, the harder it would be to keep the secret of Rhiannon. She'd hidden the truth for so long, she didn't want to destroy Rhiannon's memories by revealing that another man was her father. It would hurt her daughter, and she couldn't bear that.

Worse, Connor might insist on making decisions about Rhiannon's future. He had every right, especially since she had hidden his own child for so many years.

'You knew the man he once was, Aileen,' Trahern said softly. 'If you bear him any friendship at all, I ask you to help him.'

She closed her eyes. Once, he had been much more than a friend to her. He had been the man she loved.

Trahern saw her waver and closed in for the kill. 'Until the end of the summer, Aileen. Just until his hands have healed. Can you not grant him this?'

Tears gathered in her throat, but she managed a nod. As penance for hiding Rhiannon, she'd allow him to stay. And, God willing, he'd never learn what she'd done.

Chapter 5

The following morn, his brothers had returned to Laochre. Connor rested easier now that they were gone. Aileen had hardly spoken a word since she had agreed to let him stay.

'I intend to compensate you for your trouble of caring for my hands,' he said. 'Is there something you desire?'

Aileen prepared bowls of warm pottage, not answering his question. His stomach turned at the thought of eating yet another bowl of the warm gruel. If he never saw it again, it would be too soon.

'Aileen?' he repeated.

She pushed a strand of hair back from her cheek. 'No, there is nothing. I'll tend your hands, and then you'll go.'

Her voice sounded tired as she motioned for him to sit down. With a wooden spoon, she scooped up the horrible pottage and held it toward him.

'Must I truly eat that?' he asked, putting on his most charming voice. 'I thought you made honey cakes the other day.'

A gleam warmed her eye. 'You sound like my daughter

used to, when she was a babe.' Without mercy, she shovelled in the warm gruel.

He forced himself to choke the mouthful down. When she held out the second bite, he eyed it with distaste. She wielded the spoon like a weapon, poised to attack him. But he had a warrior's defence training. When she moved forward with another spoonful, he quickly turned his head. The pottage hit his cheek instead, falling to the ground with a heavy glop.

Her mouth twitched. 'You did that on purpose.'

'Of course I did.' Connor's gaze narrowed, and he watched her for the next move. She was going to try again, and he intended to be ready.

She prepared another spoonful. 'You cannot run away.'

He moved sideways, but the pottage landed upon his neck as he dodged the spoon.

A laugh burst forth from her. She pinned him to the ground, her body forcing him motionless. He couldn't help his own laugh, feigning weakness. 'I surrender.'

She relaxed a moment, a genuine smile transforming her face. Exactly what he was hoping for.

He seized the advantage. With pottage covering his face, he lifted his head and smeared his cheek against her own. Wet gruel caked her face and she emitted a sound of disgust. 'I thought you surrendered.'

'A battle strategy. And it worked.'

'It wasn't fair.'

'I don't fight fair, *a stór*.'

'This calls for vengeance.' She smeared another handful of the mess upon his face, but he nipped at her fingers and she jerked back.

The softness of her curves pressing against him made him once again aware of her body. Aileen Ó Duinne was most definitely a woman, and one who intended to win this battle. He eased himself to a seated position, her bottom nestled in his lap. His body tightened with arousal.

Wild dark curls had fully escaped her braid, framing a face covered in pottage. Her sage green eyes brightened with teasing. 'You look like a babe learning to feed himself.'

'I'll need you to wash my face,' he said softly.

She got up from his lap, and brought back a dampened linen cloth. She knelt beside him and touched it to his cheeks and mouth.

'You forgot your own face.'

At the reminder, she folded the cloth again and cleaned away the mess. She missed a spot at the corner of her mouth, and he imagined kissing it away, tasting her smooth skin. She intrigued him. Though she had not the traditional beauty of the women he liked, Aileen had captured his attention.

'I think I have a way of making the pottage more palatable,' she suggested.

'Offer it to your sheep?'

'No.' She brought forth a container of honey to sweeten the gruel and stirred some into the pottage. 'Is that better?'

'A little.' He accepted the offering as a truce, and was pleased to see her smiling again.

Changing the subject, he said, 'I was serious about my earlier offer. There must be something I can grant you in return for my care.'

She shrugged. 'You cannot give me what I want most.'

'And what is that?'

'I want to be the tribe's healer again. But I can't change that, can I? They believe I'm cursed.'

'Then change their foolish superstitions.'

'It would be easier to turn rocks into rain. They believe what they want to believe.'

'Show them the truth.'

'Connor, I cannot hold them down and force them to accept my care.'

He raised an eyebrow. 'You're quite good at holding a man down and forcing him, I'd say.' The reference to their pottage war returned a smile to her face.

Connor sat down upon one of the pallets, the dry corn husks rustling beneath him. Aileen cleared away their wooden bowls, straightening the hut. It was as if he made her nervous. The more he dwelled upon it, the more he believed he'd done something to offend her.

Long moments passed, and Aileen swept the floor, behaving as though he weren't there. Unused to being ignored, Connor stood. 'Is there aught I can do to help?'

'You can rest.'

'I am not a weakling, Aileen.'

The closer he drew to her, the more anxious she behaved. Women were not usually afraid of him. He came up behind her. The strong fragrance of rosemary clung to her hands while she stripped the needles free of the plant. Lightly, he touched his bandaged hands to her shoulders. 'Are you afraid of me?'

She expelled a half-laugh. 'Do not be foolish. You could not harm me if you wanted to.'

'Then why are you shaking?'

'I am not.' Aileen set aside the rosemary. Connor used his

broken hand to turn her toward him. Her river-green eyes stood out in a fragile countenance. He wondered what it would be like to unravel the rest of her thick braid and let the wild curls spill down her back. Better yet, to thread his hands through the softness and to kiss her lips.

A strange tension gripped him when he realised he could not even move his fingers, much less use them to touch a woman. And this woman clearly did not want him.

He admitted it was a first for him. Most women laughed, enjoying his teasing. But Aileen kept him at a distance, offering nothing more than a healer's relationship with her patient.

'We were friends once,' he offered.

Her mouth tilted in a false smile. 'Not truly, Connor. I helped your dog, but that was all. You had eyes only for Lianna.'

Sadness coated her voice, along with the tinge of wistfulness. He hadn't seen Lianna in nearly seven years. Truth to tell, he had not thought of her since he'd arrived.

His patience waned at Aileen's refusal to accept his friendship. Connor moved away and used an elbow to push the door open. 'I shall see you at the noon meal.'

'Where are you going?'

'Out to walk in the fields.' The door clattered shut behind him, and as he trudged along the familiar path, his frustration expanded with each step. He needed to get away from the enclosed spaces, to stretch his endurance.

He had not reached the boundary of her land when he heard her call out to him, 'Connor, wait.'

Aileen strode toward him. She wiped her hands on her skirts. 'I spoke in haste. Do not tire yourself too quickly.'

'And how will sitting in a hut help me grow stronger?' The idea of remaining indoors upon a pallet was maddening. He moved towards her until she was forced to look up into his face.

Her eyes held uncertainty, her mouth frowning. A moment later, she softened with a new idea. 'I must tend my garden today. You can sit out of doors if you wish.'

'Might I?' She was behaving as though he were helpless, a man who would collapse if he so much as took a few tottering steps. Yet he had gone into battle many times, leading raids against other tribes and defending their lands from the Norman invaders. 'No, thank you.'

'I want a horse,' she said suddenly.

'What?' Her sudden change in subject confused him. He thought of the gelding his brothers had left behind.

'Not yours,' she said hastily. 'You'll need that one to return. But I'd like a horse of my own.'

He stared, uncomprehending.

'You asked what I wanted in return for keeping you. I'd like a horse.'

If she had asked for a warrior's ransom, he'd not have been more surprised. 'What do you need a horse for?'

'That is my business. You asked, and I answered. Now, if you do not mind, I must tend to my garden.'

'Horses are worth a great deal.'

'As are your hands. If you wish to grant me a gift, that is what I want.'

He didn't understand her desire for such an animal, but he could not promise such wealth without a few conditions of his own.

'I will meet your terms if my hands heal enough to wield

a sword again.' He tried to flex the bindings holding his wrist. A deep ache shot through him with the effort.

'I can make no promises—'

'Then I will give a lesser payment for your care. If you restore my hands, I'll grant you a horse.'

She wavered, but at last nodded. 'There may be some exercises where we can train your wrists and hands to be strong again.'

'Good.'

She started to walk away, but he stopped her. 'I am not your enemy, Aileen. I am no threat, nor would I ever bring harm to you.'

'I know it.' But even as she spoke, she shielded her expression. She reminded him of a wild mare, easily startled.

'There is no need to hide from me.'

Aileen raised her gaze to him. 'I am not hiding from you, Connor.'

'There is something else,' he mentioned. It was an indelicate matter, but one he could not avoid. Perhaps it was good that she disliked him so, for then it would not bother her.

Aileen waited, her face questioning. Connor offered his most innocent look, the one most maidens sighed over. 'I am in great need of a bath. I smell like a swine.'

Without waiting for a reply, he whistled and made his way towards the cottages in the distance.

Aileen ripped weeds from the earth, attacking them like a horde of invaders. She longed to dump a bucket of freezing water over Connor's arrogant head. Did he expect her to giggle and fawn over him, soaping his muscles as she blushed like a maiden?

She groaned. On the night she had tended his wounds, and many times since, she had seen for herself how time and training had sculpted his chest. Her most vivid imaginings could not have conjured up a more magnificent warrior. With dark golden hair and the face of Belenus, Connor still evoked long-buried feelings of desire. To touch his bare skin, washing him with only a light cloth made her body remember exactly what it was like to lie with him.

She hacked a stray clump of grass out of her lavender bed, berating herself. She was a healer, wasn't she? As a wounded man, Connor could hardly bathe himself.

When he'd touched her shoulders, it was as though her body remembered him from so many years ago. The physical contact had startled her. She didn't want to touch him, didn't want to risk feeling the sharp longing of desire.

Expelling a sigh, she wiped the perspiration from her forehead. When her garden held no more weeds, she walked toward the stream. She knelt at the water's edge and scooped up a mouthful of cool, clear water.

It was then that she saw her father Graeme walking toward her. He leaned upon a walking stick, his broad shoulders and girth revealing his weakness for fine foods. His hair held strands of grey, though he wore war braids at his temples in memory of his younger days.

She rose to her feet, tucking the stray hairs back. With a splash of water on her face, she scrubbed it clean to greet him.

Graeme embraced her with a warm smile. 'Aileen, you are looking well, *a iníon*.'

'And you, Da.'

His smile faded and her skin prickled with fear. Graeme Ó Duinne was a man she'd admired all her life, a father who spoke his mind without excuses. Somehow she suspected his presence boded unwelcome news.

Her father put a hand upon her shoulder. 'Seamus informed me that you have been looking after Connor Mac-Egan. Is that true?'

'Yes. He needed care, and I gave it.' She sent her father a penetrating gaze. 'Unlike others who would let a man suffer rather than accept help from me.'

'Seamus lost a great deal. He is a father who is not thinking clearly.'

She knew it, but bitterness cloaked her heart. 'He should open his eyes to the son he has instead of dwelling upon the past.'

'He cannot.' Graeme shook his head. 'And neither should you dwell upon the past.' Her father cupped her cheek, his eyes turning serious. 'You have suffered the loss of a husband, daughter. I know you grieve for him, but it is time to put it behind you. You wish to bear other children, do you not?'

The shadow of sadness passed over her heart at the mention of it. How many times had she wept at her inability to bear Eachan a child? A kind man he had been, the kindest. He had taken her in, spoken to no one of her shame. Tears sprang to her eyes, and her throat closed up. 'I do miss my husband.'

'You should marry again, Aileen. When the *aenach* begins, many will seek a wife. You need someone to take care of you.' Fatherly concern drew out the wrinkles in his face. 'It is for the best, now that you can no longer be the healer.'

Aileen wanted to cry out, *No, it isn't for the best.* But she would not disgrace herself by begging. It wasn't the prospect of a husband that hurt so deeply. It was the loss of her heal-ing as a means to help others.

The idea of never visiting the sick, tending their illnesses, and watching them heal was like a razor to her gut. And they wanted her to give it up.

Only when her father had left did she indulge herself in weeping. She cried on the way back to her small hut, letting the tears fall freely. She hadn't thought of Eachan in so long, but the mention of marriage brought all the grief back. A twinge of loneliness tugged at her heart.

When she reached her small hut, she leaned against the door and wiped the tears away. She ducked beneath the bundle of wool hung above the frame and went inside. Her gaze fixed upon the small wooden tub in the corner that she used for bathing. She could hardly imagine a tall man such as Connor inside it, and suddenly her earlier apprehensions grew stronger.

Temptation and mixed dreams filled her imagination, thoughts for which she chided herself. Connor MacEgan was a man who had hurt her once before, never knowing how he'd crushed her tender feelings. This time, she would not fall prey to such a man again.

'Graeme Ó Duinne, have you lost your wits? Why on earth would you trouble our daughter with nonsense about wedding again?'

Graeme chuckled, sitting back with satisfaction. 'She's been alone for too long. I am just giving her the push she needs.'

His wife glared at him. Graeme enjoyed seeing her ire. Never was Póla so alluring as when she grew angry. Like a *bean-sidhe*, Póla advanced upon him, her grey eyes thunderous. 'And what were you thinking, leaving an innocent girl alone with a man such as Connor?'

'Our Aileen has borne a child, Póla. She's a widow, free to do as she pleases. There is no shame in her being alone with Connor.'

'What will everyone think of her?'

'Likely the same as I do. It is about time someone matched the two of them up. It may as well be meself. I intend to see them wed before the winter.'

'She's lost her husband,' Póla argued. 'It is too soon.'

'And what better man to comfort her? Our Aileen has held feelings for Connor for many years.'

He gathered Póla into his arms. 'Do you not think she deserves happiness?'

'I think you are an interfering old man who should keep himself out of Aileen's life.'

He tilted her chin to look at him. 'I've a secret, carried over this past moon that I would share with you. Can I trust you with it?'

Her face softened. 'Of course.'

'Eachan did not father Aileen's daughter. Rhiannon belongs to Connor.'

Póla's face whitened. 'I don't understand. She—they never—'

'I've a story to tell you, *a stór*.' He took her in his arms, kissing her cheek. 'And when I've finished, you'll understand what Eachan made me promise. He asked me to bring them together, for he loved Aileen so. He wanted to gift her with the man she truly wanted.' Póla's eyes grew misty, and he knew he had touched her heart.

'Fate has brought them together, and this is how I shall keep the vow I made to Eachan.'

'Our daughter is stubborn,' Póla replied, her gaze focusing in the distance. 'She may ask Connor to leave.'

'Then we will find a way to keep them together.' And Graeme Ó Duinne sealed the promise with a kiss.

Chapter 6

'You are Connor MacEgan,' a young boy said, and beckoned for Connor to come closer. The child sat outside one of the cottages, picking weeds from a small garden.

With cinnamon hair and deep green eyes, a ready smile creased the boy's face. His young arms had a light tan from the sunlight and strong muscles that had seen a great deal of use. From the waist up, he was no different from any other boy. But his right leg was gone, leaving only a stump above his knee.

'What is your name?' Connor asked, keeping his gaze away from the boy's missing leg.

'My name is Whelon Ó Duinne. And you are one of the great warriors.' The child's face lit up with eagerness.

Connor held up his bandaged hands, feeling uneasy beneath Whelon's excitement. 'I was once.'

'Can you train me?'

Connor avoided the answer he did not wish to give. 'Why do you want to be a soldier?'

'To fight the Norman enemy, of course.'

'Not every Norman is an enemy,' Connor said, thinking

of his brothers' wives, Genevieve and Isabel. 'Many are men and women like us.'

'Then I would only fight the wicked men.' The boy flexed his muscles, and Connor hid a smile.

'There will be time enough for that later,' he said, evading the issue.

Whelon's face strained, and he shook his head. 'I must begin now. It takes me longer than the other boys to learn a skill. If I am to be a warrior, I have no choice.'

The intensity of the boy's vow made it clear that Whelon would not be dissuaded.

'You did not answer my question,' Whelon remarked. 'Will you train me?'

'That is the task of your *aite*,' Connor answered.

'My foster-father does not believe I will ever fight.' Whelon's face darkened. 'He believes that without my leg, I can do nothing.' Small hands tightened into fists. 'I shall prove him wrong. Aileen has said so.'

Connor cleared his throat, disliking the direction of the boy's thoughts. Without a limb, a man was useless on the battlefield. No one would rely upon him. If he had no men at his side, no one to help defend him, he might as well bare his chest before the enemy's blade.

'Were I you, I would choose another path.' Though he tried to keep kindness in his voice, Connor saw the hurt upon the child's face. He turned away, walking toward the meadow.

Why had Aileen given the child false hopes? She knew nothing of fighting, nor the ways of a soldier. A warrior had to remain dispassionate when he sank his blade into a man's heart. A single misstep, a fraction of hesitation, brought death. Connor knew, for he had felt the razor's edge of a sword cutting into his own skin. The scars remained. And if this young lad tried to become a soldier, he would die.

Connor passed through the open meadow, moving toward the forest. Whelon's request reminded him that he had allowed his body to grow soft in the weeks he'd spent with Aileen.

The need to train, to stretch his limbs and regain his strength, burgeoned within him. He started to run, his weakened legs flexing with the effort. There were ways he could maintain his physical abilities, even before he could hold a sword. He increased the pace, running toward the secluded forest grove.

Deep in the shadowed trees, he found an area where the trees did not grow close together. He took a moment to calm his breathing, then he extended his arm as though he held a sword. Across the ground he moved, visualising the slashes in his mind, lunging with an imaginary weapon he could not grasp. Over and over he went through the familiar motions, until his body reacted through instinct and his mind drifted.

Sweat dripped from his brow, his legs burning as he feinted right, then left. He could not let the injury defeat him. If it meant compensating with his legs, so be it. In time, he would use the sword Trahern had loaned him.

Thoughts of Whelon invaded his concentration. The child had his own form of compensation for his leg. Whelon's sculpted arms revealed a great deal of strength, far beyond that of an ordinary lad. Could he not learn to fight? His memory shifted to warriors he'd known, men who had lost limbs and returned to battle.

But then, these were seasoned men, accustomed to pain and loss. They knew the risks and could adapt. Whelon was only a child. He could not train in the same manner as one who had known fighting all his life.

Even as Connor's feet moved with the swiftness of experience, the aching of unused muscles crept forth. At long last, he sank to the ground to rest, his lungs constricted.

Connor stared at the bandaged splints. They hid his injuries, and though at times the skin itched, he rarely felt the aching pain any more. Although Aileen had promised to remove the bandages soon, the urge overcame him to see how his hands had healed.

Using his teeth to free the bandages, he unwound them until the splints fell to the ground. Though his skin was a pale grey colour, the texture did not bother him as much as the gnarled bones. His fingers had not grown straight, the right hand resembling an animal claw more than a human limb.

He could not bend his wrist, nor move his fingers more than a hair's breadth.

Despair warred with his anger. He had held on to this hope, that somehow Aileen held the skill to heal him. Now, he doubted such was possible. She had saved his life. But for what?

He should have ignored his hatred and gone to see the Ó Banníon healer. He should have put away his pride. Instead, he'd trusted Aileen.

He could not help but cast a small portion of responsibility upon her. If the elderly healer Kyna had lived, could she not have spared his hands? Aileen had not the experience of time.

As the sun dusted the edge of the tree branches with light, the morning waxing into afternoon, he feared his future as a soldier had ended. The grief of loss festered inside his mind, for he could not see how he would ever grip a sword, much less fight against an enemy. Logic and willpower raged against one another. If these hands belonged to another man, as a commander he would not allow the soldier to fight.

The thought of never lifting a sword again meant giving up his dreams. How could he lead a tribe when he lacked the strength to do so? A hollow feeling thrust itself into his mind, anger infusing him.

He could not give up yet. He'd rather die than surrender. No matter the cost, he swore he would regain his former strength. Even if it brought his death.

The welcoming aroma of lavender and rosemary filled the interior of Aileen's hut. She recalled the nights when Eachan would sit with her, sipping a warm drink. Of course, he preferred a strong dash of poteen mixed with it. Sometimes he would take her hand, caressing her fingertips before coaxing her to bed.

A smile tugged at her mouth as she remembered. He had been a gentle lover, bringing her sweetly to fulfilment. Always courteous of her needs, they had found a pattern of comfort within the marriage. The thoughts of Eachan deepened the void of loneliness welling up inside her.

Tonight she would prepare a *craibechan* of chopped bacon mixed with vegetables from the garden. Connor's comments about her poor cooking skills had chafed at her pride. She would prove him wrong. While she chopped the meat, a muffled pounding sound at the door caught her attention.

'Aileen!' Connor called from outside.

She unlatched the door. Connor entered, and upon his face Aileen saw the lines of frustration. He kept his hands behind his back, hiding them from view. She understood his chagrin at not managing the simple task of entering the cottage.

'Did you have a nice walk, then?' Signs of fatigue shadowed his face.

Connor held up his hands, the bandages gone. Though he said nothing, accusation glowed in his eyes.

'Why did you remove the bandages?' She spoke sharply, her own anger rising. By taking them off too soon, he endangered his healing. 'You should not have removed them. The splints keep your bones together. They need more time.'

When he didn't answer, she reached out to his hands. He jerked away, his face lined with fury.

'Is this your healing, then?' Connor demanded, holding up his right hand. His skin had healed, but the bones would never be completely straight. She had done all she could for him. He could regain motion, though perhaps not the same range of movement.

'Sit down.' She refused to justify herself, when he only wished to rage at her.

'What did you do to me?' he growled.

'I saved your ungrateful life. Now sit down so I can mend the damage you have done,' she commanded. Without waiting for a reply, she gathered fresh linen and searched for wood to splint his fingers.

How could he be so foolish to remove the bandages this early? Each day was critical for the bones to knit, particularly those in his wrist. His misshapen fingers did not matter. The true damage had harmed his wrist, and this affected all movement.

He remained standing. Aileen sensed an indefinable emotion from the tall warrior. The sun had brought colour into his skin, and his harsh face remained unyielding.

She took his wrist into her hands, his muscled forearms

corded with wrath. As she bandaged his hands and wrists, his gaze grew cold. He spoke not a word, his silence damning.

When at last she had finished, she moved back to the forgotten vegetables, picking up her knife. Her hands shook as she sliced them, but she hid the trepidation behind her task.

'I met a boy this morn,' he said at last. 'Whelon is his name.'

Aileen's knife slipped, and she nicked her finger. She pretended as though he had said nothing. 'Did you now?'

'*Rinne mé.*' Connor took a step closer, but Aileen could not retreat. 'How did he lose his leg?'

'He was hurt in a small skirmish with the Normans. He was bleeding badly, and the men made a tourniquet.' She paled, closing her eyes at the memory. 'They did not use it properly, and when I removed it, his flesh had already begun to rot. I had to remove the leg to save him. He would have died if I hadn't.'

'I have seen a sickness as you've described. Men who have lost a great deal of blood often lose their limbs.'

Aileen closed her eyes, trying to block out the boy's screams from her memory. The men had held him down, and with every move of the blade, it was as though she were cutting her own limb off. By the gods, never did she want to perform such a task again.

'Whelon wishes to become a soldier,' Connor revealed. 'He asked me to train him.'

A fragile smile touched her mouth at the thought of strong-willed Whelon. 'That has been his dream for a long time.'

'You should not encourage him,' Connor warned. He held his hands toward her. Only a thin edge caged his fury.

Aileen set down her knife and faced him. 'There is always hope.'

'No. Not for him. And not for me.'

'Your hands are not as bad as you believe. Broken bones require time to heal.'

'I won't become a burden upon my family.' There was anger and despondency in his voice, though he attempted to keep his tone neutral. 'Or to you.'

'You are not a burden.' She reached out and took his forearms in her palms. 'If you have needs, ask and I will do what I can to help you.' But already she could see the resignation upon his face. If he gave up on himself, never would his wounds heal. A grain of despair filled her at the thought.

Connor moved closer until it became impossible to concentrate on the vegetables. She laid down the knife, wondering what he wanted.

Icy grey eyes bore into her. His newly bandaged hands rested on the surface of the table. 'I do have needs, Aileen. But not ones you can fulfil.'

The accusation in his deep voice was meant to intimidate her. Instead, the rich sound seduced her, making her notice every detail of his handsome face. His mouth tempted her, firm and yet soft. He wore his dark gold hair pulled back with a leather thong, but there were no war braids plaited at his temples. More Viking than Irish, she'd always thought. A small scar rested at the base of his chin, where beard stubble could not grow.

'If you do not ask for my help, I cannot know what your needs are,' she said gently. 'There is no shame in asking.'

He looked away and she saw the pride in his stance. He would not ask, she realised.

'Why would you try to convince a crippled child that he could be a soldier? Or tell a man with broken hands that one day he will fight again?'

'I have faith,' she argued. 'My healing herbs can do much to help others. And yet there are still miracles I cannot explain.'

Aileen lifted his damaged hands into her own palms. 'I have held a child born two moons too early in the palm of my hand. He should have died. Instead he grew up to be Lorcan, the boy who found you in the fields.'

Gently she touched the bandages, as if her skin's warmth could provoke healing. 'I have seen men live from battle wounds that should have killed them instantly. I believe in a greater power than my own.'

'Pagan gods?'

She read the doubt upon his face. 'Both the gods of our ancestors and the Christian God have given hope to many. I'll not grow into a bitter old woman by crushing the hopes of those I heal.'

'And what are your hopes, sensible Aileen? Wealth beyond your dreams? Marriage to a king?'

She braved a laugh. 'I am not that foolish.'

'What do you want, then?'

'I want to be a healer again,' she said. 'I want them to stop blaming me for what happened.'

'And what did happen? Why won't Seamus allow you to heal?'

Her own grief of loss smothered her. She lifted her eyes to his. 'Whelon is Seamus's son.'

'I thought he only had daughters.' Connor frowned. 'I suppose he was born after I left?'

She nodded. 'Whelon was one of his favourites. It has been two years since I removed his leg.' She expelled a hurt laugh. 'Seamus blames me for the poison.'

He moved to stand beside her. The remark gave her comfort for it meant he did not side with Seamus. 'Is that why he does not permit you to treat anyone else?'

She shook her head. 'It was not until three moons ago that he forbade me to touch another tribe member. His wife Riona bore him twin infant sons. But it was too soon for them to be born.' Aileen didn't try to hide the tears that slid down her cheeks. 'They died a few days later. Seamus believes it was my fault.'

Connor reached out, as if to take her hands in his. But he glanced down at his bandaged hands, realizing he couldn't. He lowered them.

'Is that the curse they speak of?'

She shrugged. 'I know not if I am cursed. Some days it feels as though I am.' She wiped her tears away, using the corner of her shawl. 'My father wants me to marry again. Perhaps the gossip about the curse will disappear if I do.'

'Whom would you wed?'

She shook her head. 'Few men would have me, save Riordan.'

'I don't see why that would be so. You've a pretty face and you'd make a man a good wife.'

Her face reddened at the mention of her face. 'Don't tease me. I know I am not comely.'

'Yes, you are,' he said. Drawing closer, she could smell the musky scent of forest and man. His eyes turned smoky. 'And aside from your cooking, any man would be lucky to bring you into his home.'

'My cooking?'

'Completely inedible. One would think that a woman with your herbal skills would know what to do with meat.'

'There is nothing wrong with my cooking!' She couldn't

believe he would insult her so. 'You were not well enough to eat anything, save pottage.'

'The mutton you cooked for my brothers was not bad, that I will grant you. But the fish soup was enough to make me want to crawl into a grave.'

She swatted him with the drying cloth. 'You are a wicked man, Connor MacEgan.'

'Prove yourself to me, then. Cook a sumptuous feast.'

Her lips curved. 'I might.'

Aileen noticed that Connor ate every morsel of the *craibechan*, though he teased her by pretending to choke. She had to feed him the mixture, but he'd refused the spoon.

'Why?' she demanded. 'Do you wish to eat like a barbarian?'

'I learned my lesson the last time,' he said softly. 'You burned my mouth when you fed me with a spoon. If you use your hands, then you can't burn me, can you?'

Her cheeks flushed. She'd been angry the last time, while they dined with his brothers. 'I won't burn you.'

'Use your hands,' he directed again.

'So be it. But I warn you, it will be messy.'

'You can bathe me afterwards.'

A flush of desire sparked at his words. She fed him a small bit of the meat and carrots. The touch of his lips against her fingertips sent a shiver through her.

The predatory shadow of a beard lined his cheeks, and his mouth was firm and sensual. She tried to eat as well, but her appetite had gone. With each morsel of food she gave him, her traitorous body reacted.

By the gods, this man tempted her. She wanted to lean

forward, to kiss him the way he'd claimed her mouth years ago. Never had she forgotten the way he'd made her feel, the way her body surrendered beneath his as he'd filled her.

When she fed him the last bite, she jumped to her feet, furious with her own lack of control. She cleaned up the dishes, and reached for her broom to sweep the hearth. Though the floor was already clean, she swept it to clear her mind free of him.

'Aileen?' The rough edge to his voice pulled her sensibilities into pieces. 'I would like that bath now.'

'Of course.' She hung the heavy cauldron above the fire and went outside to fetch water. The cool breeze eased her flaming cheeks while the sky held clouds of moisture. It would rain this night. She took deep breaths, calming the storm of anticipation. Connor did not want her. He stayed only for her healing skills. To think that he might desire her was naught but foolish longings better suited to a young maiden.

She carried two wooden buckets to the stream, wishing she could plunge into the icy water to calm her feelings, so long had it been since she'd lain with a man. Time had not lessened her desire for Connor. Now that he was here, it only grew stronger.

She made several trips to fill the cauldron, then stoked the flames to bring the water to a boil.

'What is that for?' Connor asked.

'You asked for a bath. I am heating the water, unless you would prefer it cold.'

'I like it warm.' His voice was low, dark with the same desire she felt.

'Very well.' She tried to behave as though it didn't matter.

'And you? Will you bathe as well?'

Her skin broke out in goose flesh, her legs weakening at the thought of him watching her bathe.

'I will. After you have finished.' She pulled out the small wooden tub, dragging it to the centre of the room. It was only large enough to sit in, with knees drawn up to the chest.

Connor pictured Aileen's naked body, rivulets of water spilling over her breasts. A strange awareness seized him. He hadn't thought of her in that way before, cloaked as she was in her *léine* and woolen *brat* about her shoulders. Now she unbound her dark curling hair, combing it before the fire. The flames crackled upon the hearth, warming her skin.

Suddenly a cold stream sounded far more welcome. She was acting nervous around him, and for some reason it pleased him. When she'd fed him the *craibechan*, he'd seen her blush. But Aileen was no virgin. She had known the pleasures of a husband, and desire roared through him at the thought of sharing her bed. He wanted her, wanted to touch the smooth porcelain skin and kiss the sadness from her face.

'Do you miss Eachan?' he asked suddenly.

She nodded. 'He loved me. I only wish I could have borne him a—' Her words broke off, and she looked stricken, as though she wanted to take back the words. 'I wish I could have borne him another child,' she managed. 'Rhiannon was our only daughter.'

Aileen's face turned crimson and she turned toward the cauldron. She dipped buckets of hot water, pouring them into the tub. Steam rose from the water, and she added a scattering of green herbs.

'Am I to be boiled and seasoned like a roasted fowl?' Connor teased.

'It is only mint and a few other herbs for healing. Do not bathe your hands,' she warned. 'After the bandages come off, you may wash them.'

When the tub was filled with water, Connor eyed it with suspicion. 'I cannot fit into such a small space.'

'You can if you kneel.'

Connor had his doubts, but he saw no alternative, save standing before her naked. A concern rose in his mind. 'Will others think less of you, if I stay here?'

Aileen shook her head, regarding him with a frank appraisal. 'They already think less of me as a healer. I cannot see how their opinion matters any more. And I am not a young maiden who has never seen an unclothed man.'

Her reminder shot another blade of desire into his groin. Eachan had lain with Aileen, touching the softness of her skin. He had cupped those heavy breasts within his hands, running his thumbs over the nipples. Connor shifted in his seat, uncomfortably aware that it had been many months since he'd last been with a woman.

Aileen allowed her *brat* to fall from her shoulders and lifted her earth-coloured overdress off. She wore only a thin cream-coloured *léine* that clung to her slender waist.

'Are you planning to join me in the water?' he asked lightly.

She smiled and shook her head. 'There would not be room for me, and well you know it.'

'You could sit upon my lap.' Though he meant the words as nothing but flirtation, his imagination conjured up a sexual vision of Aileen straddling him, her womanhood pressed against his rigid length.

'It is warm in here,' Aileen said. 'And I've no wish to get my overdress wet.' She came closer and began unlacing his tunic.

The soft touch of her hands moving across his chest inflamed his lust. The knowledge that he could not touch her with his injured hands made it worse. It was torment, having a woman's hands upon him and not being able to act upon his own desires.

'What of Riordan?' Connor asked, trying to dispel his need. He lifted his arms, realising that if Riordan knew of this arrangement he would be furious.

'Riordan holds no claim over my decisions. He is not my husband.' Aileen reached for his trews, but Connor stopped her.

'And what if he becomes your husband?'

She stopped. 'I am a healer, bathing a man who cannot do it himself. There is no shame in it.'

At the touch of her palms upon his hips, his erection grew even harder. Her fragrance of fresh herbs and femininity undid him. He suppressed a groan, stopping her from lowering his trews. 'If you wish, I can—'

'You can remove your own trews?' she asked mildly.

Though her words were not a taunt, it reminded him of the unwanted weakness. Aileen stripped him of his clothing, averting her gaze from his manhood.

Connor stepped into the bathing tub, kneeling down to hide himself from her. Though she behaved with the appropriate courtesy, her ministrations bothered him. He should have been able to enjoy the hot water, the hands scrubbing away the dirt.

And yet, her palms moved with sensuality over his skin,

with a startling familiarity. He had the oddest sensation that she'd touched him intimately before, though he knew it was impossible.

He was grateful that the tub hid the remainder of his body, for he could not shield his reaction to her.

A curl of her hair fell against his shoulder, a silken strand that teased him. He had the urge to thread his hands through her hair, pulling her down for a kiss.

And yet, he could not touch her. The Ó Banníons had wrought a fitting punishment upon him, unjust though it was. He could no longer caress a woman's skin.

'You may stand now,' Aileen said softly.

Connor remained motionless. Her fingertips rested upon his shoulders, drops of water sliding down his arms. She held the cloth against him, and the temptation of her touch made him want her more.

'I want to kiss you,' he said huskily. Her lips opened in a startled reaction. The invitation hung between them, but she did not move away.

Connor closed the distance. She tasted of strawberries, a tart sweetness that tantalised him. She held herself so very still, not turning him away, but not kissing him back either. There was a soft innocence about her, and yet she had been another man's wife.

Connor tried to coax her mouth to open, to let him slide his tongue within, but she pulled back. Her shoulders rose, her breathing unsteady. She desired him, too. Her mouth beckoned for another kiss, while his body wanted far more.

'I thought you—you said—' Though her face blushed fiercely, she stammered, "You did not want me.'

Connor halted her with a dark gaze. 'I want you far more

than is good for either of us.' With that, he stood, letting her
see the full length of his arousal.

Aileen stepped back, averting her shocked gaze. 'You are
right. It would not be good for us.'

He expected her to flee, to chastise him for kissing her.
She did not. Instead, she said nothing of his erection but drew
the soapy cloth over his thighs, down his legs. His lungs compressed, his body craving the feel of her naked skin against
his own.

'I mean no offence,' he said by way of apology. 'It has
been a long time since…' He didn't know quite what to say,
hoping he could ease the disquiet. 'I suppose it would have
happened with any woman.'

Aileen frowned, and he thought he detected annoyance
in her expression. 'Perhaps.'

She poured a bucket of warm water over him to rinse, and
wrapped a drying cloth around him. Connor accepted her
assistance while stepping out of the tub.

She rubbed him dry with brisk motions, nothing at all
untoward by them. In time, his aching subsided and she
brought him a clean tunic and trews.

'These belonged to Eachan. They may not fit, but you
may wear them while I tend to your clothes.'

He accepted them, and, true to her word, the tunic pulled
tight against his chest. 'My thanks to you.'

She seemed ill at ease, and he knew he had to say something to reassure her.

'Know that I would never force my attentions upon you,
if they are unwanted,' he said.

'I know it.' In the dim light of the hut, her complexion

appeared paler than usual. He wished he had not acted on impulse.

'But you should not do that again.' She mustered her courage and looked into his eyes. 'It is better if I am only a healer to you.'

A fleeting pain eclipsed her face. He wanted to reach out to her, to discover the mysteries she hid behind a mask of shyness. But he respected her desire not to lie with him.

'I will return to the sick hut for the night,' he said. He struggled to open the door with his bandaged hands, moving outside. For a long time he stood in the moonlight, the night air cooling his desire.

But as he closed his eyes, he heard the water lap against the tub when she entered it. His imagination conjured up carnal images of a woman's body, supple skin and lush curves. Inwardly he cursed as he returned to his own pallet.

He did not sleep well that night, his thoughts dwelling upon her.

Chapter 7

'Póla Ó Duinne, you simply *must* tell me what has happened to Aileen.' Riona Ó Duinne's hands fairly flew across the weaving loom, while the other women brightened with interest. 'My husband Seamus is furious about what she did to Connor. I cannot believe she would try to treat his wounds.'

'She saved his life,' Póla pointed out. She bristled at the criticism of her daughter and jerked the *feith-géir* across the threads. 'Just as she saved Whelon's.'

Riona's face hardened. 'It would be better for Aileen to find a husband.'

'And so she will. My Graeme intends for her to wed Connor,' Póla claimed. 'He thinks to be a matchmaker, he does.'

'Connor and Aileen?' Riona scoffed. 'She's reaching above herself if the thinks to wed a warrior like him. He'd not have her.'

'I would have him myself, Mother,' Grania giggled. 'A more handsome man I've never seen.'

Riona shook her head and smiled. 'You'd do well to remain chaste for your future husband, Grania. But if you speak to your father, he might consent. The MacEgans would make a powerful alliance, after all.'

Outside the cottage, Riordan overheard their laughter. He had come to speak with Póla, but their gossip about Connor had caught his attention. Riordan's skin crawled at the thought of Connor touching Aileen. Fury such as he'd never known poured through him.

Aileen was his. Hadn't he been there when Eachan died, consoling her? Hadn't he helped keep her land tended, helping her plant the corn for this next season? She had been grateful to him.

Riordan abandoned his intention to speak with Póla. He had wanted advice on how to pursue his courtship further. Now he saw that they had greater ambitions for their daughter. Connor MacEgan belonged to the *flaiths*, the noblemen who reigned as chieftains. To wed a man such as Connor would raise Aileen's stature even more than her own rank as a healer.

But he loved Aileen. She had ever been in his thoughts, even while she belonged to Eachan. His own wife had died in childbirth, but he knew how to bide his time. One day Aileen would welcome him into her bed, into her heart. She would ripen with his seed and bear him a child.

As he crossed the meadows, a soft rain fell upon him, dampening his tunic. Riordan smiled, allowing the rain to soak through. Aileen would invite him into her home to warm himself before the fire. He could say that he'd come by to inspect her animals, particularly the new lambs born that spring.

And when he came to her, he'd not allow Connor MacEgan to usurp his place. Póla Ó Duinne was wrong. Aileen cared for him, and in time her friendship would turn into love. He would make sure of it.

Aileen raised her shawl to cover her hair as the rain intensified. She led one of the sheep with her, for it had escaped the pen. In her other hand she carried a wooden mallet to repair the broken fence.

The walk back to her land was slow, for the sheep kept stopping to graze along the way. Aileen did not mind, for it gave her the chance to dwell upon her thoughts. She ran her hand across the rough wool of the animal, nudging the ewe forward.

It was less than a sennight until she could remove Connor's bandages. Though he could not perceive the magnitude of the healing, she was well pleased with the outcome. He would regain use of his hands, though perhaps not enough to fight again. Pride filled her at the thought.

She had an old pig's bladder she could fill with water. By squeezing it, he could flex his stiff fingers. In time, he would be able to care for himself once more.

Her skin warmed at the memory of last night. She had never seen Connor fully unclothed before, even on the night of Bealtaine. His body could have been one of the legendary statues of a god, carved of smooth marble. Though she had not touched him in a wanton manner, her mind had envisioned another sort of night, one where he claimed her body with his.

The sheep lowered its head to nibble a patch of grass, and Aileen rested her hands upon the creature. She didn't realise how much she had missed lying in a man's arms. Although her husband Eachan had pleased her in the privacy of their bed, he had never quite diminished the memory of Connor.

She hadn't forgotten Connor's arousal nor his embarrassed remark that it would have happened with any woman. He was right, of course. She was glad she had not succumbed to her desires. A man such as Connor knew not how to be with one woman. Hadn't he flirted with Grania and the others?

Aileen nudged the sheep again, pulling upon the rope halter. In the distance, she saw a figure moving toward her. The rain had slowed, enough for her to recognise Riordan. She lifted her hand in greeting.

'Good morn to you,' Riordan spoke, taking her hand and squeezing it lightly. Aileen returned the gesture of friendship, forcing herself to truly look upon Riordan. For so many weeks he had come to visit with her, helping her when she needed him. He was the sort of man who would make a good husband, not Connor.

Aileen forced a smile on to her face. 'What brings you here, Riordan?' It was apparent from the direction of his path that he'd come with the intention of seeing her. The sheep lowered her head again to eat.

'I came to look upon your new lambs and to see if you needed aught.'

'I am well, thank you.' Aileen gestured toward the sheep. 'This one thought to leave her pen and go off to seek her fortune. I'm going to mend the fence.'

'I'll help you, if you like.'

She shrugged, offering a smile. He meant well. 'Yes, I would like that.'

Once the sheep was safely back inside the pen, Aileen

held the wood in place while Riordan hammered the peg to close the gap in the fence. They worked in silence, but she sensed he wanted to tell her something. When they had finished, at last he revealed his concern. 'You are alone with MacEgan now with no one to protect you.'

'Protect me?' She couldn't understand why he would be afraid. 'There is no need to fear for my safety. Connor has never threatened me in any way. His bandages come off in a few days and soon after that, he will return home.'

'I'm glad to hear it. I do not like the thought of you being alone with a warrior of MacEgan's reputation.'

Aileen shook her head at Riordan's unfounded worry. 'His hands have not yet healed. There is nothing to concern you, or anyone else. He has not touched me.' But her face burned at the thought of giving Connor his bath.

'And do you wish for his touch?' he asked with a sudden intensity. He took her hand again, this time with a possessive grip.

His motion startled her. 'No, of course not. He is no different than any other wounded man.' Even as she spoke the lie, Riordan's hand tightened upon her. A coldness filled her at his jealousy. For the first time, she grew frightened of him.

'I like it not, Aileen.'

'You are hurting my hand,' she said. He released her immediately. Aileen rubbed her fingers, her thoughts troubled. Never had she seen Riordan behave in this way. He had always been gentle and a friend to her.

With reddened cheeks he lowered his head. 'Forgive me. It is only that I care for you.'

She tried to be flattered by his jealousy. 'I know it.'

'I have kept my distance out of respect for Eachan,'

Riordan said. He softened his voice, pleading with her. 'But you must know that I want nothing but your happiness, Aileen. Fate has granted me a second chance at winning your heart. I'll not let it pass.'

He reached out to cup her cheek. She knew he planned to kiss her, and she forced herself to endure the touch of his lips upon hers. He was a good man, a man she might wed one day.

Or perhaps at the *aenach*, if her father got his way. Whom else would she wed? No other man would consider her as a bride.

In his eyes, a hunger lay waiting. Aileen tried to allay her apprehensions, but his touch did not evoke a single response. Not the way Connor had.

She shivered, thinking of her hands passing across Connor's rigid shoulders, the hardened male skin that made her ache for him.

Riordan misinterpreted her shiver and deepened the kiss. Aileen kept her mouth closed when he tried to bring his tongue inside.

It did not matter. She had not held any feelings for Eachan when they'd wed, but in time she had felt affection toward him. It would be the same with Riordan.

She tried to kiss him back, but her mouth froze. It felt wrong somehow.

Riordan drew back, his eyes hooded with anticipation. She recognised his ardour and her own lacklustre response.

'You must know how you tempt me,' he said, his hands trailing down her spine.

'I buried my husband two moons ago.'

'But he was sick before that. How long was he abed?'

'A full season,' she admitted. The sickness that had

claimed her husband's life was not one she could heal. She had seen the wasting disease before, an illness that no prayer or medicine could fight. Eachan had known it, too.

'Let me woo your heart, Aileen,' Riordan insisted. 'I'll not ask you to give any more than you are able.' He drew her palm to his lips.

The gesture was one Eachan had made toward her, many a time. She had been a foolish girl long ago, dreaming of Connor's embrace. She had denied her heart then, accepting Eachan's suit. It had been a good marriage, though she had not given birth to any more children.

But she wanted another child, wanted to fill her home with them. Riordan could grant her that, if she would allow it. Surely in time, he could cause her heart to tremble in the same way Connor did?

Connor would leave, and, unless she could prove her worth as a healer, she'd have no choice but to marry. It might as well be a man who loved her. 'Have patience with me,' she whispered, 'and eventually you may have what you seek.'

The joy upon Riordan's face evoked such a terrible guilt. He believed she cared for him in the same way, that it was only grief that made her hesitant.

Aileen allowed his arms to enfold her, though her hands remained at her sides. She closed her eyes, willing herself to close off the memories Connor had rekindled.

The chieftain of the tribe, Seamus Ó Duinne, embraced Connor warmly. 'You're looking better, lad.'

He had journeyed to his foster-father's ring fort after Seamus had sent word to him. It had been almost seven years since he'd been here, and the dwelling looked much the same. His foster-mother had hung woven tapestries upon the whitewashed walls, and in the corner an elabourately carved bride's chest stood.

Connor followed Seamus into a private chamber, where he gestured for him to sit down. 'Riona is out visiting today. She'll be most disappointed that she missed you.'

Connor smiled at the mention of his foster-mother. Riona would cluck and fuss over him like a hen.

'Thank you for answering my summons. We have much to discuss.' Seamus sent him a thoughtful look. 'In a few days, this season's *aenach* will begin. I intend to bring your case before the *brehons* to seek their judgment. The Ó Banníons must answer for your injuries.'

A servant poured a cup of wine into a silver chalice. The Brehon courts were held at every public gathering, and the occasion of the *aenach* was no exception. The local fair, although it provided a means of celebrating and feasting, was also a time for more serious matters of justice to be debated.

'I've no wish to bring the case before the courts,' he argued. 'Brehon laws will enact a fine, nothing more.'

'It is the way of our people.'

'But it is not enough. Not for what happened to me.'

A pretty maid sat down beside him and lifted the cup to his lips. Connor drank the spiced wine, the rich flavour a welcome change from the mead he was accustomed to.

'What is it you want?'

'Vengeance. An eye for an eye.'

Seamus shook his head, his displeasure evident. 'The *aenach* is the place to discuss judgements. Do not let your anger sway you from the right path. If the Ó Banníons did this to you, then the case is a simple one.'

'Not so simple,' Connor said. His skin tightened with frustration. 'Flynn Ó Banníon will claim that I lay with his daughter Deirdre. Without her consent.'

'And did you?'

Connor leaned forward, letting Seamus see the darkness of his resentment. 'You know the answer to that already.'

Seamus nodded, steepling his hands. 'If what you say is true, the Ó Banníons will claim that you owe his daughter the *corp-díre* for stealing her virtue.'

'But he owes me the same for bringing harm to my hands. The fines will nullify each other.'

'Can her lie be proven?'

'It is her word against mine.'

'Hmm.' Seamus took a deep sip of his wine. 'Your reputation among the women does not help the matter. Too many could understand how Deirdre was seduced.'

'I never laid hands upon her.'

'As you say. But it will be difficult to prove. A full body price will be demanded.'

'I do not want *corp-díre*,' Connor said, lowering his voice. 'I want the Ó Banníon's death.'

Seamus's face grew sharp. 'You speak foolishness.' He signalled for the maid to leave their presence. When they were alone, he added, 'This is a matter for the courts to decide.'

'A throng of arguing lawyers will not bring back my hands.'

'And murder will?' Seamus questioned.

'It will make me feel better.'

His foster-father shook his head. 'Always a dark temper

you had, Connor. But the blood of the Ó Banníons would bring nothing but war.' He stood and led Connor outside.

'How are your hands? Will you be able to fight again?'

'We do not know. But I have seen the wounds—' His voice broke off. His twisted fingers could never grip a sword. Flynn Ó Banníon had destroyed him, as surely as if he had taken his life.

'I will ask the monks to say prayers on your behalf.' Seamus said. 'And my offer to you stands, should you wish to dwell with us.'

'I prefer the isolation of Aileen's hut.'

Seamus frowned, but did not voice an opinion. He walked alongside him to the door. 'What will you do if Flynn Ó Banníon comes to the *aenach*?'

'The *brehons* can pass whatever judgement they wish in the courts.' A dark smile tilted at his mouth. 'My own form of justice shall come later.'

'Are you ready?' Aileen asked. The days had passed, and it was now time to remove Connor's bandages.

He held his hands out to her, and Aileen unwound the bandages slowly. Upon his face, she read the doubts. One by one, she eased the splints free. At last, she revealed his hands.

Although the skin still held a waxen grey colour, the fingers of his left hand were aligned. She bent each knuckle to check the movement. 'Does it hurt?' she asked.

'They are stiff.'

She curved his hand into a fist, brightening when she saw that the fingers lay parallel to one another, just as they should.

The right hand looked far worse. The fingers were not of the correct length, and she knew it was due to the massive crushing of the fingers.

Connor attempted to flex his wrists. The left hand moved freely, while the right wrist moved only a little. 'It will improve in time,' she reassured him.

Beneath his expression she saw a grim fury. 'How long?'

She shook her head. 'That, I cannot know. It depends on many things.'

He moved his fingers, struggling to push them back into their former flexibility. The right hand had little motion, and his frustration worsened.

'I cannot fight like this.' He reached for a wooden cup, his fingers refusing to curl around the vessel. 'I'd not be able to hold a sword, much less wield it.'

'As I've told you, it will take time.'

'I do not have time, Aileen. Nearly two moons of my life I've wasted while Flynn Ó Banníon grows fat and content.'

'You cannot think to fight him.'

'I intend to sink my sword into his heart for what he has done.'

'And when you do, you believe you will win? You haven't the strength for such a fight.'

'Then that is your fault.'

'Mine?' She could not believe he dared to accuse her. 'I was not the one to harm you. I saved your hands.'

'If you had more experience as a healer, perhaps I'd be able to hold a sword again.'

'More experience?' His arrogance infuriated her. Kyna had trained her in healing since she was a young girl. She remained confident in her skills, no matter what the villagers claimed. And this warrior dared question her? 'Any other healer would have cut your hands off. You would have bled to death.'

'I'd have been better off dead than to live like this.' He strode outside, shoving the door open. The wood crashed behind him, rocking against the door frame.

Aileen's anger made her tremble. She picked up the wooden drinking cup and hurled it at the wall. The satisfying thunk made her wish she could have struck his head. Connor had no idea how badly he'd been wounded.

Her wrath increased as she picked up the bandages and splints, casting them into the fire. As the flames took hold and burned, she tore a length of cloth into strips for bandages. The act of destruction gave her a means to release her anger.

Connor was an impatient man. He could not understand what he'd been given. All he could see was his loss.

The twisted fingers of his right hand would for ever remind him of his deformity. He could not see past it. His vanity would not allow it.

Tears stung her eyes. Somehow, she had believed there was more to Connor MacEgan than a handsome warrior. It seemed she was wrong.

Chapter 8

Connor returned to the forest grove, the afternoon sun warm upon his face. He reached down and lifted a thick fallen branch with his left hand. With effort, he managed to hold it, though his wrist ached. He rotated his wrist in slow motions, gritting his teeth against the pain.

Lunging forward, he tried to use the makeshift sword. A surge of aching fire ripped through the unused muscles, but he forced himself to continue.

He had tried to bring Trahern's sword, but he lacked the strength to drag it from the sick hut. Rather than damage the blade, he had left it behind. He would spend the first few days rebuilding his unsteady grip.

Though the branch felt awkward in his left hand, at least he could grasp it. When he tried to transfer the limb to his right palm, the branch clattered to the ground.

Frustration and doubts undermined his confidence. At last, he sat down against the base of an oak, his hands raw with the effort of fighting. He wiped the sweat from his brow, noticing the trickle of blood from his palms. Aileen would have to treat the blisters.

The thought of her sobered him. He hadn't meant to voice his opinion aloud. She did possess great skills as a healer, but it wasn't enough for him.

He'd wanted a miracle. When God had not granted him that boon, he had lashed out at the one person who had tried to help him. He regretted his words, but they were true. He did question her skills, her experience. If she were older, would he have more strength in his hands?

A soft crackle and thump drew his attention. He reached for the branch, but relaxed when he saw it was the boy he'd met earlier. Whelon, he remembered.

'What do you want?' Connor asked.

The boy used a pair of crutches to move forward, the motion rustling the leaves. He studied Connor and his gaze fell upon the stout limb. 'What happened to your sword?'

Connor did not wish to admit his inability to bring Trahern's blade from the hut. Instead, he told a version of the truth. 'It was stolen from me. By the same men who crushed my hands.'

'Normans?'

'The Ó Banníons,' Connor corrected.

Whelon extended his hand. 'May I hold it?'

With his left hand, Connor raised the limb to the boy. It was the same height as the lad and as thick as his wrist. Whelon extended it, the ghost of a smile upon his face. 'This is how you train?'

The boy's intense longing humbled him. Why would the child dream of a warrior's training when he lacked a leg to stand upon?

'It is part of it.'

'Teach me.' Whelon offered the staff back to Connor.

He faltered, not wanting to offend the boy. 'I do not think I can. Your leg—'

'I have one good leg.'

'You do. But a swordsman must have good balance and footwork to succeed in battle. I fear that—'

'You are afraid I will die, if I try to learn the ways of the sword,' Whelon guessed. 'You needn't fear. I can learn balance.'

'There is also endurance and speed.' Connor refused to cloak the truth. If the boy wanted training, he had to confront the reality of his skills.

'Endurance I have,' Whelon argued. 'I travelled this far to meet you.'

'How did you know I was here?'

'I saw you coming from Aileen's cottage. And I watched you train once.'

Connor didn't like the idea of being watched, much less by a lad with false notions of his abilities. He shook his head. 'I cannot train you.'

Whelon looked as though he wanted to argue, but he held his tongue. A pitying expression crossed his face. 'I thought you might understand. I suppose I was wrong.'

The boy did not look back, but used his crutches to hobble out of the forest. At the edge of the horizon, the sun rimmed the meadow with crimson and gold. Connor rose, stepping over the fallen branch. Whether a man lacked a leg or the full use of his hands, the outcome was the same. He had no right to be a warrior.

But with a phrase, he had killed the boy's hopes. Did that

make him any better than the Ó Banníons? Guilt balled inside him, and he wished he'd held his tongue. Whelon was a child, not a man. It wasn't right to deny the boy a chance to try.

'Whelon!' he called out sharply, running to the edge of the woods. At the base of the hill, the boy turned his head.

'At dawn tomorrow. Meet me here.'

The blinding joy upon the boy's face startled him. For a moment he understood why Aileen wanted to grant hope to the child.

He sighed. They would make a pair, the two of them. A boy without a leg, and a man without hands.

Hope was a rare thing, lost by so many. Though he might be making the gravest of mistakes by allowing the boy to dream, a warmth encircled his heart.

Aileen stepped forward into the circle of small huts, her nerves taut. She wanted to see her cousin Bridget, whose baby would come at any time now. Bridget had not asked to see her, but Aileen hoped she would not refuse.

Frasier Ó Duinne's hammer rang upon the anvil, smoke rising from the hearth as he shaped horseshoes. He stared at Aileen but did not greet her. The tension wound tighter within her stomach.

Inside, Bridget sat beside the fire, talking to an older woman with dark hair. With her swollen belly, Aileen could tell it would not be long now. She judged the size of the child, noting that Bridget had lost the smooth roundness of mid-pregnancy. Her stomach bulged with protruding knees and elbows.

'Hello, Bridget,' she greeted her cousin. Both women stopped speaking and regarded her.

'Have you met Illona, our new healer?' Bridget asked.

Bitterness choked her, but Aileen managed to accept the Ó Bannion woman's embrace and kiss of greeting upon her cheek. Illona seemed to be the age of her mother, with fine lines edging her eyes.

'I understand you were once the healer at Banslieve,' Illona said. The direct question held no trace of cruelty, but it touched a raw nerve. Aileen wanted to cry out, *I am still their healer*. Instead she nodded.

'How are you feeling?' Aileen asked, forcing her attention back to her cousin.

'The babe will come very soon,' Illona said. 'No doubt within a few days.'

'My cousin can speak for herself,' Aileen said.

Bridget looked uncomfortable. 'I am tired. I have not slept well these past few nights.'

'May I see?'

Bridget hesitated, her glance flickering toward Illona. The woman nodded, and a ball of frustration took root within Aileen. Why would her cousin seek permission from a stranger?

But she bit her tongue, forcing back her anger.

The baby's head was correctly positioned downward, and Aileen held her hands upon Bridget's stomach. In time, a flicker of movement confirmed that all was well.

'Does the babe move within you often?'

Bridget shook her head. 'It has grown quiet these past few days. It moves when I lie down at night, but rarely during the daytime.'

The stillness often foretold an impending birth. Many a time, Aileen had to reassure a terrified mother who was pregnant for the first time that such was to be expected. There was little room left in the womb.

But Bridget had borne three children already and her eyes held the serenity that all would come to pass as it should. Her labour would be swift, Aileen knew. The other babes had come within hours, and this child would be no different.

'If you would like to assist in the birth, I shall send for you,' Illona offered. 'Another pair of hands is always welcome.'

'Perhaps.' She clenched her hands to keep her temper in check. The woman had simply stepped into her place, and now she expected Aileen to assist her, following her bidding?

Aware of the tension between the two women, Bridget interjected, 'Will you attend the *aenach*, Aileen?'

'*Rachaidh mé*. I shall participate in the women's council.' Though as a council member, she could listen to grievances and suggest resolutions, it wasn't enough for her. She wanted to be there as a healer, to meet with the other women and discuss treatments. To have that taken from her was akin to losing the best part of herself.

'You will see your daughter Rhiannon there, of course,' Bridget added. 'That must make you happy.'

Aileen had forgotten. Of course Lianna would bring Rhiannon. All members of the Ó Duinne tribe attended the *aenach*, without exception. The feasting, merchants and games encouraged everyone to attend.

'Yes, of course,' she murmured. Inwardly, panic rose up inside her. Would Connor recognise Rhiannon as his own child? Should she say anything to Lianna? Or was it best to keep Rhiannon away from the *aenach*?

Her mind blundered through the mess of the coming days. Why hadn't she thought of it sooner? She dreaded having to explain her deed to Connor if he guessed. And surely he would, for Rhiannon had her father's eyes and face.

Her fears coiled like a viper, striking at her heart. She could not avoid Rhiannon at the *aenach*, nor did she want to. Though it might bring her stolen moment into Connor's awareness, there was naught she could do about it.

His cruel words from this morning came back to haunt her. Like Seamus, he blamed her for his loss. If he found out what had happened on the night of Bealtaine, he would be furious. Though she did not care if he lashed out at her, she had to protect Rhiannon.

As Rhiannon's true father, he had rights under the law. He could demand that Rhiannon be sent to his family for fosterage until she reached the age of fourteen. After that, he could arrange her marriage to anyone. Rhiannon's entire future would lie in his hands, and Aileen could do nothing about it. She refused to stand back and let him make decisions without her counsel.

If he found out, she doubted not that he would be furious. The question was, did she have the courage to tell him before he learned the truth himself?

It was growing late, and she said farewell to Bridget. She could not bring herself to say anything to Illona. As she journeyed home, the anxiety of seeing Connor deepened.

Though she tried to prepare herself, her stomach burned at the awkwardness of sharing a meal with him. Again, she wondered whether or not to tell him about Rhiannon.

Her face grew hot at the thought of admitting she'd

switched places with Lianna. Would his face transform in disgust? Would he hate her for deceiving him?

She thought of the way he'd kissed her the other night, kindling feelings she'd thought were long gone. He was no longer the inexperienced boy whom she had loved, but had become a dangerous warrior. If she allowed him to make love with her, the old feelings of longing might return.

She should know better than to trust her heart to Connor MacEgan. Though he tempted her, he would leave soon. And when he left, she didn't want her family life ripped asunder.

Aileen lingered on the journey home, the sun waning into dark purple clouds. In the sky the mist of an approaching rain swelled and evoked the bountiful scent of earth. When at last she reached her land, wisps of smoke rose from the chimney of her small hut.

Inside, Connor sat upon the floor, his long legs sprawled before him. His hair was damp, as though he'd come from swimming in the stream. A bead of moisture rolled down the side of his face, evoking the memory of the night she'd bathed him. She closed her eyes, willing the sensual image away.

In his hands, Connor held the pig's bladder. He squeezed it, focusing all of his attention upon the exercise. His face tightened as he tried to bend his fingers. She should make a healing brew to ease his pain, perhaps with honey to sweeten the bitter taste.

But then, why should she make anything for him, when he had spoken so harshly to her this morn? He deserved nothing from her.

She thought suddenly of the new healer Illona, and it hurt

to think of her replacement. No matter what the villagers believed, in her heart she would always remain a healer. And this, she decided, was why she would make the drink for Connor. Because it was the right thing to do, to take away another man's suffering when she held the means.

Aileen removed her *brat* and set it aside. Connor stood when she drew near, in a silent gesture of respect. It did not make her feel better; instead, it heightened her anxiety about what she would say to him.

'*Dia dhúit*,' she greeted.

Connor returned the greeting and reached to take her hand. His left hand held hers in a light grip. He was trying to conceal the effort it took for such a small movement. Even still, her trained eyes noted the tension in the muscles of his forearm. Then she saw blisters upon his reddened palm. What had he done to himself?

'I said words this morn that were unkind. I would ask your forgiveness for them.'

Regret lined his tone, but it was the slight caress of his thumb against her palm that dissolved her anger. His grey eyes offered an apology, and her focus turned to his mouth.

The shocking memory of his heated kiss slid under her skin. When he released her hand, she could still feel the warmth of his palm, and God help her, she wanted more.

'Am I forgiven?' He shot her a sensual smile that would send most maidens into a swoon. In response, Aileen straightened. By Danu, she had more sense than that.

'I don't know. I have not decided yet,' she answered.

'I thought that might happen. It is why I've brought you a gift.' Connor crossed to the far end of the hut. He lifted a package wrapped in cloth and extended it toward her.

Aileen did not know what to say. Though his apology was sincere, behind the words lay the unspoken truth. He did question her skills, believing she had not the experience of Kyna. He could not see the presence of any motion at all as a miracle, only a loss.

Aileen forced herself to swallow her pride. There had to be peace between them before she could reveal her own secret. 'You did not need to bring me a gift. I accept your apology.'

'Open it.'

When she unfolded the linen, inside lay a length of dark green ribbon. Made of silk, it was the sort of gift a lover might give to a woman.

Such an irony, for they had been lovers, and he knew it not.

'My thanks to you,' she managed.

'Your mother Póla suggested it when I spoke with her earlier. She thought it might be a fitting gift.' Connor's mouth tilted up in a chagrined smile. 'Though my own mother preferred golden jewellery. Had I the means, I would have given you that instead.'

'This is lovely.' Aileen tucked the ribbon away and hid her embarrassed gaze from him. Connor managed to make her behave like a flittering girl. His commanding presence had not diminished even a little, despite his wounded hands. He leaned up against the wall, and she noticed the way his tunic stretched across his broad chest. Not an ounce of fat clung to his deeply chiselled muscles.

She wanted to run her hands across that chest, to taste his kiss once more. She wanted his bare skin against hers.

Aileen shook the pleasurable thoughts away, trying to pull herself back together.

'I brought fish,' Connor said, pointing to a string of trout hanging near the door. 'I tried to clean them. Unfortunately, I made a mess of it, so I stopped.' He lifted his hands in chagrined surrender.

'How did you catch them?'

'Though I would like to say it was my own doing, young Whelon and his friend Lorcan brought them to me this afternoon. They gave me the fish in return for my promise to train both of them tomorrow at dawn.'

'You?' Had he claimed his intentions to walk upon water, she could not have been more surprised. 'How could you train the boys?'

While they spoke, she gutted the fish and scaled them. Using salt and freshly crushed herbs, she rubbed the seasonings into the fillets.

'I may not be able to demonstrate the skills, but I am capable of training men.'

'They are boys, not men. Children who will grow up to tend the crops and harvest them, not slaughter one another.' Aileen spitted the fish, hanging them to roast over the fire.

'There is no harm in it. And it is all I can offer them.' His defensive tone forced her to hold her tongue.

When the fish had finished cooking, Aileen set the fillets upon a platter along with a thick slab of bread and crisp spring peas. They ate seated at the low table, their knees a careful distance from one another.

'Do you require my help to eat?' she asked.

'No.'

Aileen offered him an eating knife, which he accepted. Connor struggled to slice a portion of the fillet, his left hand sawing at the fish.

Uncomfortable silence expanded to fill the space.

'Will you attend the *aenach* tomorrow?' Connor asked at last.

'Of course. Everyone does.'

'I suppose there is always a need for a healer when the games take place.' He grimaced. 'Especially with the men trying to kill one another for the sake of a maiden.'

'I am not allowed to heal any more,' she said softly. Without intending it, unwanted tears sprang to her eyes. 'I am sorry, but it infuriates me. This is who I am. I cannot stop being a healer, any more than—'

'Any more than I can stop being a warrior?'

The soft query made her stop. For the first time she understood his loss. Silently she took his hands in hers, tracing the twisted bones, the angry reddened skin.

'I swear to you, I did everything in my power to heal your hands.' She lowered her head, wishing he could somehow see the truth. 'I hope it was enough.'

'So do I.' He reached out and gently dried her tears. Though he seemed self-conscious of his misshapen hands, she did not care. She covered his hands with her own. Lightly stroking his skin, she saw his expression transform. He appeared predatory, a warrior bent upon conquering.

Then he hesitated, as if gathering his own control. 'Perhaps on the morrow you will find a new husband to care for. There are many competitions for the men.'

She released him and stood, understanding that he did not intend to kiss her. It must have been her imagination, thinking that he might want her. She shielded her embarrassment.

'The men try to prove their strength,' she admitted. 'Such idiocy.'

'Is that how Eachan won your heart? By showing his skills in a competition?'

She paled at the mention, for he could have been no further from the truth. Instead, she brushed off his insinuation, saying only, 'No. He was the only man who asked me to wed.'

'I have my doubts of that. I've seen the way Riordan looks at you.'

'He had already wed someone else.'

'Then that was his loss.' His words were sincere, making her all the more uncomfortable. Before she could speak, Connor rose and approached behind her. 'There will be sword fighting tomorrow in the contests.'

'Not for you,' she warned. Though she did not believe Connor was foolish enough to attempt it, many men would seek to challenge him. Some would welcome the chance to see him humiliated in a mock fight. Riordan, she realised, could be one.

'I have a different battle to face,' he said, but did not elabourate.

As have I, she thought. Connor stepped toward her, his arm reaching around her waist. In the soft glow of the lamp, he appeared like Belenus himself, the sun god. Ash-grey eyes seared hers with unspoken desire.

The feel of his arm around her waist, his face only a heartbeat away from hers, made her skin prickle. The pine scent of him filled her senses. His firm mouth bent down, hovering above hers. She could feel his breath against her lips.

'Would you pull away if I kissed you again?'

She held deathly still, afraid of his kiss and yet more afraid of his power over her. Should she steal this moment with him and seize the pleasure she wanted?

'Why would you want to kiss me?' she asked.

'You are a beautiful woman.' He brushed a featherlight kiss against her mouth, enough to tempt her. Her clothes felt heavy against her skin, her breasts tightening with need. Inside the intimacy of the hut, the air seemed charged with heat. Against her stomach, she felt his desire and the answering response of her damp womanhood.

She closed her eyes, wishing she had the strength to push him away. Or at the very least, ask him to return to the sick hut.

'We shouldn't,' she whispered, tasting his mouth even as she spoke the words of protest.

'No, we shouldn't.' And he took her lips, kissing her deeply. The heady touch of his tongue against hers, along with the heat of his mouth, invoked every memory, every stolen moment from Bealtaine. She wanted him even more now, this man whom she had once loved.

Trembling, she broke off the kiss. His strong muscular body pressed against hers, his heavy thighs supporting her shaky legs. If she spoke the word, he would make love to her.

And what if this night resulted in another child? Would she lie about that, too?

Guilt and cowardice warred inside her, as his lips roamed the column of her throat.

Tell him. Her heart urged. He had offered forgiveness for what he'd said and given his friendship freely. Surely he would not harm his own daughter, though he might be angry. If she ever intended to tell him, now was her moment.

She took a step backwards, praying with every fibre that he would not condemn her.

'Connor, do you remember the last year of your fosterage? The night of Bealtaine when you—'

'I remember.' Anger creased his face. 'It is not a night I wish to speak of.'

His words cut her down as surely as any sword. She picked up the broken pieces of her courage and forced herself to finish. 'There is something I must tell you about it. About Lianna and…and the night you honoured the gods.'

She steadied her breathing, grateful for the dim interior of her hut. He could not see the humiliation, the fear within her.

Despite it all, she held no regrets. Though it had been wrong to hide the truth from him, she now had a beautiful daughter. Her only child had been conceived that night.

'When you lay with Lianna—'

'Do not speak to me of that night.' He leaned forward, revealing an icy rage she had not known he possessed. It was as if he knew already what she was about to say. His grey eyes turned to frost, the cool demeanour of a mercenary. 'I have tried for many years to forget each moment of it. It was naught but a mistake.'

Her nails dug deeply into her palms as his words struck an invisible blow. She had loved him that night, believed their lovemaking to be a fitting offering to the gods. Even as the fields ripened with a rich harvest, so too had her body.

As she went through the motions of cleaning up after the meal, Aileen held back the tears. Had she been such a poor lover on that night when she'd welcomed him into her arms? It had awakened her to the wonder of love. But for him, it had not been the same.

Though she had told him nothing, Connor had made one thing very clear. He would not welcome the knowledge of his daughter, nor would he dismiss Bealtaine as one festival among many.

She would not speak of it again, nor admit what she had done. If he accused her about Rhiannon, she would deny it, as would Lianna. No matter what happened at the *aenach*, she had to protect her daughter.

Chapter 9

Whelon stumbled as the two boys sparred with makeshift swords. Lorcan struck hard against the wooden branch, showing his friend no mercy.

Connor corrected Whelon's stance. 'Keep your eyes on Lorcan. Never look down, for that will be the last time you lay eyes upon an enemy. You'll find his sword in your belly.'

Whelon wore a wooden staff attached to the stump on his right leg. Though it was serviceable, Connor questioned the wisdom of sharing his knowledge with the child. Whelon had not the ability to join in a battle. His dream of becoming a fighter could never come true.

And yet, Connor found satisfaction in teaching the boy. He saw the fierce pride upon Whelon's face, the need to prove his skills. It was like watching himself as a child.

With both hands, Whelon spun and struck Lorcan's branch from the side. The blow caught Lorcan unawares, and he sprawled to the ground.

A smile spread over Whelon's face, and he reached down to help his friend up.

'Well done,' Connor said.

The boys sparred again, emitting loud battle cries. The training had transformed into play. Connor allowed the boys to continue their game. His hands ached from the previous day's training, more blisters swelling upon his palms. He had not spoken of it to Aileen after last night.

He picked up a branch, using his foot as leverage to snap off the extra twigs. The fingers of his right hand still would not move to his liking, forcing him to use the left. Though he had trained to fight with his weaker hand, he far preferred the right hand.

Connor forced the fingers around the branch, gritting his teeth to control the movement. Tendons tightened and stretched, his wrist shaking while he attempted to move the branch in the manner of a sword.

While he engaged in the exercises, he thought of Aileen once more. She had wanted to tell him something about Bealtaine, and he'd refused to hear it. It reminded him of the morning afterwards, when he'd found Lianna bare-breasted in Tómas's arms. It was a moment of humiliation he'd never forgotten, and he had no desire to dredge up the past.

Now, it was Deirdre Ó Banníon who evoked his wrath. Were she a man, he'd have challenged her for offering such lies to her father.

Connor swung the branch at a tree, shattering the wood. The impact sent a blast of pain through his wrist and arm, and he gasped. The boys turned from their play, but he shook his head so as not to concern them.

He knew not if they'd asked permission to come, and it was time for them to join the preparations for the *aenach*.

Their foster-parents would be searching for them. Connor sent them off, promising another lesson in a few days' time.

'You are coming to the *aenach*, aren't you?' Whelon asked, his young eyes hopeful.

'*Tá*. But I'll not compete in the games.'

'No one expects you to,' Lorcan remarked, releasing another shrill battle cry. He walked alongside Whelon, content to move at his friend's slower pace.

Connor examined his right hand when the boys had gone. Such an act of foolishness, to think he could wield a sword in the way he had always done. The weakened muscles refused to yield to his bidding. Upon his wrist and palm, he studied the scars of past fights. Nicks and slashes covered both sides. Each was a reminder not to lose his attention upon the fight. Some were earned in battle, those more valued than the others. He had lived, while others died at his hand.

As he passed through the forest, pushing his way past the smaller branches, his thoughts moved to the Ó Banníons. Today the Brehon courts would hear the case and decide upon a judgement.

Seamus Ó Duinne believed he should accept the *corpdíre* and settle the matter. Connor preferred an eye for an eye. Or hands for hands, as it were. He increased his gait, sprinting across the field toward Aileen's hut. The exercise satisfied his longing to exert every last muscle.

When he reached Aileen's hut, he saw her standing outside with her animals. In the coolness of the fading dawn, the sky held clouds the dark colour of fleece. There would be rain this day.

He slowed at the apex of the hill, watching her. Dark strands of her hair streamed in the morning wind, while she fed the animals. She poured a bucket of grain into a small trough, guiding his own horse's mouth into it. Her hands moved over the animal's skin, and he froze at the sight. As if she sensed his presence, she turned to him.

Something within him halted. For over two moons, he'd dwelled with this woman and he hadn't seen how breathtaking she was. With clear skin and sage eyes that saw through him, there was something ethereal about her.

Her blue woollen overdress accentuated the creamy white *léine* beneath, her feet bare. As he strode towards her, she smiled in greeting, but the smile did not quite reach her eyes.

'What did you want to tell me about Bealtaine?' he asked.

The bucket fell from her hands, the grain spilling upon the ground. A startled look overcame her, a fear that she masked quickly. 'You would not believe me if I told you. It does not matter now. I suppose some things are better left in the past.'

He didn't believe her. Her rushed speech, and the way her gaze would not meet his, made him suspicious.

He leaned down and righted the bucket, his fingers struggling to curve around the wood. Though he tried to make his hands grasp the handle, he was forced to lift it with his forearm.

'It bothers you. What happened that night?' He'd been so absorbed in his own anger that day, he recalled seeing her pale, frightened face that morn. Had someone forced her? A darkness curled in his stomach at the thought of someone harming Aileen.

Her cheeks were crimson, but she accepted the bucket. Shaking her head, she tightened her lips into a thin line. 'I tell you, it does not matter.'

The resignation on her face kept him from asking again. Instead, Connor walked beside her while she finished the remainder of her morning chores.

'Mass will begin soon, along with the opening ceremonies. We must make haste.' Aileen opened the door to the hut, holding it out to him while she gathered her *brat*. She wrapped the warm shawl around her head, crossing it over her shoulders. Connor donned his own mantle, raising it to shield himself from the soft morning rain that had begun to fall.

Aileen handed him a basket, which he accepted, hooking it over his forearm. She had laboured for most of the night and morning preparing honey cakes for the *aenach*. Connor lifted the corner of the cloth, his mouth watering at the sight. Fragrant steam rose from the basket, of warm pastry and sweet honey.

'Do not think of stealing one,' Aileen warned. 'Unless you wish to have your hands broken once more.' A note of teasing underscored her remark. Connor preferred it to the wounded look he'd caused. He'd rather see her smile.

'Am I not a guest in your home?'

'A burden, more like. For the past few moons I've done nothing but wait upon you hand and foot. Feeding you, tending your wounds—'

'Bathing me.' He could not resist needling her with the reminder of that night. As soon as he spoke of it, Aileen whirled upon him.

'What is it you're about, Connor MacEgan? Are you wanting to take me into your bed?'

She stared hard at him, eyes blazing. Her full lips were

reddened, her dark hair contrasting against her pale skin. As soon as the words left her mouth, his body responded. He would not mind taking her into his bed. To feel her soft skin bare against his own, to taste her mouth.

'And if I said I would?' He acted upon his desires, kissing her the way he'd been wanting to. Her lush, full lips played against his own, and he moved his hands over the swell of her hips. Even as his body responded, a voice inside warned that he was opening a door he should not. She was the woman who had seen him at his weakest moments. He had chosen to stay with her because she would not entangle him the way other women would.

Aileen trembled in his arms, her kiss tentative and sweet. He tasted the rain against her lips and moved his mouth to her ear. She inhaled sharply. Her palms covered his chest, her thumbs stroking the ridged muscles. The simplicity of the gesture made his body tighten.

Belenus, he wanted her. And though it might be wrong, he sensed that she needed him, too. They could enjoy each other, could they not? He drew back, watching the clouded desire in her eyes. 'What must I do to earn your trust?'

'I will not share your bed, Connor MacEgan. I've more sense than that.' She gave him a strong push, and he backed away. Frustration punctuated her stride, and he forced himself to cool his ardour. She was afraid of him. Or possibly her own feelings. He needed to lighten her mood.

'Set your mind at ease, Aileen. I've no plans to seduce you here upon the morning grass.'

She shot him a suspicious look. 'I would not put it past you.'

'The dew does tend to make your clothing rather wet,' he teased. 'Most uncomfortable.'

She released an exasperated 'Humph.'

With feigned seriousness, he asked, 'Where would you prefer that I take you?'

This time, she understood his jest. Pausing in her walk, she tilted her head to one side. 'Upon a pallet. A soft one with sheets made of woven silk.'

'Have you never made love outside, then?' From the way her skin flushed, he guessed not.

'Have you?'

He only smiled. 'Should you desire it, you've only to ask it of me.'

'That day will never come, Connor MacEgan. You may find yourself another woman to seduce this eve.'

Strangely, he did not want another woman. He'd rather steal this woman away during the moonlit hours. Men and women of the tribe frequently paired off on nights such as this one, to make love beneath the stars. It harkened back to their pagan forefathers. But Aileen refused to lie with him. Was it because she was afraid? Or did he repulse her? He glanced down at his misshapen hands before hiding them in a fold of his mantle. Stiffening his shoulders, he followed her and wondered what her refusal had truly meant.

When they reached the fairgrounds, Aileen separated from his side to join the women in setting up the vast array of food. Several men had slaughtered both swine and cattle alike, while others worked to dig a roasting pit. The mingled scent of blood and smoke pooled in the air while the men and women worked to clean the meat. The rain had stopped, but the sun hid behind grey clouds.

Twelve large tents stood to provide shelter and a space

for gathering. In the distance he saw groups of children seated at the feet of a poet, listening to stories. The light sound of pipes and harp music joined with the throng of voices.

Familiar faces surrounded Connor, wishing him good morn, voices bidding him welcome. But one man cast him a look akin to murder. Riordan approached with a driven purpose upon his countenance.

'MacEgan,' he said by way of greeting.

'Riordan.' Being of a taller stature, Connor possessed the advantage of height. Riordan did not take well to being looked down upon.

'Aileen has done all she can to heal your wounds.' Jealousy hardened the man's face. 'You should return to your own people. Your presence bothers her.'

'It bothers her?' Connor questioned. 'Or does it bother you?'

'Hurt her, and you will answer to me.' A darkness tinged Riordan's threat. He did not allow Connor to reply, but moved toward the long trestle tables where Aileen worked alongside the women.

Connor resented the man's threat. Never had he harmed a woman. He longed to sink his fist into Riordan's stomach, to feel the satisfaction of a fight. Though he recognised the words as idle jealousy, his hackles rose when he thought of Riordan being near Aileen.

As he strode through the throng of people, he caught sight of a familiar banner. A grave chill spread over him. The *méirge* held the colours of the Ó Banníon tribe. Somewhere among them was Flynn Ó Banníon, the man responsible for his injuries.

He stared at the crowd, searching to find his enemy. A cool trance seemed to settle over him, the need for vengeance outweighing all else. He reached to his side, forgetting that he had left his sword in the hut. The absence of the weapon reminded him once again that he was not ready to face the Ó Banníons in combat. But his time would come.

The priest Father Maen raised his hands, the dark brown folds of his sleeves falling to his sides. He waited for silence when all the tribesmen had gathered. Then he invoked a Latin blessing, calling for the folk to pray for fruitfulness in both harvest and in family. Connor joined the tribe in their response of 'Amen', but his gaze remained locked upon the faces of Ó Banníon men he had once called his friends. Now, nothing of that camaraderie remained. There was still no sign of Flynn Ó Banníon, the chieftain.

After the prayers, the folk dispersed into groups for storytelling and the games. Children raced, shouting and laughing as they moved amid the dogs and animals. A few elders began games of chess with pieces carved of ivory and black stone. Connor kept a wary gaze towards the Ó Banníon tribe, but none spoke to him.

He walked through the crowd, passing among merchants who vied for his attention. He had brought along a few pieces of silver from the purse Trahern had given him. Though it would not be enough to purchase more than a few trinkets, he found himself moving toward the horses.

A fine black *Ech*, its skin sleek as midnight, caught his eye. Such a warhorse might cost a chieftain four hundred cattle in exchange. The steed tossed its head, the silver bridle flashing in the morning light.

'Brought over from Wales, he was,' the vendor boasted.

'Fastest animal for riding you'll find. Good bloodlines. The Norman king wanted this one.'

'He is very fine,' Connor acknowledged, 'but I am looking to gift a woman with a horse. She does not need an animal better suited to royalty.' Nor did he have the silver to purchase such a steed, not even with help from his eldest brother Patrick, the King of Laochre.

The merchant's eyes gleamed. 'Then it might be you'd be wanting a gentler animal, like this one.'

Connor examined the grey mare. The bone structure proved to be good, although the mare seemed more interested in grazing than in trotting or walking. 'She is tame, I see.'

He stroked the animal's coat, intending to walk away before the merchant began bargaining.

'Flynn Ó Banníon will be anxious to see you,' a low voice said.

It was Niall, a man he'd once called friend when he'd fought alongside the tribe. Slightly taller than himself, Niall had trained with him on more than one occasion. They were evenly matched, which made the sparring good practice for both of them. Though Niall's hair was a darker gold than his own, he had been like a brother to him.

Connor tensed, his glance moving toward Niall's sword. The man caught his look. 'I played no part in what was done to you. Had I known, I would have tried to stop them.' Niall's expression was solemn. 'I am sorry for it.'

Connor wanted to believe him. Niall had never been known to deceive others. Always had he spoken the truth. 'Does Ó Banníon believe I am dead?'

'No. He knows you are alive. Seamus Ó Duinne asked him to answer the *brehons*.'

Connor ignored the merchant's pleas to stay and inspect more horses. He walked alongside Niall, moving toward the food preparation tables.

'I've no wish to see him.'

Niall shrugged. 'That I can understand. When you confront him, it will be your word against his.'

To Connor, it did not matter what Ó Banníon claimed. He preferred to settle his vengeance outside of the courts. 'Do not reveal my presence to him yet.'

'It does not matter what I do. He will know where you are within moments. Look.' Niall pointed toward a blonde-haired beauty who was staring at both of them.

Connor met the gaze of Deirdre Ó Banníon. Shock transformed her expression into fear. Good. She had reason to fear him, after her treachery.

'I'll leave the two of you to speak,' Niall offered. 'I am certain you have much to say.'

Connor made no reply, his gaze trapping Deirdre. She glanced around, as though searching for an escape. He allowed none, willing her to stay rooted in place.

Her golden hair was neatly braided, sun-kissed auburn highlighting the strands. Clear green eyes rivalled the hills of Éireann with their striking colour. A beautiful woman was Deirdre, and a powerful one with her position as the chieftain's daughter.

With a light smile, she began walking toward him. He considered avoiding her, but a cold rage simmered within him. Her lies had caused his punishment. As she moved towards him, her hips swayed seductively. Deirdre twined her arms about his neck and pressed herself close. 'Connor MacEgan! I cannot believe it is you.' With a sensual smile, she added, 'I have thought about you often.' Her breasts rubbed against him, her hands moving down his back.

'As have I.' The thought of wringing her devious neck had traversed his imagination a time or two. He kept his posture rigid, not returning any of her false affections. If he shoved her aside, witnesses might claim he'd attacked her a second time.

She misread his intentions and pressed her mouth against his. He did not relax, his body remaining as still as an ancient stone monolith. Deirdre tried to coax a response with her kiss, but he granted her nothing. Unlike Aileen, whose innocent touch had seared him with lust. He wanted her to know that he felt nothing for her.

'Have you finished?' he asked mildly. 'Or will you claim that I took your virtue in front of everyone here?'

She paled. 'I never meant for my father to—'

'To what? Discover your lies? He believed you and punished me for it.'

'I thought he might allow us to wed.'

'And did you consider that I had no desire to wed you?' He did not hide his disgust from her. 'You think your charms impossible to resist?'

Deirdre's fury mirrored his own. 'Were you any different, Connor MacEgan? I have heard many women claim that none can resist you, especially in your arms.' She raised her hands to his chest, stroking his muscles. He stiffened as her touch moved down his arms to his hands.

She held his gnarled right hand in her palm. 'You cannot be so proud now, can you?'

'Be gone from my sight, lest you suffer the consequences.' His anger was held by a spider's thread, his hands painfully clenched into fists.

Never had he struck a woman, nor even wanted to. But Deirdre was as much to blame as Flynn Ó Banníon. Thankfully, she fled, disappearing into the crowd. She would inform her father of his presence. So be it.

Deirdre Ó Banníon was a woman spurned, and he doubted not that she would do anything to make his life miserable.

Chapter 10

'Did you expect Connor to be any different than when we were children?' Riordan asked. He had seen her dismay, watching Connor kiss another woman. Aileen knew it shouldn't bother her, but only this morn, Connor had teased about wanting her, asking her to join with him.

And sweet saints, she had wanted to. She didn't know why she had thought he'd changed. But it hurt her deeply. She had begun to hope, for a moment, that he might see her as a woman instead of a friend. Seeing him with the beautiful maiden had been precisely what she needed to close off her mind.

'Leave the food preparations for a while, Aileen,' Riordan coaxed. 'I've placed a wager on your behalf.'

'A wager?'

'Come and see.' He took her hand, and Aileen allowed him to pull her toward the games. A gentle smile edged his face, and she forced herself to grant him her attention. Though he did not make her blood race the way Connor did, Riordan was a steady man.

A fragile wisp of longing brushed at her heart. Didn't she

deserve the man she truly wanted? Was she not worthy of Connor? Why did she have to settle for a comfortable man, when what she wanted was a man to make her come alive?

Her thoughts tangled into a puzzle, for she didn't want an unfaithful man. Why had Connor kissed the woman? Or had he? She struggled to remember if he had embraced the woman, if he had returned the kiss.

Her anger sharpened. If she allowed Connor into her heart, she could not stand aside while women threw themselves at him. And it would happen. The truth was, she didn't know if she could trust him. Nor could she trust her heart to hold its distance.

In the centre of a circle, a fierce-looking tribesman flexed his muscles. The man's dark forked beard gave him a demonic appearance, his strength intimidating.

With a look of pride, Riordan said, 'I'll be fighting him for you.'

Aileen didn't like the notion, not at all. To see men strike blows at one another irritated her. She had no desire to tend broken noses and bleeding knuckles resulting from a needless fight. 'I do not think you should.'

'I can win,' Riordan insisted. 'And when I do, five silver bracelets will be yours.'

Her stomach twisted, but she mustered a smile. 'I do not need the bracelets.'

'But you deserve them,' he said. He reached out to take her hand, and Aileen resisted the urge to pull away. 'Even if I lose, I win. For I'll have a beautiful healer to tend my wounds.' He raised her hand to his lips. The soft kiss made her feel empty inside, for she felt nothing.

At that moment, Connor appeared in the crowd, a head

taller than most of the folk. His dark gold hair was pulled back with a leather thong. Grey eyes stared at her, heated with intent. Her heart beat a little faster, her skin prickling. Even if a thousand people surrounded her, still she would sense his presence.

Beneath his gaze, her anger warmed. He had kissed her this morn, offering a tumble as though she were nothing more than a serving wench. In contrast, Riordan wanted her as his bride.

She broke away from Connor's stare and pulled Riordan toward her. She held her hand against Riordan's auburn beard, pressing a kiss upon his cheek. 'For luck,' she offered.

A gleam of possession ignited in his eyes. Riordan pulled her tightly against him. He tilted her head back and kissed her lips with unrestrained ardour. Aileen accepted the kiss and tried to make herself kiss him back. Yet her lips seemed to be made of stone.

Why can't I feel anything for him? she wondered. *What is wrong with me?*

When she turned back to Connor, he had gone. Her spirits sank, for she had behaved like a silly maid trying to make her suitor jealous. Already she regretted her actions. She braced herself to watch the wrestling match, ignoring the sounds of the men grunting and trying to crush one another.

And all the while, her eyes searched for a glimpse of Connor in the crowd.

'The *brehons* are waiting to hear your case,' Niall told Connor. 'They are inside the tent.'

He already knew what the judges would say. They would levy a fine upon the Ó Banníons. But accepting payment for the loss of his hands was unthinkable.

'Is Deirdre with them?' Connor asked.

Niall inclined his head, his expression unreadable. 'She is.'

Connor's defences rose, stretching his patience thin. He lifted the entrance flap of the tent set aside for the *brehons*. Morann Ó Duinne sat upon a low stool, his long ashen beard curling almost to the ground. A shock of white hair covered his pate, and legend told that his black eyes could pierce the heart of a complicated case and bring it to justice. Two other tribe members, one from the Ó Duinne tribe and the other from the Ó Banníon tribe, nodded in greeting.

Morann's eyes studied Connor's hands before his gaze flickered to Deirdre. Demure and quiet, she bit her lower lip like a recalcitrant child. Her pale skin made her appear the victim.

They would believe Deirdre's tearful testimony, that he had taken her virtue. Connor clenched his fists, relishing the pain of it. It reminded him of what he'd lost, all because of her.

He didn't deny his own mistakes. Had he remained alone without female company, this might not have happened. He had accepted the warm embraces of willing maidens, and now he had paid the price for it.

'I have already heard the details from Seamus so I would ask Connor to explain his injuries.' Morann turned to Flynn Ó Banníon. 'Then I shall hear your grievances. We will decide upon the *eraic* fine to settle the matter.'

Flynn wore his battle armour from the tournament earlier this morn. A corselet formed from bull-hide leather stretched across his chest, scarred with the markings of swords. Beneath it, his saffron tunic was made of silk. A battleaxe hung at his side, the copper blade shining in the afternoon sunlight. An experienced war leader and chieftain, Flynn held the respect of his people as one of their greatest warriors.

For a full season Connor had fought among Flynn's
ranks, drinking in knowledge from a true master. To see him
now, an enraged leader with no remorse for his deed, only
deepened Connor's hatred.

He watched the eyes of his enemy. His need for vengeance curled into a thundering storm of anger. He wanted
Flynn to feel the crushing weight of the stones, to know the
pain he had endured in his hands. He craved justice.

But even as he stared into the chieftain's eyes, he knew
it would not happen. 'You believe her lies still, I see.'

'My daughter would never lie about a matter such as
this.' Rage deepened upon Flynn's face. 'You hurt her—'

'I never touched her.'

Quiet tears rolled down Deirdre's face. Disgust filled
him at her illusion.

'I would see your hands, Connor MacEgan.' The *brehon*
judge gestured for him to reveal his wounds. Connor extended the gnarled fingers of his right hand. None could
deny the injury.

'Have you regained full use of them?' Morann inquired.

Never would he admit his weakness before Flynn. 'I have.'

'No—' another voice interrupted. Aileen entered the tent
at that moment. Her chestnut braid hung against her hips,
her sage eyes staring at Morann as though she could influ-
ence the outcome by her very presence.

What was she doing here? Alarm rose within him, his
pride bristling.

'As the healer of the Ó Duinne tribe, I can testify that his
hands will not regain their full use.'

'I have been told that you are no longer the healer,'
Morann responded.

Aileen paled, but stood bravely. 'I tended his wounds. And I know that he deserves full *eraic* payment for the loss.'

'She is wrong,' Connor responded. Though he understood her intent, the admission made him appear weak before his enemy. He could not allow the Ó Banníons to view him as defenceless.

Morann waved a hand in dismissal of Connor's argument. 'I can see for myself the evidence. There is no need to discuss this further. Flynn Ó Banníon, do you deny that you intentionally broke Connor MacEgan's hands and wrists?'

The chieftain shook his head. 'I deny nothing. It was only what he deserved for dishonouring my daughter.'

Before Flynn could continue, Morann nodded to Aileen. 'I thank you for your testimony. You are no longer needed in this judgement.'

She hesitated, waiting for Connor to speak. 'May I listen to the outcome?'

Connor levelled an angry look at her. 'I do not want her here,' he said. The woman could not see what she had done with her interference. Did she believe she was helping him? She had publicly voiced her doubts. Connor's frustration tensed like an arrow hovering at the bowstring, poised to shoot.

Aileen's face paled at his fury, her eyes bewildered. At last she surrendered beneath his anger and left. Though it would take time, Connor refused to leave the tent until he'd unravelled the damage she had wrought with her testimony. He would fight again.

And the Ó Banníons would meet his blade and his challenge. His honour was at stake.

* * *

Outside the tent, Aileen moved through a haze of wounded feelings. Faces blurred, sounds echoed in her head. She saw a group of storytellers, strangers she had not seen before. One man coughed, a hacking sound that tore at his insides.

Aileen knew she should stop and ask if he needed help, but right now her own heart ached. She moved past the crowds, toward the edge of the meadow. When at last she stood alone, the wind whipped at her face, cooling her hot cheeks. Connor had humiliated her before the *brehons*. Foolishly, she had thought to help him.

For long moments, she watched the descent of the sun as though it were her own spirits.

'Mother?' a voice whispered.

She turned and opened her arms. 'Rhiannon, *a iníon*.' She clasped the dark hair of her daughter to her breast, hugging her fiercely. 'Tell me of your doings this day.'

Rhiannon's mouth curved with pleasure. She spoke of winning a foot race and of her excitement at the games. 'Did you see the bards? Duald says they have come all the way from Wales.'

'I did.' Aileen recalled the coughing man, wondering again if she should have stopped to offer aid.

'They will tell the tale of Brian Boru.' Rhiannon took her hand and pulled her toward the fires where a throng of folk had begun to gather. 'Come with me and listen.'

Aileen allowed her daughter to lead her toward the hillside. Small fires flickered in the evening twilight, offering warmth to those who huddled near. Already she saw couples moving toward the isolation of the forest groves. It was early yet, but as the mead flowed, more folk would enjoy a private celebration of their own.

Grateful she was that Rhiannon was far too young for such. With her straight limbs and flat chest, it would be many years before womanhood would blossom in her young body.

'I want to move closer to hear them.' Rhiannon guided her past the tribesmen, at last reaching a tight circle where the folk stood. Many small children clung to the shoulders of their foster-fathers while elder boys jumped, trying to gain a better look.

Aileen held her daughter against her, letting her palms rest upon Rhiannon's shoulders. They listened to the first play, then another. The tale of a roving friar held them in laughter, but Aileen grew distracted when she saw Connor standing to the side. He did not see them yet, and her hand tightened upon Rhiannon's shoulder.

What would he say when he met his daughter for the first time? Would he recognise his own features in her face? Aileen steeled herself for the possibility that he would loathe her for what she'd done. She had stolen a child from him, seduced him on the ritual night. She didn't want to see the hatred on his face.

'We should go.'

'But, Mother, I want to hear the next tale,' Rhiannon pleaded.

Aileen's throat tightened. She had hidden her secret for over seven years. Should she stay and face him? Or should she run? The choice was taken from her when Connor sighted them.

The air slipped from her lungs, but Aileen kept her

hands upon Rhiannon's shoulders. So be it. Let him think what he would.

'Mother, you are hurting me—'

She loosened her grip. 'I am sorry.'

Moments later, Connor stood before them. Aileen held herself upright, prepared for his accusations. His attention flickered over Rhiannon for a fraction of a second, but he said nothing.

'This is my daughter, Rhiannon,' Aileen said. She held her breath, keeping her eyes locked upon his face.

'Rhiannon.' Connor greeted her with a polite nod. 'Your mother has spoken of you before. I was sorry to hear of your father's death.'

The gentle tone, the simple offering of sympathy, turned her insides to ice. He didn't recognise his own daughter, his own blood. Tears and hysteria warred within her, for this was the moment she had feared most.

And he didn't even recognise Rhiannon. Her secret was safe, and she need not be afraid any longer. It should have been a liberating release. Why, then, did the tears bundle up inside her, threatening to break free?

'Did they pass a judgement?' Aileen managed to ask.

He inclined his head. 'Walk with me, and I will tell you.'

Aileen released Rhiannon, pressing a kiss against her temple. 'Listen to the stories, *a stór*. I shall see you this night.'

He walked beside her, waiting until they were away from others who might listen. 'Why did you interfere?' he demanded sharply. 'The case did not concern you.'

'I did not trust the Ó Banníons to speak the truth. The *brehons* should know the extent of your injuries.'

His eyes fastened upon her with cold anger. 'I am not a weakling, Aileen. Nor am I afraid to face Ó Banníon with my sword.'

'You cannot hold a sword.'

'But I will.'

She shook her head. 'Flynn would strike you down with a single blow.'

'Weren't you the one who spoke of faith? Was it not you who refused to crush the hopes of those you heal?'

His words made her cheeks burn. 'That is different. They are children, and you a grown man.'

'I am a man, yes. One who lives by the sword, and I will face Ó Banníon.'

'What do you mean?'

'Morann agreed to my request. Two moons from now at Samhain, I will challenge Flynn Ó Banníon.'

A whisper of dread crept up her spine. She envisioned Flynn Ó Banníon's blade sinking into Connor's skin. She closed her eyes, willing the unwelcome thought away.

'Why would you do this? You cannot kill him.'

'If I defeat him in battle, I regain my honour. And he will drop all accusations against me.'

'What claim did Deirdre make? Did the *brehons* believe her?'

'They will always believe a woman's pretty words and tears.' Connor's face darkened with resentment. '*Tá*, they believed Deirdre.'

'Must you pay a fine?'

'They wanted to dismiss the matter, since our fines nullify each other. I refused to accept Morann's judgement. He finally agreed to my request.'

'What if Flynn Ó Banníon wins the battle?' she asked.

'It won't matter. For the only way he can win is to kill me.'

Aileen saw the resolution in his eyes. He would sacrifice everything. His eyes were bleak, the cool grey of stone.

'Do not fight him,' she whispered. 'Let it go, Connor. You're alive. Isn't that what matters?'

'He never intended to kill me. Only to cause suffering.' He stared into the distance. 'I won't be staying with you much longer. I'll go home to my brothers, to train as I must.'

They returned to the storytellers, the words of the bard captivating the audience. As they neared Rhiannon, Connor turned back. 'Does she miss her father?'

The words caught at her heart. Swallowing, Aileen shrugged. 'She has been with her foster-father since she could walk. Tómas has taken good care of her.'

A moment of surprise flashed across his face. 'Lianna is her foster-mother then, isn't she?'

Did he still hold feelings for Lianna after all this time? Knives of jealousy cut into her heart.

'She is. They have four children between them besides Rhiannon,' Aileen added.

Connor didn't respond, but seemed resigned to her answer. They stood together on the outskirts of the crowd while the bard wove the tale of Cuchulainn.

His hand reached out and bumped against hers. Then he flinched, as though he'd forgotten his crooked fingers. Embarrassment coloured his cheeks.

'Your daughter reminds me of my mother,' he said suddenly. A light smile tipped his mouth. 'But she has your face.'

Aileen could not look at him. He had seen the resemblance and yet remained blind to the truth.

His shoulder brushed against hers, and for a moment she wished he would pull her into his arms. She wanted to lean her head against him, to feel his strength. Aileen found herself staring at his mouth, and she forced her gaze back to the storytellers.

Connor's hand moved to the small of her back. 'Help me to fight again, Aileen.'

The fierce longing in his voice sobered her. She took his disfigured hand into hers. 'I will do as much as I can for you.'

With his left hand, he drew her palm in until it touched his chest. At the contact, her body prickled with awareness. 'Will it be enough?'

She gave his hand a slight squeeze. 'I am offering you my faith. It is all I have.'

Connor drew her hand to his lips. The light kiss might have been given in friendship.

Why then, did his eyes offer promises of far more?

In the darkness, the orange flames of the fires danced an eerie pattern. Whelon used his crutches to move past the tents and the long tables to where the bards had set up their camp. Spellbound by their storytelling, he had hoped to coerce them into one more tale.

The sound of a hacking cough came from behind one of the shelters. Whelon followed the sound until he came across a man heaving with sickness.

'Are you all right?' he whispered. But there came no reply.

Whelon drew nearer and saw the man's reddened skin gleaming with sweat. The bard's glassy eyes stared as though he were blind. Another cough seized at the man, and he clutched his side in agony.

Without thinking, Whelon hobbled to the man and eased him to the ground. His arms burned with the effort, but he helped the storyteller into a reclining position.

'I'll summon the healer.'

But the man would not release his wrist. Whelon tugged, then froze as he stared at the man's face. Upon his lips, the tell-tale sores revealed the truth.

Whelon jerked back in horror, making the sign of the cross. He had heard tales of men who had died from the pox. The man's arm was covered in sores, revealed by the raised sleeve of his tunic.

He had to find Aileen. Quickly, Whelon used his crutches to get away from the fallen man.

He glanced backward at the body. Unseeing eyes stared at the sky while the man's chest no longer rose with the breath of life.

The pox had invaded the Ó Duinne tribe.

Chapter 11

'I've been looking for you all evening,' Riordan said.

Aileen turned, and he held out a wooden goblet. She had been standing alone after Connor had left to speak with Seamus. Rhiannon slept in one of the tents with the children.

When she reached out to accept the goblet, Riordan smiled. He beckoned her toward a small grove of trees, away from the crowd. Aileen followed, wondering what he wanted.

From his flushed expression, it soon became clear. She wished she had not come. Tonight, her thoughts had woven into turmoil. She now knew that she could not force herself to have feelings for Riordan.

She wanted Connor. And though she might never have him, it was wrong to lead Riordan into believing she cared.

His hand closed over hers. He lifted the cup to her lips, and she drank a sip of the spicy red wine. How could she leave without hurting his feelings?

'Is it to your liking?'

She nodded, and he raised the rim to her lips again. Instead of tipping the cup, his fingers stopped upon her cheek. With the barest of touches, he caressed the line of her face.

In his eyes blazed the fires of lust. 'It is also to my liking. I find that I've been longing for a taste of it all night.' He dipped forward and stole a kiss before she could stop him.

Her skin warmed with embarrassment. 'Riordan, I do not—'

'Shh.' He lowered the goblet and stepped closer until she could smell the wine upon his breath. He turned the cup until his lips touched the place where she had drunk. After he had finished, he tossed the goblet to the grass.

His hand snaked around her waist. Aileen tensed, putting her hands up to prevent him from coming too close. She berated herself for letting things go this far. Riordan had made no secret of his desires. It was her fault, letting him believe she wanted him to become her husband.

When he touched her, her skin felt clammy. She tried to push him away, but he kept her locked in the unwanted embrace. 'Let yourself forget Eachan, Aileen. I'll take away your grief this night. Let me lie with you.'

She shook her head, turning her cheek when he tried to kiss her again. 'Riordan, this isn't what I want.'

'It's been a long time for you, Aileen.' His hand squeezed her bottom. 'I can give you the children Eachan couldn't.'

His arrogance fuelled her anger, and she jerked his hand away. 'Do you believe me incapable of making my own decisions? I know what I want, and it isn't you. Get away from me, Riordan.'

She could not read the expression in his eyes, but his drunken demeanour repulsed her. For the first time, she grew aware of his size. He could overpower her without the least bit of effort. But she refused to let him frighten her.

'Let her go.'

Connor strode toward them, ignoring the folk who had turned their heads in interest. Public spectacle or not, he was well aware of Aileen's discomfort.

'I am fine,' she said. Though she held her shoulders with confidence, she clenched her hands together. She looked as though she'd rather be anywhere else than here.

'This is none of your affair, MacEgan.' Riordan met his gaze with a challenge.

All this day, Connor had hoped for a way to release the caged energy within him. He wanted to fight someone, to prove that he had not lost any of his abilities.

'She told you no, and you did not release her. I believe it is my affair, when a man seeks to force a woman.'

'I would never force Aileen.' Riordan's fists doubled up and he circled Connor, searching for a weak point. 'But aren't you the one who forced Ó Banníon's daughter? Quick to accuse, aren't you?' He swung at Connor, but Connor sidestepped and the fist met with air.

Riordan threw another punch, and Connor blocked it with his forearm. 'You've had quite a bit of wine this eve, haven't you, Riordan? It seems to be affecting your aim.'

'It hasn't affected mine.' A feminine fist jabbed him in the shoulder. 'I did not heal your hands, just to have you break your fingers once again.'

'He dishonoured you. And I find that I'm wanting to break a few of his fingers.'

Riordan lurched forward, but Connor's elbow connected

with his face. A sickening crunch resounded and a trickle of blood ran from Riordan's nose.

'I don't need to use my hands,' he remarked. But he paid for his arrogance when Riordan dived, knocking him off his feet. Connor tasted dirt and blood, but he quickly rolled over and leapt to his feet.

'Enough of this.' Aileen pushed Riordan back. 'Both of you are behaving like animals.'

Though she stood between them to stop the fight, Connor's eyes locked with Riordan's. He wanted to avenge Aileen's embarrassment and release his own frustrations.

She left them both behind, walking in long strides. He couldn't stop himself from watching her. Her long dark braid swung against the blue overdress. The gown flattered her slender hips, dipping at the curve of her waist.

He recalled the inviting taste of her lips. A rush of jealousy invaded at the thought of Riordan touching her, whether Aileen wanted him to or not.

'She is mine, MacEgan.' Though Riordan did not begin the fight again, Connor didn't miss the threat.

'Is she? Then why did she turn from you?'

'She turned from both of us. But you're leaving, while I'm the man who will wait for her.' With a smug look, Riordan returned to one of the tents, swaying slightly.

Connor ignored the taunt. He refused to think of Aileen allowing Riordan to share her bed, or worse, wedding the man. Riordan's attack had spurred something primitive within him. Aileen evoked his raw need to protect.

In the hour that passed, Connor's thoughts grew heated. He imagined removing the gown from her shoulders, sliding the wool across her bared skin. Would her breasts pucker in the cool night air? Would her breath shatter when he touched her? Or would she allow him to touch her at all?

As a group of actors performed a play, he found her among the audience. She laughed at a humourous part of the story.

'Aileen,' he said in a low voice.

Her face turned toward him, but she did not smile.

'I am returning to the cottage.' Hunkering down, he reached out to take her hand. 'If you've time later, I need you to tend one of my wounds.'

Her brow crinkled with confusion. 'What do you mean? I thought—'

'Someone punched me in the shoulder tonight.' He fingered the spot where her fist had connected with the hardened muscle. 'I believe there might be a bruise.' He teased her, the corner of his mouth twitching with a laugh. 'I'll wait for you.'

'You'll be waiting quite a long time,' she rebuked. Even so, he caught the flash of interest in her eyes.

For Aileen Ó Duinne, he decided the wait would be worth it.

'Aileen.' A child's hand tugged at her skirts. She turned and saw a young girl's worried face. Zaira, Aileen remembered, one of her cousin Bridget's foster-children.

'What is it? Is someone hurt?'

'No, it is Bridget. She does not look well.'

'Is it time for the babe to be born? Her time is near.'

Zaira shook her head. 'I do not know. But I fear for her.'

'Where is she?'

'Near the women's tents. She spent all day at the women's council, and now she is with the storytellers.'

Aileen walked with the young girl toward the assembly of women. Children played in front of the tents while another boy fed a dog scraps from the feast.

She wondered if anyone had thought to summon Illona, the new healer. Even the thought deepened her resentment. She had delivered babes for tribeswomen over the past few seasons. She needed no one's help for that.

But the quiet memory of the chieftain's two children invaded. She had held the tiny bodies in her hands, weeping over the loss of Seamus's twin sons. Though she had done all she could, the boys had not lived more than a few days.

And what if there was a problem with Bridget's child? It was not right to shoulder the responsibility alone. Though she hated the thought of another woman interfering, the compulsion to protect the newborn infant was stronger.

Zaira gripped Aileen's hand to pull her forward. When they entered the tent, Aileen searched until she saw her cousin.

Bridget held a hand to her swollen belly, and tell-tale signs of tension creased her eyes. Aileen watched closely until she was certain. Bridget looked to be having pains, despite her storytelling.

When the story was over, Aileen stepped past the young children and took Bridget's arm. 'When did they start?'

'A few hours ago. It may be some time yet before the babe is born. Have you sent for Illona?'

'Not yet.' Aileen turned her attention back to the young girl Zaira. 'Can you find Illona and send her back to us?'

'I don't know where she is.'

'Then ask. Tell her she is needed to help with the delivery.'

Bridget gripped Zaira's arm. 'I want to birth this child in my own hut. Not here. Tell Illona to meet us there.'

'There may not be time,' Aileen protested. 'We should—'

'No.' Stubbornness lined the pregnant woman's face. 'I swaddled each of my babes with my grandmother's blanket. It has brought luck to all of them. I'll not deny this child the same.'

Aileen started to argue, but held her tongue. What did it matter where the child was born? She could see that Bridget would not relent.

She directed her attention to Zaira. 'Do as Bridget says. And afterwards, go back to the hut. Make sure a warm fire is burning and prepare Bridget's bed.'

Zaira raced ahead to follow her bidding. When the girl had gone, Aileen assisted Bridget in rising to a standing position. 'In the meantime, I will help you,' she assured her cousin. 'This one will come faster than the ones before. Can you walk?'

'Of course.' With a bemused smile, Bridget took Aileen's arm, accepting the support. 'You seem concerned.'

Though there was always an element of danger, helping women deliver babies was a task Aileen enjoyed. To help guide a new life into the world, hearing the newborn squall and wrapping the tiny infant in warm swaddling clothes—it somehow made her own barrenness easier to endure. Were it not for Rhiannon, she would have none to call her own.

She knew her daughter slept in one of the tents, along with the other children. Though she wished Rhiannon could attend the birth, it was better for her to remain here.

Bridget stopped walking a moment later, breathing slowly. Her eyes closed with the effort of the contraction, and she gripped Aileen's hand for support.

Inwardly, Aileen counted the length of time between contractions and feared the expectant mother would not make it home in time. She searched for a kinsman, someone to bring a horse. At last, she caught sight of one of her brothers.

'Cillian!' she called out, waving to him.

Her brother turned and smiled at her, crushing her into an embrace. Beneath his mantle, she realised that he had changed since his apprenticeship. His arms held the strength of manhood, his smile confident. 'It has been a long time, my sister. Are you well?'

She nodded, explaining Bridget's situation. Cillian glanced at the woman, his brows furrowing. 'I thought you were not allowed to heal any more.'

Aileen didn't lie. 'That is true. But I cannot leave her like this while waiting for Illona. She won't make it back to her hut without a cart. I cannot put her on horseback. Can you help us?'

His expression grew serious. 'What of the new healer? Is this not her responsibility?'

'I sent for her.' At the warning in Cillian's eyes, she waved her hands. 'Bridget is our cousin. Seamus will not mind if I help her until Illona comes.'

'He forbade it, Aileen.'

'The new healer is a stranger and an Ó Banníon, no less,' she argued. 'I am Bridget's family.'

Her brother sighed and shook his head. 'I do not know, Aileen.'

'Please, Cillian. Bridget needs us.' Even now, the expectant mother's pains grew closer together. Aileen gripped his hand. 'She will not make it home without our help.'

Finally, he relented. 'If I had any doubts in your abilities, never would I agree to this. I will bring a cart to help you. And I'll make certain Illona comes.'

'Thank you.' She kissed his cheek, and he ruffled her hair.

'What's this I hear about you and Connor MacEgan?'

Her face flushed scarlet. 'Nothing that would interest you.'

He laughed. 'Our mother will tell me anything I wish to know.'

'And none of it will be true,' Aileen argued, while her brother went off to find a horse and cart. She breathed easier when she saw Cillian hitching a mare in the distance. Now she needed to find Frasier and tell him of his wife's labour.

She spied Lorcan near a table heaped with pastries and waved to the boy. 'Lorcan! Bring Frasier to help me with Bridget. Her babe will come this night.'

Lorcan reached out for an almond pastry. He stuffed it into a fold of his tunic before hurrying toward the crowd to find Bridget's husband.

Bridget swayed, and Aileen strained to hold her upright. With each step, she recalled her own agony giving birth to Rhiannon. And yet, a frisson of excitement bloomed within her. She would endure childbirth again in a heartbeat, should God bless her with another babe.

'We will be there soon,' she soothed the labouring mother.

'If I do not deliver this babe in the field,' Bridget responded. Tight lines of pain etched deeply at the corners of Bridget's mouth. A vicious contraction gripped the woman, and Aileen coaxed her through it.

'I'm glad you are here, Aileen,' Bridget breathed. 'Even if Seamus has forbidden you to be our healer, I've always trusted you.'

The words eased Aileen's mind, and she warmed to them. Moments later, Cillian arrived with the cart and horse.

Lorcan had not yet returned with Frasier, but Aileen trusted the boy to fetch him.

The cart rumbled across the meadow, Bridget clutching at the curve of her stomach. As the torches faded into the distance, Aileen found herself thinking of Connor. He had gone to their hut, promising to wait for her. Though she recognised his intent, she didn't know how she felt about it.

Not that any of it mattered. She had to remain with Bridget until the birth, and Connor would give up waiting for her. It would be dawn before she returned home.

The cart stopped before the stone hut, and Cillian helped carry Bridget to the straw pallet. Zaira had a pot of water hanging above a warm fire.

'Should I stay until Illona arrives?' her brother asked.

'No. But thank you for your help this night.' She dropped her voice to a whisper. 'And for letting me do this.'

Her brother departed, and Aileen worked with Zaira to ease Bridget's labour. Frasier arrived at last, but though he had attended the other births, his pallor was far more ashen than Bridget's.

'I don't want you here,' he said brusquely. 'We must wait for Illona.'

'She is not here yet,' Aileen reasoned. 'And I don't think Bridget intends to wait. Would you rather she give birth alone?'

Frasier tensed, but shook his head. 'Seamus says you are cursed by the *sibh dubh*, Aileen Ó Duinne. I'll not let you near Bridget. Not after what happened to his sons.'

Aileen longed to shake sense into the man. 'I delivered each of your three children, Frasier Ó Duinne. No harm came to any of them.'

'That was before the curse.'

'There is no curse,' she insisted. Her own frustration tightened within her. A child would soon be born. Selfishly, she wanted to be the healer to bring it forth.

Another cry burst forth from Bridget, and desperation lined Frasier's face. He would do anything to take away her pain.

'Do you want me to leave?' Aileen asked softly. She prayed he would not accept the offer.

Frasier's shoulders slumped forward. 'There isn't time, is there?'

She shook her head. 'The babe will not be long now.'

He blanched, contemplating the consequences if she left. Aileen took his hand. 'I swear to you, I will take care of her. She is strong and healthy. All will be well. And Illona will come.'

'Bridget will not like it if you leave.' With reluctance, he let her stay, pacing back and forth. Aileen was grateful that their other children were sleeping in the tents at the *aenach*, away from their mother's distressed cries.

Over the next hour, she sent Frasier outside the hut for numerous unnecessary tasks. The activity kept him from hovering over Bridget. At last, Illona arrived. The woman did not countermand Aileen's orders, but instead worked alongside her.

Time blurred into a haze until at last Aileen called for Frasier to help Bridget into a squatting position. He supported his wife's body while she pushed. Infinity compressed into a single moment as Bridget strained. Sweat beaded upon her forehead. She closed her eyes to focus on the task while Aileen invoked a rhythmic healing chant. The soft words flowed, familiar words Kyna had spoken and passed down to Aileen whenever a new life was about to come forth.

Illona's voice merged with hers, and the two women joined together to guide the birth. The small head stretched against Bridget's womb, sliding into Aileen's hands. She eased the shoulders forth and cleared the young mouth. The only sounds in the hut were chanting, Bridget's harsh breathing, and the sudden cry of a newborn.

Aileen lifted the child on to Bridget's stomach. Tears slid down her cheeks as she relived her own daughter's birth. 'She is a beautiful girl, Bridget.' It never failed to enchant her, seeing a child emerge into the world.

'She is,' Bridget agreed, stroking the infant's head. Illona tied off the babe's cord and severed it.

'You did well, Aileen. I could not have done better myself,' Illona complimented her.

Aileen accepted the words of praise, but they were a reminder that she had been replaced by someone else. She tried to concentrate upon the important matters, but already Illona had taken her place, guiding Bridget with the delivery of the afterbirth. Thanks be, there was no tearing, no need for a healing poultice.

She found a clean *léine* for Bridget while Illona wrapped the afterbirth in cloth for a later burial. When Bridget was settled into bed with her newborn, Aileen said her goodbyes to the family.

Outside, she washed her hands in the animal trough. The summer's night air had grown chilly, and Aileen shivered, rubbing her arms. Whispers of starlight glittered in an ebony sky while the rasping of crickets invaded the stillness.

Aileen lifted her *brat* over her head and wrapped the warm folds of the woollen mantle across her shoulders. The exhilaration of welcoming the infant into the world made her smile. She walked the distance to her hut, thankful for the blessing of an easy birth.

To her surprise, she saw Connor open the door to her hut. His large frame filled the entrance, and he held out a wooden cup of mead to her. Aileen accepted it, drinking deeply.

'Lorcan told me of Bridget's babe. Did it go well?'

'It did. She has a beautiful daughter.' Aileen's smile widened at the memory of the tiny fingers wrapping around her thumb. It meant even more that she could assume the role of healer for her cousin, even if it was just for a moment.

'You are up late,' she remarked.

'I promised to wait for you.'

A thrill of premonition enveloped her as Connor led her inside. It was like crossing through the years to the girl she had been on the night of Bealtaine. But this time, he was inviting her to join him. Her skin grew warmer, her heart beating faster. Did she want this? Did she want him, knowing that he would leave her once again?

A pot of warmed water hung over the fire, and he poured it into a shallow basin. 'Sit down,' he invited.

Aileen sat upon the wooden bench, unsure of Connor's intentions. He knelt before her and took her feet into his lap. His left palm traced the outline of her foot. Though the twisted fingers of his right hand should have repelled her, sensual shivers emerged at the touch of his callused palm. She understood the effort this cost him, the level of concentration. Steadily he lifted handfuls of water over her bare feet, washing them in an age-old custom.

'You don't have to do this,' she said.

'I want to.' He brought her hands to his shoulders while he caressed her soles. Years of fighting had moulded rigid lines of strength into his arms.

She pushed away her body's response to him, willing herself not to look at his firm mouth only a breath away. 'I am nothing to you but another woman, Connor. And that isn't what I want.' She stood, not caring that her gown grew sodden in the water.

'You are wrong, Aileen.' He rose, his silver eyes casting a spell upon her senses. 'More than any other woman, I want you this night.'

Broken shards of memory cut into her. He hadn't wanted her, not when she'd tried to gain his attentions as a girl. She didn't fool herself into believing that he wanted her now.

Before she could stop him, Connor leaned forward and kissed her. She tasted mead upon his mouth, the heady rush of sensation. His tongue teased hers, and though her mind begged her to stop, she opened to him. Tentatively, she tasted him with her own tongue. Droplets of water dampened her gown and he pushed the *brat* from her shoulders, letting the shawl fall to the floor. Fire permeated her skin, and all the while she melted against the warmth of his mouth upon hers.

'Aileen,' he whispered, reaching beneath her gown. He wanted to remove her overdress, but she shied away from him.

'Do you want me to stop?'

Her heartbeat thrummed beneath her breasts, and she

hesitated. Caught between reason and desire, she fought against her body's need for him.

'I don't know what I want,' she said honestly. 'You're going to leave.'

He cupped her cheek. 'It doesn't mean we can't enjoy each other until then.'

She closed her eyes, not wanting him to see her indecision. 'What if I asked you not to leave at all? Would you give up your revenge?'

Slowly, he shook his head. 'I cannot stay, Aileen.' He raised his misshapen right hand. 'I need to be the man I once was.'

His words crumbled any hope she might have held. His pride was more important than all else.

His hot mouth kissed the soft place in her neck, sending shivers into every pore of her skin. For a moment she allowed temptation to overcome reason. He lifted the overdress aside, lowering the folds of her *léine* until it hung at her waist. Bared before him, he pulled back to look at her.

'Your skin reminds me of this water,' he said huskily. 'Smooth and warm.' He lifted a handful of the wetness, letting it pour over her breasts. Her nipples puckered at the sensation of droplets spilling over.

Then he bent to take her breast into his mouth, and she could no longer remember the reasons why this was wrong. Though it was a night when men and women shared lovemaking with one another, coupling in the darkness, Connor MacEgan was a dangerous man. With his words and his touch, he lay siege to her heart.

By the sweet saints, he knew how to seduce her with his mouth. He suckled against her, pulling her deep into his mouth until her womanhood grew wet in response.

Don't, her mind begged her, even as she tilted her mouth to his. She kissed him with the memory of their shared passion, of the magic of Bealtaine. Her body ached to feel him filling the emptiness inside.

Take him, her body urged. And God forgive her, she needed him this night.

Chapter 12

She lifted his tunic away, grazing his skin with her thumbs. Battle scars marred his torso, and he inhaled when she traced her fingers down his chest. The touch of her hands inflamed him.

Aileen stepped out of the basin, and Connor knelt to dry her feet. Though he struggled to control his hands, he could not caress her beautiful long legs in the manner he wanted to. Instead, he used his mouth to kiss a path up her shapely calves, up to the smooth skin of her thighs. She trembled at his touch. Though she was a widow and a mother, she reminded him of a young maiden with her shyness.

Truth be told, she reminded him of the first time he'd made love to a woman. On the night of Bealtaine, he had touched breasts as soft and firm as these.

'Is it true,' he murmured, 'that you were in love with me once?'

A startled look crossed her face. 'No.'

'Not even a little?'

'Not even that much,' she said.

'You're hurting my feelings, Aileen Ó Duinne,' he teased, kissing the curve of her breast.

'You have no feelings, Connor MacEgan. Any woman is good enough for you,' she teased. Her voice sounded brittle, and he drew back to look at her.

'Not just any woman.' He didn't like the way she made him sound. He might flirt with women, but he didn't tumble them. Others teased him, but he'd never before cared about what they said.

This woman made him care. It bothered him that she saw him like this. Weakened, like a broken fragment of a man. She had bathed him, fed him, as though he were a little child. He'd rather die than cower behind her skirts, facing his enemy's sword.

The next time he saw Aileen Ó Duinne, she would see the warrior he'd always been. But for this moment, he wanted to show her just how much he craved the taste of her.

He took possession of her mouth, his kiss more demanding. He captured her nape with the curve of his arm and the sweet scent of crushed rosemary emanated from her hair.

He had to know, from her own lips, that she desired him. He needed to touch her, to watch her body rise with pleasure.

But instead of opening her arms to him, she shivered. Gone was the pleasure he'd kindled in her eyes. In its place, he saw wariness.

'What do you fear?' A dark suspicion rained down upon him. 'Did Eachan ever harm you?'

'No, never.' She pulled the sleeves of her *léine* over her shoulders. With her body covered, she swiped at the tears. 'But I cannot lie with you. Nothing has changed.'

'I don't understand. Tell me.' In her eyes, a deep sadness

lurked. Her pain did not extinguish his need, but he refused to let the matter go. 'Why is it wrong? We hurt no one by enjoying each other.'

'It would hurt me.' She swiped at her cheeks and turned away. 'I can't be with you, Connor. I thought I could let go of the past, but I can't.'

Before he could summon a reply, she opened the door to her hut. The night air breezed inside, causing the hearth to flicker. 'I need you to leave.'

He didn't argue. After collecting his tunic, he strode outside. Her words had slashed his pride, and he found it difficult to look at her. It was the first time a woman had turned him away.

It bothered him more than he'd thought it would. Somehow she had placed him in the same regard as Riordan. He didn't like it, not at all. But why?

Had he repulsed her with his hands? He stared at the deformity that had once been his right hand. The bruising had faded, but the bones would ever remain twisted. He struggled to make a fist, but the fingers would not line up straight. The motion burned, straining tendons and flesh into a position that was no longer natural.

Of course she would look upon him with disgust. How could she tolerate making love to a man who could not touch her? It stung in a way he didn't want to admit. Losing his ability to fight was one matter. But losing the desire of a woman was another.

Fumbling with the ties of his tunic, he slipped the garment over his head. He didn't bother trying to fix the laces. It wouldn't do any good.

Poised at the entrance to the sick hut, he waited. His

hands pressed against the hard stone while the familiar scent of thatch mingled with the night air. Had he imagined her response to him?

She had kissed him, allowed him to remove her *léine*. For long moments she'd endured his touch before at last the tears escaped. He felt a fierce need to assuage her pain, to drive out the demons of her past.

The question was, had he become a demon himself? Was he now a man no woman would want?

Aileen sank before the hearth, the tears flowing freely down her cheeks. He didn't understand, couldn't know the vicious aching inside her.

She did want him. More than anything else, she had wanted to welcome Connor into her arms. But what had that gained her the last time, save a broken heart? And a child.

Connor MacEgan would never make her comfortable. He got beneath her skin in a way she couldn't understand. For the past few years, she'd forgotten him and gone on with her life. But from the moment he came back, her feelings had sparked into flames.

If she took him as her lover, she'd lose her heart again. She had no doubt that Connor would leave. He'd return to his family, and she'd be alone again. No, she couldn't spend a few nights of pleasure with him. It might be only bed sport to him, but it meant a great deal more to her.

He was also the father of Rhiannon, a secret bond that would ever draw them together. It still bothered her that he hadn't recognised his own daughter.

Perhaps it wouldn't have meant so much if she'd had other children. But Fate had cursed her since Bealtaine. After

Rhiannon, she had lost two other children. One son, then another. Both had been stillborn.

Eachan believed it was his fault, that he was too old to father children. After they had wept over the deaths of their sons, he'd offered not to touch her again if it would save her the pain. She had refused. How could she deny him the comfort in her arms, after all that he'd given her? Inwardly, she had prayed that God would grant her a child. She'd held out hope for nearly seven years before the illness made it impossible for Eachan to touch her again.

She stared into the glowing hearth, not bothering to move to her sleeping pallet. The cold ground suited her mood. Exhaustion preyed upon her mind until she could no longer think clearly.

Her body regretted turning him away. She wished she could have seized the moment and given in to her needs. At the thought of his kiss, the way his mouth had moved up the skin of her thighs, waves of aching washed over her again.

Should she go to him? Lead him into her hut and touch every firm muscle, every ridge and scar of his flesh? Her hand moved to cup her own breast, the nipple tightening with memory. A bittersweet smile creased her lips.

If she did, she'd only fall in love with him again.

The moon slid behind a cloud, a soft amber light casting its rays over the grasses. Dawn would come soon. In the moist air, Connor sensed the coming rain.

A distant noise caught his attention. Hoofbeats travelled at a swift pace. Connor slipped inside his hut and reached for his brother's sword with his left hand.

The cold metal hilt warmed beneath his palm, and he

stepped back outside. Whether or not the approaching rider meant any harm, he intended to be prepared.

But as soon as Connor saw the young boy clutching the mane of an elderly mare, he sheathed the sword in its scabbard. Whelon's small shoulders leaned forward, as he struggled to slow the horse's gait.

'What is it?' Connor asked.

'One of the bards,' Whelon gasped. 'He died. I saw his arms, and they were covered with sores. Aileen should come.'

Connor quelled the icy chill that struck him. He had seen such illnesses before. The invisible demons of the disease could strike any man down and render him dead within days.

'Wait here.'

He opened Aileen's door without knocking, and she jerked with surprise. 'We must return to the *aenach*. One of the bards has died.'

'How?' Aileen did not argue but grasped her basket, packing it with dried herbs and bandages. 'Are you certain he is dead?'

'He died from the pox. Whelon saw the sores.'

Aileen whitened, but gathered her *brat* around her shoulders. She reached to gather a stone vial and made the sign of the cross. He understood suddenly that it was holy water she took with her.

'You should begin praying now that the demons will not strike us down,' she urged. Though she kept up the appearance of calm, he recognised her fear.

Inwardly he mirrored her sentiments. The pox did not reveal itself immediately. Sometimes days or even a sennight would pass before they would know which persons would suffer.

'Say nothing to the others,' Aileen warned. 'I do not need a host of villagers falling into panic.'

'What about the other healer, Illona?'

Aileen's shoulders lowered, her face sombre. 'We will tell her, once we have seen the body. I need to see the sores first to be sure. If it is the pox…then we'll send for Illona.'

Connor helped her mount behind Whelon. 'I'll follow you soon.'

Slapping the mare's flanks, the pair rode back towards the grounds. Beneath his breath, Connor murmured a prayer. He mounted the horse left behind by his brothers and spurred it onwards. Raising his eyes to the darkened skies, he wondered who would be spared.

And who would lie beneath the cold ground.

When Aileen reached the *aenach*, Whelon led her to the place where the bards had set up camp. Connor arrived shortly after. Confused, he stared at the place where a tent had been. Save a fallen rope and trampled grass, there was no sign of the men.

'He was there. I saw him.' Whelon's eyes held disbelief. 'Where did they go?'

Aileen knelt to take a closer look. She did not doubt Whelon's word, for the boy had never told an untruth before. And if it were indeed the pox, the men had reason to flee.

'Wait.' Connor gestured in the distance. 'Do you smell that?'

She followed him, running past the rows of tents until they were a goodly distance away. The acrid scent of burning flesh made her want to gag. It did not take long to find the source. Within a makeshift stone hearth, far from the grounds of the *aenach*, lay the charred remains of a body.

Aileen made the sign of the cross, silently praying for the

man's soul. She held her distance, but the blackened skin gave no evidence of the pox.

'Tell me what sores you saw,' she said gently.

Whelon tore his gaze away from the body. His face was pale, stricken with fear. He was no stranger to death; none were. But his mouth trembled.

'He had sores on his arms, the size of small berries. His cheeks were red, and I heard him cough.'

Aileen recalled the man she had seen earlier. Though the severe cough harboured the signs of a serious illness, she had not seen any pox sores. Perhaps Whelon had been mistaken.

'What do you think?' Connor asked.

She shook her head. 'Without seeing the sores, I don't know. Many illnesses appear similar. It might not be what we think it is.'

Please, let it not be. She had heard stories of entire villages who had fallen prey to the pox. The few survivors were scarred for the remainder of their lives.

'What should we do?' the boy asked.

Aileen draped her arm around Whelon's shoulders. 'You should go home to your foster-father. He'll box your ears for making him worry so.' She ruffled his hair. 'Get some rest.'

'What of the man?' Whelon wanted to know. 'We can't just leave him there.'

'I'll take care of it,' Connor said softly. Aileen met his gaze and was grateful for his offer. Soon the folk would rise from their tents and might discover the death. The storytellers had long gone, and their intent to hide the body was clear. They would not be looking for their companion.

'Thank you,' she said, reaching out to touch his arm.

His steady grey eyes flared for a moment, then cooled. 'You should get some rest yourself.' He pulled away, and Aileen remembered suddenly that she'd asked him to leave.

Her head swam with muddled thoughts. Though she knew she had made the right decision, telling him to go, she didn't like the way he was looking at her now. A cold distance had fallen, an invisible shield she could not break through.

She helped Whelon mount the mare once again. The boy leaned against the mane, his small body drooping with weariness. She turned back to watch Connor, even as his figure grew smaller in the distance. She wanted to keep her promise of helping him heal. There were ways to mend the torn muscles, to speed his progress toward fighting again. It would take many weeks yet, but perhaps he would let her try.

Her mind conjured up different splints to help adjust his motion, exercises Kyna had taught her would rebuild torn muscles. She would heal Connor MacEgan's wounds fully. And she'd not weaken to temptation, no matter what happened.

In the meantime, she prayed that they would be spared from the demons of sickness.

Another sennight passed, and Connor tested the weight of the sword with his right hand. Aileen had forced him to wear splints at night, keeping pressure on the joints. He had made no further advances toward her, and she did not mention the night she'd turned him away.

His wrist ached with the effort of holding the sword, but he kept his pain silent. It did not escape her notice.

'Try the other hand,' she urged.

Connor switched hands, and took a few practice swings. Aileen stood nearby, but her presence distracted him. She wore an overdress the colour of moss, the *léine* beneath it a lighter shade of green. Her hair was bound by a single braid crossing above her forehead like a crown. The dark curls spilled across her shoulders, and, as always, she smelled of the rich herbs she tended.

His desire for her hadn't weakened. If anything, he wanted her more. He slashed the sword, moving his wrist against an imaginary enemy. A white-hot aching tormented his wrist, but he forced himself to continue.

'Enough,' Aileen bid him, and he sheathed the sword. 'Let me see your fingers.'

He held them out, and she stood near, pulling on each of the joints. 'These need to be splinted again.'

Her thumbs stroked his knuckles, massaging the soreness. His breath caught at the tender gesture. 'How does that feel?' She pulled gently at each of his fingers, her skin cool against his callused palms.

'It aches.'

She frowned, leading him back into the sick hut. An array of splints and bandages awaited him, and she adjusted the fingers of his right hand. 'I'm going to bind this one again. Don't use it for a few more days and it might be I can align the muscles.'

She wrapped his hand, her attention upon his palm. Yet a spiral of heat rushed through him. It tormented him, not being able to touch her. As she reached for one of the gnarled fingers, she winced. His cheeks reddened with embarrassment, for the finger looked more like it belonged to an animal than a man.

'You lied to me,' she said softly. 'You're in far more pain than you've said.'

'A warrior is accustomed to pain. It matters not.'

'I can give you a potion to ease your suffering.'

'I don't need to sleep my days away, Aileen.' When she'd finished tying up the splints, he softened his tone. 'How are Bridget and her baby?'

A wistful smile edged her face. 'The baby is sweet. She's fallen asleep in my arms a time or two.'

'You see them every day?'

She nodded. 'I've said to Bridget it's to look in on them, but, in truth, I want to hold the babe. It's been so long since I've held Rhiannon.'

'You should have more children,' he said.

Her smile disappeared. 'I would need a husband for that. And I've no wish to marry at the moment.' Her face flamed, and Connor recalled Riordan's unwanted attention.

She suddenly tilted her head. 'And why is it you've never married?'

'I've no land,' he said. 'Few chieftain's daughters would welcome such a poor prospect as myself.'

'Surely your father would have given you a little property.'

Connor shrugged. 'The land he gave was hardly more than a small plot. I gave it back to my elder brother. I receive income from the rents, but I haven't a fortress of my own.'

'Do you need one? Can you not be happy as a farmer?' There was a hint of teasing beneath her question.

'I wish I could.' He knew he should not want more than he had. But it bothered him that his brother should have command of a vast fortress and thousands of acres of land, while he could not hold the same. His fighting skills were strong enough to become a king himself. But he'd never dream of challenging Patrick for the honour. He respected his eldest brother too much.

'What will you do after you leave?' she asked. There was a trace of pity in her voice, and he stiffened.

'Return home. Train until I must face Ó Banníon.'

'And if you lose?'

His smile held no humour. 'I'll be dead, and it won't matter, will it?'

'This is not a fight to the death, Connor.'

'It will be.'

He did not wait to see her reaction, but used his left hand to open the door. To his surprise, a group of boys waited for him atop the hillside. Their ages ranged from young Lorcan to a few lads old enough to be a squire. Some held wooden swords, a few possessed daggers, and the smallest lad proudly held a stout tree limb.

'Your army regiment is here,' Aileen remarked drily.

Lorcan stepped forward, a wide smile creasing his boyish face. He pushed a lock of dark brown hair to the side. 'I come with a message from our chieftain. Seamus Ó Duinne wishes for you and Aileen to dine with him this night.' He bowed at the completion of his message. 'What reply should I send?'

Connor exchanged a look with Aileen, who inclined her head. 'We accept the invitation of our chieftain.'

'Be there before sundown,' Lorcan urged.

From their eager stance, Connor asked, 'Was there anything else you wanted?'

One of the elder boys stepped forward. 'We'd like you to train us, sir.'

He didn't know what to say. Aileen moved beside him and touched his arm. 'You wanted a purpose for your life, other than being a farmer. It seems fate has answered your request.'

Chapter 13

'The tree branch weighed more than he did,' Connor finished. Aileen wiped the tears of laughter from her eyes. After spending the day watching the ragged group of boys attempting to swat each other with wooden staffs, she didn't know when she'd been more entertained.

Connor had not scolded or reprimanded them, even when two of the boys began chasing one another with the staffs. He'd simply disarmed them and forced them to sit on the grass, watching the others. It was punishment enough, not being allowed to participate.

The older boys received more serious attention. Connor had corrected their stances, offering advice on which motions would bring down an enemy. They listened, and not one had voiced a question about Connor's injuries. All seemed to accept that he would redeem his fighting abilities in time.

Connor's left hand brushed against hers, and he took hold of her palm. Aileen accepted the touch, though her heartbeat stumbled. He kept talking about the boys' training as if the gesture meant nothing. Aileen tried to relax, but she was distracted.

Stop behaving like a giddy young girl, she warned herself. But his touch unravelled her senses. Before she knew it, they were standing at the gates of Seamus Ó Duinne's ring fort.

The rocky stone walls encircled a group of outbuildings, while the chieftain's house lay beyond the inner curtain wall. Though the *donjon* was not as large as some she'd seen, the fortress showed signs of wealth.

Inside, fresh rushes were strewn over the threshold. A servant accepted Aileen's scarlet cloak, and Riona Ó Duinne rushed forward to embrace Connor.

'It's pleased I am to see you, a *dalta*.' Riona Ó Duinne ruffled Connor's hair as though he were a young lad.

Aileen repressed a smile at the affectionate term. Connor MacEgan would ever be viewed as Riona's son, no matter that he was not her own flesh and blood.

To Aileen, she gave a curt nod. The message was clear: her presence would be tolerated, but not welcomed. There was no kiss or embrace, and Aileen pretended as though she thought nothing of it.

'Hello, Riona,' she said.

The woman did not return the greeting. To Connor she offered a warm smile. 'I saw you at the *aenach*, but I've been wanting more time with you as I said to Seamus. I told that man who calls himself my husband, I'd not be sleeping with him until he brought my boy back for a visit.'

Seamus rolled his eyes. 'Stop your prattle, woman, and let the man come and eat with us.'

Riona patted Connor's arm, a smile lighting up her eyes. 'Come, then.'

Connor turned back to Aileen and extended his hand. She took it, though aware of Riona's displeasure. For a moment, she wondered why she had been invited.

Connor led her to sit upon a wooden bench just inside the home. The chieftain's house was only a single level with a large interior. Partitions divided up the house into smaller chambers for sleeping, while the largest area was used to greet and entertain guests.

'How are your hands?' Seamus asked Connor.

'They grow stronger with each day,' he said. And it was true. With Aileen's help, he now noticed subtle progressions. Each night she adjusted the splints, and his range of movement had improved.

Seamus grunted. 'Good.' His gaze sharpened upon Aileen. 'Bridget and Frasier told me you delivered their new babe.'

'I did.' She raised her chin, meeting his gaze squarely. 'Bridget has a healthy daughter.'

'You were forbidden to heal.'

'My cousin needed my help.' Anger blazed in her expression. How dare he reprimand her for helping her family? She was tired of defending herself, tired of being blamed for what had happened to their sons. It broke her heart to remember the tiny, frail bodies of the babes. She wished there were some way to undo the past.

'Illona told me that you did well while you were there.'

Had his words become more gentle? Or was she imagining it? Seamus's gaze moved to Connor's hands. 'After that night, Illona was told to return to Dunhaven, upon the order of Flynn Ó Banníon. Did you know of this?'

Aileen shook her head, suppressing the rush of hope that

filled her. 'No, I did not know it. I thought she would stay among us.'

'When Flynn learned of Connor's presence, he forbade her to stay.'

Suspicion coloured her tone. 'Why do you tell me this?'

He glanced at Riona, whose face was pale. 'Until Samhain, I will grant you the right to be our healer once more. If you prove your worth, you may remain as such.'

'No!' Riona burst out. Rigid pain creased her eyes, her face white with emotion. 'You cannot let her, Seamus. Not after what happened to my sons. They died because of her.'

Aileen shook her head, unable to speak. She recognised the raw grief, the mother's pain. If something happened to Rhiannon, would she not feel the same? There were no words to take away Riona's anger. Only time could heal it.

Seamus took Riona's hand, caressing it. 'You need not fear, *a ghrá*. She'll not harm anyone.'

He leaned forward, his face fierce with warning. 'But one death during your trial period, Aileen, and you will leave us. Is that understood?'

'I am not God. I cannot prevent a natural death,' she argued, extinguishing the hope rising within her. 'If a man's soul is called, I can do nothing.'

'No deaths brought by your own hand.'

'You ask the impossible. No healer can make such a promise.'

'Then I will send for someone else.'

'You would force me to leave, if I fail?'

'I would.' His stern countenance convinced her of it. 'Until you prove yourself, our people believe you to be cursed. They'll not trust you again, if aught goes wrong. I cannot say what they would do to you. It would be for your own protection.'

Aileen felt as though she were clinging to the edge of a crevasse. She wanted so badly to accept his offer, this second chance. But if she failed during the trial period, she might have to leave her home and family.

The memory of the storyteller's death haunted her. Though she had not seen any signs of the pox as of yet, it might come.

And if it did, there was no one else to help them, save herself. More folk would die if she did not agree. There was no choice but to accept Seamus's offer. Though it was a grave risk and only for a short while, she needed to be a healer again. 'I will do it,' she whispered.

'I beg of you, Seamus,' Riona intervened. 'Think of what happened to our sons.'

'That was not her doing,' Connor interrupted, placing his hand upon Aileen's shoulder. 'Do not blame her for their deaths.'

Warmth blossomed inside her at his reassuring touch. It meant a great deal, hearing him defend her skills.

'She ruined Whelon's life as well.' Riona's face grew enraged. 'He was meant to be a leader like his father. What else is left for him, if he cannot fight?' She began to weep quiet tears.

Connor exchanged glances with Aileen and stood. He put an arm around Riona and spoke softly to her. Aileen did not hear what was said, but the words must have brought Riona comfort. The older woman wiped her eyes, her pallor ghostly white. 'Forgive me,' she said. 'I will return in a moment.'

Seamus's shoulders lowered as he stared at the corridor where his wife had departed. 'It hurts her still. She mourns the boys and cannot abide to look at Whelon.'

'But Whelon lives,' Aileen said softly. 'You have that.'

Weariness cloaked Seamus. 'It is not enough for her.'

He signalled for two servants to bring basins of water.

Sitting beside Connor, she caught his glance. Though another servant's hands moved across her feet, her skin erupted in goose bumps. Connor's silver eyes grew heated, and she thought of his hands upon her. As if to rekindle the vision, he covered her hand in his.

She breathed in deeply, inhaling his clean male scent. Awareness of him slipped beneath her defences. Beside him she felt small. Though he'd been injured, his frequent training exercises kept his body strong. His chest filled every inch of the tunic he wore, and she sensed the power radiating from him. On a battleground, he must have been a formidable opponent.

Before she could collect her thoughts, the servants dried their feet and they walked barefoot upon a straw mat to the cushions lining the floor.

Riona returned, her eyes reddened from weeping. She stood beside her husband, who handed her a silver goblet. 'Please, sit down,' she bade them.

The low table was covered in cloth, and they accepted two goblets of wine. Aileen took a sip, and the sweet blend took her by surprise.

'Where did you get this? It is the best wine I've ever tasted.'

'I traded for it,' Seamus admitted with pride. 'A man came from Saxony, and a finer wine I've never tasted.'

'And too much of it you've tasted,' Riona argued. 'Between the wine and your poteen, it's a wonder you haven't pickled your insides with as many barrels as you've drunk.'

Aileen hid her smile behind the goblet. She sat beside Connor at the table, their knees brushing. A harpist entered the room and began to play a light melody as the servants brought in the first course of food.

The evening progressed as though within a dream, for she was aware of Connor's eyes upon her. Aileen found herself conscious of his every move. He offered her choice pieces of the roasted pork, his fingers brushing against hers as he passed the meat to her.

She fought her body's reaction, wishing he did not tempt her so. At this very moment, she longed to feel his embrace, to taste the warmth of his mouth. She wanted his kiss against her throat, her breasts, even touching her most secret place. Her gown had grown overly warm, and she drank the remainder of her wine to press away the unwanted feelings.

The haze of the drink buzzed in her ears, but at one moment she stared at him. By the blessed Belisama, he was handsome. His gold hair was pulled back with a leather thong, his warrior's face strong and chiselled. Her attention was drawn to his mouth, the masculine lips that had brought her so much pleasure.

She closed her eyes, as if to shut out the temptation.

'Do you want more?' he asked, holding the pitcher of wine. His voice allured her with its low timbre. Dark grey eyes burned into hers, mirroring her own desire.

'Yes,' she whispered. His returning look seared her as he filled her cup. Despite her lightheaded state, she was aware of her actions. She was a grown woman with needs. And here was the man she'd always dreamed of, looking at her with the same desire. She should take what he offered, even at the risk to her heart. It might be her only chance.

Seamus coughed, drawing her attention back to their host. 'I want to ask why you've challenged Flynn Ó Banníon.'

In her chieftain's gaze, Aileen saw the concern. He knew, as she did, that if Connor raised his sword against Ó Banníon, he would be defeated.

'If it is a question of payment—' Seamus said.

'No. He owes me a fine, as well. The *brehons* wanted an even exchange.'

'Then why will you not take it?'

Connor's expression darkened into shielded rage. 'Because it is my honour we speak of. I have done nothing against his daughter. If I accept this agreement, I am admitting a false guilt.'

Seamus's face coloured, but he shrugged. 'Why should you risk your life over a mistake?'

'Because I want my vengeance. He took away my fighting skills, my ability to support a family.'

Aileen's heart constricted. There was his true reason for wanting to face Flynn Ó Banníon. He didn't believe himself to be a man any more, nor could he have the family he wanted. His hands had not been crushed. It was his dreams.

She suddenly saw past his shield of pride. Just as she was willing to risk everything to be a healer again, he would sacrifice his life for honour.

If he regained his strength, would he become a chieftain or a king? Would he reign over a land with sons to train as he had Lorcan and Whelon? Her eyes blurred, for she could envision the dream as surely as though it were her own.

But if he failed, he would pay the ultimate price. 'What if you die?' she whispered, her throat closing up with tears.

His gaze hardened to stone. 'I am already dead, Aileen. But in this way, I can die knowing that I faced my enemy. I'll not die a coward.'

The finality in his voice made her understand that nothing would stop him from this battle.

He didn't have the strength, not against a master swordsman like Flynn Ó Banníon. Even without his wounded hands, such a battle was an invitation to death. She knew he would fail.

'You'll die a fool,' she whispered, unable to listen any more. She rose from the table, blinking back the hot tears. 'I am sorry, Seamus and Riona, but I must go.' She refused to look back at Connor.

Outside, she passed through the gates, hearing the night sounds of a fire crackling and muted conversations. She accepted a torch from one of the soldiers and walked into the open field. The fire cast a golden glow against the grasses, and this time she gave rein to her feelings. Silent tears slipped down her cheeks. She couldn't bear to think of Connor dying.

Footsteps moved behind her. She did not move, knowing it was Connor who followed.

'Why is it, I wonder, that you have worked to help me regain my strength when you believe I'll die?'

'Because I promised,' she responded. Turning, she added, 'And I keep my promises.'

He touched a hand to her shoulder. 'Wait. Please.'

She paused, allowing him to face her. 'What more do you want from me, Connor?'

'I want to know why my death would bother you so.'

Moonlight spilled over him, illuminating his face. She swallowed back the tears. It was too late to guard her heart from him. The thought of Ó Bannon striking a death blow against this man, the father of her child, quite simply devastated her.

She was in love with him.

'It would be a waste of my healing,' she lied. 'I went to all the trouble to mend your bones, when you only intend to get yourself killed.'

'Is that the only reason?' he asked, raising his palm to her cheek. He wiped away the tears, his touch burning deep into her heart. She wanted so badly to go into his arms, to feel his warmth surrounding her.

She gathered herself together. 'No. It's not the only reason.'

Not awaiting a reply or an excuse, she turned from him. Quickening her strides, she left him standing alone. Her blood pounded in her veins, her face crimson with embarrassment. She hadn't wanted to admit that she cared, especially when the only feelings he held for her were lust.

She blinked through the tears, knowing that nothing she did would turn him from the path he'd chosen.

In the shadows, she heard the sound of movement, but did not look up. She had humbled herself enough tonight. If Connor wanted to speak more to her, he could do so in the privacy of the sick hut.

A strong hand covered her mouth, another hand reaching for her breast. Shocked, Aileen dropped the torch. Another man picked it up, a stranger she hadn't seen before.

The man holding her tore at her *léine*, and Aileen fought against him, freeing her mouth. He held her fists, his grip bruising.

'Connor!' she shouted. 'Help me!'

The man jerked her savagely off her feet, knocking her to the ground. He pinned her, his heavy body pressing her down. Aileen screamed, and saw Connor draw his sword. The other assailant blocked him, the metal clanging. Seconds later, her attacker released her. He picked up the torch and swung it at Connor. The two men circled him, one meeting Connor's sword, the other moving behind. Aileen stumbled to her feet, searching for a rock or a weapon.

Nothing. She ran toward one of the men, calling out a warning to Connor. The other villain struck a vicious blow, and the sword crashed from Connor's hands. He ducked to avoid the slash of a fiery torch, rolling away from the men. When he reached for the sword, his right hand could not raise the weapon.

'Run!' he gritted out, rising to his feet. He darted past one of the fighters, narrowly avoiding the slice of a sword.

The next moments moved in a blur. Aileen saw another figure racing toward them. Metal clashed against metal, and the man howled in pain as the blade slashed his skin.

She saw Riordan, wrenching an attacker away from Connor. His fist connected with the assailant's face in a solid blow, blood dripping down. The other man appeared dazed, hardly struggling.

Aileen picked up the fallen torch, holding the flames as a weapon.

'Get out of here,' Riordan commanded to the attackers, lifting his sword as if to strike a killing blow. In the fire-light, his fierce visage appeared barbaric. The men did not argue, but fled.

Then he turned, and the cruelty disappeared. 'Are you all right?' he asked gently.

Aileen held the torn pieces of her *léine* together, trying to shield herself from his gaze. 'Yes.'

He pulled her against him, his heavy body protective. 'It's all right. No harm was done.' He stroked her hair, and Aileen trembled in his embrace. She wanted to pull away, but his firm grip would not allow it. In the darkness, she saw Connor rise to his feet. He said nothing to the pair, but continued on toward her land.

It was then that Aileen noticed they were nowhere near Riordan's hut. How had he heard the attack? It was late at night. Discomfort festered in her thoughts.

She was grateful, but at last she extracted herself from his arms. 'Thank you for your aid. How did you come to be here?'

Riordan shrugged. 'One of the lambs wandered out of the pen, and I came to look for it. I suppose it was Fortune that made me hear your need.'

He leaned in and touched his forehead to hers. 'I couldn't bear it if anything ever happened to you, Aileen.'

'Forgive me, Riordan.' She ran a few paces away, her stomach burning. The effects of the wine curdled her insides, coupled with her fear. Her knees buckled, but though she clutched her middle, the contents of her stomach remained where they were. Her head spun with dizziness, and she forced herself not to be sick. Riordan helped her back up, but she couldn't stop shaking.

'I'll walk you home,' he said.

She let him, her mind numb. Was Connor all right? He'd disappeared, not speaking a word to either of them. When she tried to remember if he'd been hurt, the events blurred. Riordan was speaking to her throughout the journey home, and she was dimly aware of responding.

When they reached the door, he tried to take her into his arms. She accepted his embrace, for her legs would not hold steady. She drew balance from him, still trembling.

'You are frightened. I can stay with you tonight,' he offered.

'No.' She shook her head. 'I'd rather be alone. And Connor is here if—'

'He did well defending you,' Riordan scoffed. 'I could see that for myself.'

The derision in his voice turned her cold. 'Please, Riordan. I just want to sleep.' With a pointed look, she added, 'Alone.'

'If you have need of me…'

This was not working. She took his hands in hers. 'I am grateful for your help this night. Truly I am.' She expelled a sigh.

His face coloured with pride, and she understood suddenly that this was what he'd sought. Her approval.

'Tomorrow morn, perhaps you'd like to walk with me?' he invited.

She forced a false smile on to her face. 'I'll see how I feel in the morning.' For now, she just wanted to be left alone. She needed to see Connor, to know that he was all right. But if she let Riordan know it, he'd never leave her be.

Finally he left, closing the door behind him. Aileen reached for a jug and poured herself a cup of mead. She drank the amber liquid and fortified her strength.

When she was certain Riordan had gone, she left her hut to see Connor. She opened the door, but there was no fire, only cool darkness.

'I don't want you here, Aileen.'

His voice was like granite, harsh and unyielding.

'Did they harm you? Let me see—'

'No.' He kept away from her in the shadows. 'You need not concern yourself on my behalf. They did not harm me.'

The stillness stretched onwards, and he asked, 'What about you?'

'I am not hurt.'

'It was good that Riordan was there.'

And yet, she could not understand how Riordan had come to be there at precisely the right moment. 'It was.'

'Go back to your hut, Aileen.'

'Not yet.'

The intimate darkness granted her a kind of courage she might not otherwise have. She stepped forward, touching her palms to his face. His warm skin, the rough planes of his jaw, drew her to him. She leaned down and kissed him.

His firm mouth did not kiss her back, so she put more of herself into it, taking his lips and deepening it. She threaded her hands into his hair, and suddenly she broke through to him.

He kissed her back, his mouth unleashing the full force of passion. His tongue met hers, and she gripped his neck to keep from losing her balance. His hands kept still at her waist, but his mouth devoured hers.

Her body awakened, and she needed to be with him. She no longer cared that he was going to leave her, planned to give himself over into Death's hands. For this night, she craved his touch.

And then he broke away. 'Leave me, Aileen.'

'I don't want to.'

He leaned in, nipping a kiss against her lips. 'You were right to turn me away the other night. It's better if we don't travel down this path.'

'I was wrong,' she whispered. 'But you frightened me. When I'm with you, I can't stop myself from feeling this way.'

'You saw what happened.' His voice was bitter. 'I couldn't protect you from those men.'

'There were two of them,' she argued. 'You were outnumbered.'

He expelled a sigh. 'Half a season ago, they would both be lying on the grass, their life blood spent. It would have taken me only seconds to run my blade through their hearts. They would never have touched you.'

'I don't believe it.'

He raised his injured hand to her face. 'These hands are no longer whole, Aileen. I'm not the man you deserve.'

He kissed her again, but she recognised it as a kiss of farewell. 'I am going to return home to my brothers, to finish my training. Riordan can protect you the way I can't. And he cares for you.'

Hurt rage bubbled forth. 'I'm not going to wed Riordan. He isn't the man I want.' She held him, but he did not return the embrace.

'I cannot be the man you want either, Aileen.' He took her hand and led her to the door. 'Go.'

With her heart beaten and broken, she closed the door behind her.

'You did not have to cut me,' the stranger argued, hissing as he tended the wound upon his arm.

'Then your reflexes are slow,' Riordan remarked. 'You should have raised your sword quicker.'

He tossed a bag of silver at their feet. 'There is your payment. Do not show your face in these lands again.'

The man pocketed the pieces, grinning. 'A good wage. Pity I couldn't have touched the lass a little more. A pretty bit, she was.'

Riordan swung a fist, but the man ducked. He'd spent a great deal on these two, but it was worth it. Connor MacEgan hadn't been able to rescue Aileen. She now knew how weak the warrior was, how unworthy MacEgan was of her affections.

In her eyes, Riordan knew he'd become a hero. Hadn't she embraced him? Hadn't she agreed to walk with him? His mind filled with thoughts of her loving him.

And best of all, he imagined Connor MacEgan falling beneath Ó Banníon's sword. How he would love to be there to see it when it happened.

Chapter 14

The next morning, Connor was gone before sunup. Aileen saw his belongings were still in place, and she breathed a little easier. He hadn't gone yet.

She packed her basket of healing herbs and walked toward the cluster of cottages. She did not know how the villagers would react, though Seamus had granted her permission to visit them. A fist of apprehension curled inside her stomach, worry that they would not want to see her.

The noise of wailing caught her unawares. A woman stumbled forth from one of the wicker huts, her long black hair hanging against her shoulders. Her voice cried out in grief.

Aileen recognised the woman as Maive, and she rushed forward. 'What is it?' As soon as she touched Maive, she felt the burning signs of fever. 'Come and lie down.' She guided the woman back into the hut, but Maive struggled.

'He's dead.' She pointed toward the bed where her foster-son Padraig lay.

The boy's eyes were glazed, his body lying upon a straw pallet. Aileen knelt beside him, and saw a multitude of red spots covering the boy's torso. An invisible wall of fear cut off her breath. Her worst fears had come to pass. The pox was here. Though she had memorised every word Kyna had taught her, she had never seen the illness herself. Cold fear sliced at her confidence. Would Seamus hold her responsible for Padraig's death?

She closed off the thought. It was too late to worry about that now. She could not abandon Maive in her time of need. Though she could not save the boy, she could still help the mother. Repressing her instincts to flee, she took a step back from the child. 'How long has it been since he died?'

'A few hours.' Maive's hands shook, and she began to sob. 'He had the fever for two days. Then he complained that his head hurt, and I sent him to bed. This morn, he was covered in the pox, and he did not rise.'

Aileen led the woman to her own pallet. 'Lie down and let me look after you.'

'I'm going to die.' Maive wept, letting Aileen ease her down. 'What is the use?'

'Not everyone dies from the pox,' Aileen reassured her. She dampened a linen cloth and wiped Maive's forehead. 'I'll make you something to ease your pain. Try to rest.'

Maive turned her face toward Padraig. Aileen saw the direction of her gaze and she picked up a woolen *brat*. Without speaking, she drew the shawl over the boy's body.

'I will pray for him,' she said.

The woman's face transformed with wrenching pain. 'He was a good lad.'

'Where is your husband?' Aileen asked.

'Gone. He left us, when the demons brought sickness

here.' Maive emitted a sigh of disgust. 'I hope the gods strike him with the illness, the coward.'

Aileen picked up her basket and searched inside until she found the stone vial of holy water. She poured a little on to her fingers and anointed Maive's forehead. 'I will do what I can to drive the demons forth.'

Even as she tended Maive, she remembered the burned body of the storyteller. Surely he had brought the demons of pox upon them. From the old healer Kyna's instructions, Aileen remembered that the demons tended to move among the bodies of those nearby.

'Has Padraig played with any of the other boys recently?' Aileen asked. She filled the iron cauldron with water and set it to hang above the fire.

Maive's voice grew softer. 'He played with Whelon a few days ago. He wanted to go with the other boys to see Connor MacEgan, but he was not well enough.'

A deep chill pervaded Aileen's skin at the mention of Whelon. It had been Whelon who had discovered the fallen storyteller. And if Padraig had fallen prey to the illness after visiting Whelon…

Her heart sank. By the saints, let it not be true. She closed her eyes. The water bubbled in the pot, and when it was ready she prepared the drink. She lifted the cup to Maive's lips. The woman drank, but it was difficult for her to swallow. Aileen wiped her forehead again and saw the traces of small lesions beginning to form.

She needed help. If the sickness began to spread throughout the *tuatha*, she needed someone with her to tend them. Illona was gone, forbidden to help her.

Connor. The name was a prayer on her lips as she assured

Maive she would return. Aileen lifted the skirts of her gown and rushed across the meadow to the forest where she knew he trained. The oaks rose high above the meadow like sentries guarding the hidden clearing. But Connor was not there.

She raced towards the sick hut, more than afraid she would find him gone. Would he have left so soon without saying farewell? Last night he had forced her to leave him. The thought of finding an empty hut filled her with despair.

Her sides ached, but she pressed onwards. The morning sun cast a sharp glare, and she shielded her eyes. When at last she reached her land, she wanted to weep with relief.

Connor stood near the animal pen, leading a mare the colour of snow. Young and seemingly gentle, the mare allowed Connor to take her around the circle.

'You said you wanted a horse,' Connor remarked, holding out the reins.

She had forgotten about it completely. At the time, it had been an offhand thought, a gift she had never thought to receive. The mare dipped her head to sniff Aileen's hand. She patted the animal, her throat seizing with emotion. He'd remembered.

'I don't understand,' she said, her voice breaking. Why had he bought the horse now? Was it meant to be a farewell gift?

He placed the reins in her hand. 'I hurt your feelings last night.'

Aileen guarded her emotions, not letting him see the anguish brimming in her heart. She met his gaze with honesty. 'Yes, you did.'

'I never wanted that.' He reached out to caress her hair, touching the strands as though they were silk. 'Over the past few moons, I've said many things that I wish I could take back. I've spoken in anger and in haste.' He let his hand drop to his side. 'You never deserved to be treated like that. I wanted to atone for my mistakes. It isn't enough, but it's all I can give you.'

'You could have given me a memory,' she whispered.

He closed the distance and kissed her lightly. In his grey eyes, she saw regret. 'You're better off without me, Aileen.'

Silence descended between them. She swallowed hard, pain filling up inside her. 'How did you manage it? The cost of a horse is very dear.'

'I made an agreement with Seamus. My land in exchange for the animal.' He shrugged. 'Not that I had very much to offer.'

'You cannot do this,' she argued. 'It's all you have.' She couldn't understand why he would make such a sacrifice.

'I won't be needing the land, Aileen. Both of us know it.' He cupped her chin with his disfigured right hand. 'And I wanted to keep our agreement. As a healer, you need a horse for your duties.'

The strangling tide of grief spilled over. She knew, after this day, Seamus would banish her. How many more deaths would there be? She closed her eyes, praying for mercy.

'The horse was for Whelon.' She blinked back tears, remembering the dream she'd held for him.

He stared at her with confusion. 'Whelon?'

She nodded. 'He wanted to be a soldier. But he cannot run, so I thought he could be a messenger or a sentry. The horse was for him. To give him legs because I had to take one from him.'

'You gave him his life,' Connor said. 'It was enough.'

Life. Her mind shuddered with the terror of the pox. 'We

have to go to him. A boy has already died from the pox. They played together.'

Connor understood her need. 'Gather your supplies and I'll prepare the horse. We'll ride.'

She had forgotten her basket at Maive's, but she used a bundle of cloth to collect more herbs. She gathered a vial of spikenard oil, fresh garlic bulbs and ragwort. Within moments, she raced outside. Connor helped her atop the mare and mounted behind her. As they rode back to the cottages, she leaned into his strong arms.

'Thank you,' she whispered, though from the wind he could not hear her. To have him at her side meant everything. She drew strength from him, and for a moment she closed her eyes, wishing he could be with her always. She ached, knowing that he would leave.

When she stopped at Maive's hut, the woman was sleeping. Aileen wiped Maive's feverish brow once more, then lifted Padraig's body into her arms. She carried the still form behind the hut, and Connor dismounted to help her. Though she believed the demons of sickness had already left Padraig, she did not want his body near his mother. Gently, she covered the boy with the *brat* once more. Later they would bury him.

'We must go to Whelon,' she urged. She collected her basket, adding the cloth bundle of herbs. Connor lifted her up again, and within moments they rode across the fields toward the dwelling of Whelon's foster-parents.

Connor leaned forward, his mouth at her ear. 'You'll save him, Aileen. Do not fear.'

His words of confidence could not quite convince her.

Though she had faith in her healing abilities, the pox was a sickness more powerful than any she had ever faced. In her mind, she centred her focus upon the old healer Kyna's words: *Not everyone dies*.

She had to hold fast to that hope, to believe that she could cure Whelon. Perhaps it was not too late.

Smoke rose from the chimney, offering the frail chance that someone was caring for the boy. Aileen knocked upon the door, hardly waiting for the call to enter before she opened it.

The hut was empty, save Whelon. There was no trace of his foster-parents Brenda and Laegaire, nor his foster-siblings. Though a fire burned in the hearth, they had abandoned him.

If Seamus knew that his son was left alone, his wrath would be unthinkable.

Aileen pulled back the layers of blankets from Whelon. His small face was flushed with heat. Upon his cheeks, lesions had begun to form. In her mind, she remembered Padraig's limp body, his eyes staring in death.

She needed to tell Seamus, to let him know. But then her fears returned. What if Seamus found out about Padraig? He might not let her treat Whelon. And Riona... Her heart ached to think of the mother's grief.

She couldn't let him die, no matter what.

'Aileen?' Connor's voice broke through her fear, and he gestured toward the basket of herbs. 'Shall I boil water for you?'

His question snapped her back into reality. Whelon needed her. And she must do whatever was necessary to fight for his life.

'Yes. I'll need it later to make a willow bark drink for him.'

Aileen unlaced the boy's tunic and ordered Connor,

'Sponge his body with water to bring down the fever. I'm going to treat the rash.'

Aileen selected the vial of spikenard oil. The intense perfume of the root filled the air as she poured a small amount over her fingers.

She rubbed his skin with the oil, hoping it would cure the rash. Silently, she murmured a healing chant, one to drive away the demons of sickness. She massaged the oil into his skin, down his torso, and even upon the stump of his leg. He shivered as though attacked by unseen enemies.

When the willow bark had finished steeping, Connor held Whelon's head upright while Aileen eased the drink down.

Hours passed as she continued giving him the brew, then easing the oils into his rash. And still his fever rose hotter. She stared at the door, then at Connor. 'I cannot believe they left him here alone.' Though she had never called Brenda and Laegaire her friends, the callous act of abandoning a child enraged her. Their fear of the illness had overcome any affection they had felt toward Whelon.

'They might have gone to fetch help. Or the priest,' he said. But both of them knew the truth. The couple had thought of no one but themselves.

'We have to tell Seamus,' Connor said.

'I know.' She poured more of the oil into her palm. 'But let it be after I've done what I can for him.'

Connor helped her make more willow bark brew, silently offering his support. Only an hour ago, he'd gone at her bequest to check on Maive. The woman held on to life, and he'd brought her more brew, along with some of the spikenard oil. He had also found another woman to look after Maive.

Not everyone dies, Aileen reminded herself. Maive's survival offered a grain of hope. And still Whelon's fever did not break. It seemed that more and more lesions erupted on his skin, no matter what she did.

When night slipped across the horizon and only the light from the fire cast a glow upon them, Connor put his hand upon her shoulder. 'Are you not afraid the illness might strike you?'

'No more than you are afraid to lift a blade to an enemy. It's what I do.' But she was a warrior of a different nature, one who could not meet her enemy face to face.

'I had the pox as a child,' he said. 'Though I do not remember it, I remember my mother's tears.'

'You are not scarred from it,' Aileen remarked.

His lips lifted slightly. 'Not in places you can see. Unless you have a better memory than mine.'

At the reminder of seeing him naked, she tensed. She had thrown herself at him last eve. He hadn't wanted her, told her they should not lie together.

She bit her lip, wondering if she should have admitted the truth. That she'd seduced him once before.

'It is late,' Connor said. 'Would you like to rest? I'll keep watch.'

She shook her head. 'I can't sleep. Not at a time like this.' Surrendering to sleep would be like offering Death a foothold. She'd not be distracted for a single moment. 'But if you are weary, you may wish to sleep.'

'No. If you remain awake, I'll be here to help you.'

She cast a glance toward Whelon, who slept. Then she closed the distance, taking his face between her hands. 'Few men would do what you have done for me this day.'

'I have little to lose,' he admitted. He pulled her close, stroking her hair. Aileen wanted to weep at the tender gesture. Why did she have to love this man? It tore her apart, knowing that he valued his honour more than his life.

More than her.

She broke the embrace and went to stand by the fire. She filled the pot with more water, wishing she knew what to say. In the end, she said nothing. All she could do was savour the few moments they had left together. He'd be leaving soon.

A few hours before dawn, Whelon began to stir. His eyes brightened when he saw them. Aileen sat beside him, Connor opposite.

'You're here,' he whispered, a soft glow of happiness shining in his eyes. 'I hoped you'd come.'

Aileen smoothed the hair from his forehead. 'Would you like some broth or water?'

Whelon shook his head. He regarded Connor solemnly. 'I thank you for my training.'

Connor shook his head and took the boy's hand in his. The misshapen fingers covered Whelon's smaller hand. 'You still have much to learn.'

The brightness in Whelon's face swelled. 'I have learned all that I can.'

'Bring me the holy water, Aileen,' Connor ordered. The intensity of the command made her falter.

'No. He's not going to die.' She refused to relinquish her hold upon the boy's life. 'I won't let it happen.'

'It's all right, Aileen,' Whelon said. His cracked lips turned upwards. 'I'm going to be a true warrior now.'

Tears bled a path down her face. 'You can be a warrior here.'

'Not a whole one.' Whelon lifted his eyes upwards. 'Let me go, Aileen.'

Connor marked him with the holy water, murmuring the words of Last Rites beneath his breath. Aileen joined him, tasting the salt of her tears.

Pure unrelenting joy shone from the boy's eyes. Peace descended over his face, and he took Connor's hand and Aileen's. With exertion, he placed the two together. Aileen's fingers interlaced with Connor's.

And with that, the boy breathed his last.

Chapter 15

Inside Aileen's hut, glass shattered. Connor stood back, silent while she struck down clay and leather vessels of medicines and herbs. With tears streaming down her face, she curled her fist and smashed against the unyielding wicker frame of the hut. Curses spilled forth as she vented her rage upon the wood.

'Aileen.' He used his strength to subdue her, holding her in his arms. 'Don't.'

'He shouldn't have died.' Fury blazed in her eyes, the colour turning thunderous. She sank to her knees, her shoulders slumped low. In the shadows, she trembled with exhaustion and grief.

'Look at me.' He sat beside her, taking her hand. Her skin was icy. 'It wasn't your fault.'

He wanted to take away her pain, to ease it somehow. But words were not enough.

She looked up, her expression that of a broken woman. 'I keep thinking that, if I had learned more from Kyna. Or perhaps if I'd tried a different combination of herbs. Maybe—'

'No. You did everything you could.' He bade her rise and embraced her, offering the comfort of his arms.

'Connor?' she whispered. She tilted her chin, her mouth only inches from his. Belenus, he wanted to kiss her. But if he gave into the fierce need, he would not stop. 'Will you help me to forget all of this?'

Aileen took a step backwards, her dark hair spilling across her shoulder. His mind conjured up sinful images, but he could not pull his gaze away. She pulled her hair to one side, then lifted her overdress away. Clad in the sheer white *léine*, her silhouette tempted him to give into his darkest desires.

His honour held by no more than a breath of reason. 'I am leaving Banslieve.'

'So am I. Seamus will force me to leave.'

'I won't take advantage of you this way.'

She bared one shoulder, then the other, until her *léine* slid to the floor. Naked, she looked like an ethereal goddess, beckoning for him to worship before her. Her nipples held the deep red of a woman who had given birth, but her waist was as small as a maiden's. A silken web of dark hair guarded her womanhood.

'You said you wanted me, once before. Is it still true?'

His manhood hardened in response. He ached to take her in his arms, to taste the sweetness of her flesh. 'What are you doing, Aileen?'

He didn't like the way she was behaving, as though she had nothing to lose. Beneath her bravado lay a woman who had been deeply hurt.

'You know what I am doing, Connor. What will your answer be?'

He wanted to tell her no. He wanted to take the honourable path and leave her untouched. There could be no future for them.

Instead, he crushed her mouth to his, knowing it was wrong. His hands roamed across her beautiful skin, and he gloried in the ability to finally touch a woman. This woman.

Her tongue reached out to his, in a slow, seductive touch. She yielded to him, her heavy breasts tightening with the same need he felt.

He knew it was wrong to make love with her, when it would only make it more difficult to leave her behind. He broke away, offering her one more chance to end this seduction.

'Why, Aileen? Why do you want to do something we'll both regret?'

'Because I need to feel alive. This night, with you. And then I'll let you go.'

She untied the laces of his tunic and lifted the moss-coloured garment away. 'Give me a memory. For we both know this is the last night we'll see each other.'

Her hands moved over his muscles, tracing the battle scars His breath caught when she lowered her lips to his chest.

The needling sense of familiarity caught him. Her touch, her body. There was something about her, a memory beyond his reach.

With her hands, she tugged at his trews, pulling them downward until she exposed his nakedness. His manhood jutted forward, long and hard.

'I need to touch you,' he gritted out. 'Do not move.'

She stood before him, and he palmed her bottom, bringing her close until her breasts touched his chest. He took her nipple into his mouth, tasting the hardened tip. A sigh caught in her throat, her neck arching with pleasure.

His own body ached to fill her, to drive his length inside her sweet depths. He parted her thighs, and inserted a finger, feeling her wetness surrounding him.

'Connor,' she moaned.

He was losing his mind. Perhaps it was this place, the darkened shadows evoking memories of long ago. But he'd swear he'd made love to Aileen before.

He trailed a path of kisses down to her stomach, lowering her to the ground.

'I've waited for this,' she said. 'I've wanted you for a long time.'

By the gods, though he knew it was wrong to take her this way, his resistance was gone. With his tongue, he tasted her honeyed femininity. Spasms of fierce need made her body shudder. He watched her body seize with pleasure while he tasted, nipped at her until waves of release stole her breath.

'Enough,' she begged, and turned him on to his back. Her hair spilled over his chest, soft and sensual. His erection was excruciatingly hard, but he wanted to make this moment special for her.

When she lowered herself on top of him, he closed his eyes to fight the release urge. She moved slowly, driving every inch of him deep inside her. Her tight well squeezed him, and he reached up to take her breasts in his hands.

Past and present merged, and he remembered every moment of Bealtaine. Sweet gods, but the last time he'd felt such intense pleasure was when he was barely a man.

He grabbed her waist, increasing the tempo until her body

slammed against him. Desire roared through him, and he rolled her onto her back, lifting her knees to allow him to go deeper.

With each thrust, he claimed her as his own. Her breathing was fast now, her body shuddering and clenching with release. It wasn't enough for him. Faster. Deeper. Stronger.

Aileen had lain in his arms that night. He was sure of it.

'Bealtaine,' he gritted out. 'It was you, wasn't it? That's what you wanted to tell me.'

She lifted her hips, opening her eyes to meet his. 'I took Lianna's place.'

Her confession twisted at his heart. He should be relieved to learn that it had not been Lianna who had turned against him. But somehow, the new knowledge invaded his trust in Aileen.

He increased the speed, until she sobbed out in pleasure. At last, he spilled himself deep within her womb.

He stayed inside, her legs wrapped around his waist. Burying his face against her neck, he fought the confused feelings of betrayal.

'Connor?' she whispered, kissing his cheek. He withdrew from her, still shaken by her admission.

He pulled on his trews, no longer blinded by desire. Though his body was sated, questions filled his mind. Why had she lied to him? Was it simply a night of stolen lovemaking?

'I want to know exactly what happened that night.'

Aileen pulled on her *léine*, suddenly self-conscious of her nakedness. Inside the hut, the fire had died down to muted coals.

'Lianna was not a virgin.' She closed her eyes, reliving that night so long ago. 'She asked me to lie with you, and I agreed. In the darkness, we thought you would not know.'

'You played me for a fool.'

The edge of his voice cut her like a blade. Aileen tried to hide her feelings. It hadn't been that way at all. But how could he understand the yearnings of a girl only sixteen years of age? She'd been so afraid, but she'd done what she thought was right.

'I believed if she fulfilled her part, the harvest would suffer. It would—'

'You played her part because you wanted to lie with me.'

She could not deny it. 'Yes.'

Beneath his accusing eyes, she struggled to maintain her composure. Tonight, she had cast aside every inhibition, anything to avoid the grief threatening to suffocate her. She'd needed him so badly.

But now, he looked at her as though she'd betrayed him. The angry glare of a warrior bore into her, of a man who didn't like being used.

'Tell me this, Aileen.' He imprisoned her wrist. 'What else did you wish to reveal about Bealtaine?' The glint in his eyes robbed her of breath.

'N-nothing.'

'Rhiannon is my child, isn't she?'

Aileen couldn't answer. It didn't matter what she said, for already he knew the truth. Her skin turned numb with fear. A tear rolled down her face, granting him the answer he sought.

'Damn the both of you,' he said, rising to his feet. His voice turned to thunder. 'Did you enjoy laughing behind my back? Give Connor any woman and he'll not know the difference. Is that what you said?'

He jerked the rest of his clothing back on, and Aileen

covered her mouth with her hands. 'No. We never talked about it.'

'I saw Lianna the next morn. Naked in Tómas's arms. I thought she'd betrayed me. But it wasn't her. I had no cause to be angry with her.'

His eyes were black with hatred, and Aileen wished she could take the confession back. But it was too late. He wasn't going to forgive her.

Blood rushed to her face, and she couldn't stop shivering. Right now she wanted to flee, to seek the solace of the night and weep for all she'd lost. But she had made her own fate. It was time to face the penalty for her stolen night.

'I don't regret what I did,' she said. How could she? Rhiannon was her treasure, her very heart.

'I have a daughter,' he said. 'One who was raised believing her father was another man. And you find no shame in that?'

'I tried to tell you. Twice.' She reached out, but he would not look at her. 'You refused to listen to me.'

'And now? What do you expect me to do? Go and tell her who I am?'

She paled. 'Don't. It would only frighten her.' She had never seen Connor so angry, but her protectiveness toward Rhiannon fortified her courage.

'You want me to pretend as though she doesn't exist?'

'That would be for the best.' Now, it was more clear than ever that she couldn't have Connor back in her life. His words bruised her heart, and she would not shatter Rhiannon's safe world with the truth.

'I won't have my daughter believing her father abandoned her.' Cold steel eyes glared at her.

Strange, how one revelation could transform a man so. Only a moment ago, she had lain naked in his arms, both of them sated from lovemaking. Now in his visage, she saw hatred.

'You abandoned me,' Aileen whispered. 'That day in the rain, when I first tried to tell you. You didn't want any part of me.'

Her anger boiled inside her with the need to spill out all the feelings she'd held back over the past seven years. 'Poor, plain-faced Aileen, in love with Connor MacEgan,' she taunted. 'I knew it would horrify you to learn that you'd shared my bed. You made that clear from the first. I wasn't about to let you hurt Rhiannon.'

'I would have helped you take care of her.'

'No, you wouldn't.' She closed her eyes. 'You wouldn't have believed me. And I had Eachan to take care of us.'

'She deserves to know the truth.' He crossed his arms, trying to intimidate her.

She'd have none of it. Her maternal hackles rose up. 'Are you going to give up your fight against Ó Banníon?'

'No.'

'Then there's no need to tell Rhiannon about you. You won't be there to watch her grow up.' By Danu, why couldn't she stop the tears from filling up inside her? She needed to be strong, to stand up for her daughter's needs.

'You don't believe I will defeat him.'

'I don't, no.' *Do not cry. Do not let him see you weaken.* She tightened her hands into fists, digging her nails into her palms.

'Then there's nothing more to be said, is there?' He strode to the door, tossing it open. With a backwards glance, he added, 'After Samhain, I want Rhiannon fostered at my home in Laochre. Deny me, and you will regret it.'

Connor slammed his fist against the exterior of the sick hut. For nearly ten years, he'd not returned to these lands. He'd cut himself off from friends and from his foster family. But Lianna had done nothing wrong. It was Aileen who was to blame for it.

He might have forgiven her if it had only been a stolen night of lovemaking. But she'd borne him a child.

He thought of Rhiannon, her wild dark hair like her mother's. Like a young colt with long limbs, she would be a tall maiden one day. Her creamy complexion rivalled Aileen's, but her eyes mirrored his own. He should have recognised it.

Beyond her appearance, he knew nothing of the girl. To have a child nearly six summers of age and to be unaware of her existence troubled him. How could Aileen hold such a secret and not tell him? He was not the sort of man to leave bastard children behind.

He gathered his belongings into a bundle, placing his brother's sword atop it. He lifted the heavy weapon with his left hand, then shifted it to his right. His wrist burned, but he gave a practice swing.

Once, he could wield a blade fluidly, without any thought. Now, it took his complete concentration to make the weapon move where he wanted it to.

He'd stayed here too long. He should have left a sennight ago. Only by training with his brothers could he defeat Flynn Ó Banníon.

After setting his belongings next to the entrance, he opened the door to let in the crisp night air. The dim starlight filtered in through the entrance, and he inhaled the scent of night.

And then, the scent of healing herbs. He closed his eyes, shutting out the memory of Aileen. His body remembered the seductive touch of her body beneath him.

Damn her for her lies. Perhaps there were some men who could father children and leave them behind, but he could not turn his back on a child. It was an act of dishonour.

He didn't know what to do about Rhiannon, save bring her to Laochre. At least then he could do something to atone for his neglect. He'd show her that he hadn't abandoned her.

His gaze fell upon a pair of splints and a ragged bandage. He held his hands up to the light. His hands were as whole as Aileen could have made them. She had kept her word and healed him.

But he still could not forgive her for the secret she'd kept.

Chapter 16

At dawn, Aileen awakened to the faint sound of voices. She rose, her body weary from lack of sleep. She opened the door, squinting at the morning sunlight. She saw Seamus, along with her brother Cillian and her father. The chieftain seemed to have aged beyond his years. Haggard lines around his mouth revealed unspoken pain.

He knew about Whelon. She could see it in his eyes. Fear and sadness clenched her lungs at the memory of the boy's death. Whelon had placed her hand in Connor's, as if to bring them together. But now, that would never happen.

Aileen pulled her *brat* tightly around her shoulders, the grey shawl offering a slight shield from the morning chill. It was like facing her own execution, for she already knew what Seamus's judgement would be. He was here to banish her, nothing else.

Her father Graeme moved forward, as if to intervene, but Cillian held him back. The door to the sick hut opened, and Connor leaned against the entrance.

He wore travelling clothes, his brother's sword hanging

at his side. He would leave today, as he'd promised. His eyes did not meet hers.

It hurt to see him, to know that he felt nothing towards her. Why had she thought it might turn out differently? And why hadn't she let matters alone? Taking him into her arms last night had been the most wonderful pleasure she'd known in seven years. It had been an act of desperation, the need to embrace someone in a moment of terrible grief. But the lovemaking came at a terrible cost. She'd destroyed their friendship.

The chieftain's face showed no mercy, and he walked forward until he stood before her. 'You know why I am here, Aileen,' he said.

'I do.' She would not cower or weep. She had made the bargain and now he would force her to leave. She raised her eyes to Seamus's. 'I am sorry for it. Would to God I could change Fate.'

'The people will not trust you as their healer any longer. They believe you brought the pox upon them.' Seamus's gruff voice held the weight of loss.

'They are wrong. I did what I could to help them.'

'You cannot stay here. They believe demons have cursed you. If you remain, they'll demand that I burn you for it.'

She drew her *brat* closer around her shoulders, afraid he was right. Though most of the folk knew her, superstitions were high. They could easily believe that the demons of illness worked through her hands.

'How long until I must leave?' she asked.

'Three days,' Seamus said quietly. 'Gather your belongings and leave Banslieve. Do not show yourself here again.'

'What about my family?' Her gaze passed to her brother and father.

'They have my permission to visit you elsewhere.'

With the judgement passed, Seamus turned away. Graeme came forwards and took Aileen in his arms, comforting her. 'I tried to change his mind, *a iníon*. But he is right. If you stay, some may try to hurt you.'

'I know.' Her voice was hardly above a whisper, but she managed to keep her emotions from snapping. 'I will be fine.'

'You can go and stay with your Aunt Noreen,' Graeme said. 'She lives just over the boundary.'

She managed a nod, clinging tightly to her father. Even as she grasped the understanding that she had to leave behind everything dear to her came the greater knowledge that Rhiannon was not safe here either. If they blamed her for the demons of illness, then they might also cast blame upon her child. She would have to take Rhiannon away from Banslieve.

Connor had ordered her to bring Rhiannon to Laochre to be fostered after Samhain. She had dismissed the idea at first, but now she considered it. There was nowhere safer for her daughter to stay than with one of the most powerful families in Ireland.

Moments later, Connor approached, greeting her father and brother. Graeme studied him with a suspicious eye. 'You're leaving today, are you?'

'I am.'

'Why don't you take her with you?' Graeme suggested with a warm smile. 'You could escort her to her Aunt Noreen.'

'Da, stop your interfering.' Aileen's face burned with embarrassment at his obvious matchmaking. How could he think of such a thing at this moment?

Connor did not return the smile. 'Aileen has done much for me, but our paths must go in separate ways. I wish her and her daughter good fortune.'

Dark shadows lined his eyes, as if he, too, had not slept. His gold hair was pulled back in a leather thong, and his blue tunic emphasised the silver of his eyes. Leather bracers encased his forearms, and tight muscles pressed against the thin fabric. He'd become the warrior again, bent upon destroying anyone who threatened him.

And she'd become a threat.

Her brother led Connor's horse from the animal pen. The saddle had already been prepared, his belongings strapped to the mare. Connor must have readied the animal for his departure earlier this morn.

'Will you break your fast before you go?' she asked.

'Not here. Seamus has asked me to join him and Riona. Then I'll depart.' He mounted the horse, his expression grim.

There was so much she wanted to say to him. She wished she could mend the ill feelings, wished she had the courage to say what she really felt.

'Wear the splints each night,' she said. 'They will help.' Awkwardness closed over her, burning her skin with embarrassment.

Dispassionate eyes stared into hers. Then he turned the horse and left.

What had she expected? A kiss farewell? Stupid she was, to believe he might come to love her. He would never forgive her. Pride meant more to him than anything else.

'Are you all right?' Cillian asked. He put his arm around her shoulders. 'Would you like me to beat him senseless for you? I can see that he's hurt your feelings, the bastard.'

She choked back a laugh, for he would. 'No.' The offer cleared her head. She wasn't going to cry over Connor MacEgan.

But she would not let him cast the blame on her. She had done what she could to keep Rhiannon safe. Now that he knew about her, the danger was worse. She would not let him control her daughter's fate, not without her own say in the matter.

And the only way to do this was to remain with Rhiannon.

'Are you in love with him, *a stór*?' her father asked.

'No. I am not a feather-headed girl with foolish dreams.'

'You were never that. But they are not such foolish dreams. He has feelings for you.'

'And if he acts upon them, I'll beat him senseless,' Cillian muttered.

Too late for that. Aileen thought.

'Da,' she reasoned, 'you're blind if you believe Connor cares anything for me beyond thankfulness that I restored his hands.'

'I am not the one who is blind,' Graeme said, patting her hand. 'But if you care for him, you'll need to go after him. Why not now? Laochre is only a few days' journey. Cillian will take you there.'

'I'll not throw myself at him. I have more pride than that.'

'I didn't raise a coward, now, did I?'

She wanted to throw up her hands in exasperation. 'This isn't about cowardice.'

'Yes, it is.' Graeme raised her chin to face him. 'You're afraid to seek what you want. Always, it's been about others, Aileen. You've given so much to so many. Take something for yourself.' His mouth curved in a half-smile, and he winked. 'A man like Connor cannot stay angry with you for very long.' He lowered his voice so that Cillian could not hear. 'Especially not if you bring his daughter to him.'

He knew. Aileen's face burned red, but she forced a nod. 'I will think about it.'

'Good. I'll give you a few moments to pack, and then I want you to come home. Your mother wants to say goodbye and give advice, and chatter your ears off.' He embraced her. 'You won't be living in Banslieve any more. But we'll come to see you often. It will be all right.'

Leaning upon his shoulders, she finally released the tears building up inside. 'I'll miss you.'

He wiped his own eyes, and cleared his throat. 'Well, you'd better get started then.'

Somehow, he'd made it bearable. With her heart bruised and battered, she glanced back at the empty horizon and wondered if she had the courage to go after Connor MacEgan.

Or if she wanted to.

It took less time than she'd expected to pack her medicines and few belongings. She'd brought a few carved wooden bowls, a hide tent, and some dried food. Nothing more than she could fit on the mare Connor had given her. She ran her hand across the animal, staring back at her small plot of land.

Danu, she didn't want to leave. Her life, all her memories, were here. She had climbed atop the roof to replace the thatching, laughing when Eachan tossed the bundles to her. It had been a good marriage, and she missed him still. Rhiannon had stumbled across the threshold, grasping the wooden frame for support when she'd learned to walk.

Her eyes dry, she swallowed hard and forced herself to look away. It was then that she saw Riordan Ó Duinne walking over the rise of the hill.

'Good morn to you, Aileen,' he greeted.

'And to you.' She forced a smile, afraid of the reason why he'd come. Certainly he'd heard of her banishment.

'Would you walk with me for a few moments?' He glanced at her horse, and then behaved as if he hadn't seen her packed belongings.

She supposed it wouldn't matter if she walked for a while. There was time yet before she went to her parents' dwelling.

She joined him, and he remained close to her side, his fingers touching her palms. 'I thought you should know that Maive lived. Only Whelon and Padraig died.'

'Did anyone else fall ill?'

'No.' This time, he took her palm in his. 'Aileen, I don't want to be parted from you. I want you to be my wife.'

Her hand felt cool in his, the touch nothing like Connor's. Once again, a steady man offered his protection. Instead of being a comfort, it unsettled her.

Da was right. She'd let her head rule her heart, never seeking what she wanted. Both times, she'd given Connor up. She hadn't spoken her heart, nor had she fought for him. She did not want to make the same mistake another time. If he turned her away, so be it. But at least she'd try.

'You have always been dear to me, Riordan. A true friend, you are,' she said gently.

Colour suffused his cheeks, as if he knew what she was about to say.

'I won't be marrying you,' she said, drawing her hand away.

Riordan took a steadying breath. 'You've already said it

was too soon to wed anyone. There is time, yet, Aileen. I can take you with me, to the home of my family in the north. Give me the chance to be the man you want.'

She squared her shoulders. 'Connor MacEgan is the man I want.' The words spilled out without warning. But they were true.

Riordan's expression darkened. 'Why do you wish to wed a man who cannot protect you? You saw what happened the night you were attacked. He bade you to run. Will you run for the remainder of your life? Think upon what would have happened, had they caught you, Aileen.'

He reached out and touched her shoulder. 'It would not have been pleasant.'

She stepped away, and he pleaded, 'I can take care of you, Aileen. Let me try at least.'

'I am sorry, Riordan. I cannot.'

And with those words, his compassion transformed into brutal wrath. 'You've shared his bed, haven't you?' he sneered. 'Like a common whore.'

She slapped him, and the sting of her hand only infuriated him more. He pushed her against the fence, his hand gripping her throat.

'I paid those two men to attack you, to show you what a coward MacEgan was,' he admitted, enjoying the shock in her eyes. 'I wasted the silver on you, it seems.'

'Get away from me.'

At last, he released her. 'Go, then. But he'll never have you. You're not noble enough for a man of his breeding.'

His words struck a barb in her confidence. Rubbing her throat, she stared at him. His sudden violence made her only the more certain that she needed to leave Banslieve.

Riordan saw her as a possession to be had, not a woman with feelings.

When at last he had gone, she lifted her face to the skies, praying to heaven that she had the courage to confront Connor. And this time, she would bring Rhiannon with her.

Chapter 17

Rain spattered against the muddy roads, but Connor paid it no heed. The stone walls of his brother Patrick's fortress loomed ahead. Over the past few days, his mind had centred upon his purpose: preparing to defeat Flynn Ó Banníon. He would gain the strength he needed, no matter the cost.

Connor slowed the gait of his horse to study Laochre. The imposing stone fortress had nearly become a castle. He hadn't realised they'd accomplished so much of the building. He had done his share of lifting stones, same as the others. Yet he hadn't appreciated the full impact until he saw Laochre from a distance. By using stone instead of wood, it would keep out the invaders. Envy struck at him, but he quelled the thought. His brother had earned the right to be king.

He kept the horse at a steady pace, watching the landscape unfold in colours of rich green. Tufts of grain lifted their heads to the sky, bowing beneath the rain. Though he should have rejoiced at coming home again, he felt empty.

The last few nights, he'd thought of Aileen. What would

become of her? Not that he should care, not after what she'd done. But he couldn't forget her beautiful face, nor the eyes brimming with unshed tears.

She'd made him feel like a callous brute. He hadn't spoken a word of farewell, for he'd truly been at a loss for words. She'd stolen a part of him, his child. Damn it all, he needed to strike her from his mind.

When he reached the gates, he greeted the guards and dismounted. A groom led his horse away, and he accepted welcoming embraces from kinsmen and friends. Patrick's wife Isabel was the first to see him in the courtyard. She flew to his side, heedless of the mud, and hugged him tightly. 'We've missed you, Connor.'

Isabel was beautiful, dressed like a queen in a crimson silk *léine* and white overdress, and Connor didn't miss her swelling middle. 'My congratulations to you and my brother. When will the new babe be born?'

Isabel's cheeks brightened with the inner glow of a mother. 'In mid-winter, I believe. Liam will have another brother or sister to torment, instead of his uncle Ewan.' While she chatted, leading him into the Great Chamber, his mind drifted back to Aileen. Had she looked like that when she'd carried Rhiannon in her womb? Had her fingers caressed the small bump as if to soothe the unborn child?

He'd caught a glimpse of his daughter before leaving Banslieve. She had done nothing more than tend the animals outside Lianna and Tómas's dwelling, but his heart had stopped cold.

He hadn't spoken a word, only watched her from a distance, drinking in the sight. Though he longed to know her, to have a bond with his daughter, he knew it was impossible.

Fate had a cruel way of taunting him. His dreams of a wife and children were beyond his reach. Though his hands had healed, he didn't know if he held the strength to defeat and kill Flynn Ó Banníon. And if he did, would he ever achieve his hopes to reign over a tribe of his own?

'Connor?' Isabel asked, drawing his attention back to the present. 'Did you hear what I said?'

He coloured. 'No. My mind wandered, I fear.'

Isabel surmised him with a sharp look. 'Let us go inside.' He could see the spinning thoughts passing over her face. Then she glanced towards the far end of the Great Chamber. 'The maidservants are happy at your return, I see.'

Connor turned and four women giggled. They stood near the perimeter of the room, women he'd admired once. Fair and dark-haired, short and tall, slim and plump, all stood poised to offer him their attentions. Once, he might have enjoyed them, but now, he viewed them as a source of irritation. He didn't even remember their names.

'I see them,' he said. 'But I've no time for this just now. I would speak with Patrick.'

'By the Blessed Mother,' Isabel murmured. 'You've gone and done it now.'

'Done what?'

'Trahern said there was a woman. You care for her, don't you?' He didn't answer, but Isabel could read through him. 'Tell me about her.'

'You are wrong,' he said. 'It's best left in the past.'

Isabel took his hand, and then she saw the misaligned bones, the crooked fingers. Though no revulsion lined her face, there was concern. 'Does she care for you?'

'Let it go, Isabel.' Though she veiled her expression, he

saw the pity in her eyes. Connor tamped down the anger rising. He didn't need or require Isabel's interference.

At that moment, his brother Patrick appeared. He wore leather training armour, and his dark hair was wet from the rain. 'I heard you had returned. Seamus Ó Duinne sent us a message that you'd given him your land.'

Connor took his leave from Isabel and followed his brother above stairs into the solarium. Patrick dismissed the ladies and waited until they were alone.

'Why did you give away your only property in exchange for a horse?'

'I had a debt to repay.'

'I'll loan you any coin you need. You know that, brother.'

'Come the festival of Samhain, I'll have no need of the land.'

'This is about Flynn Ó Banníon, isn't it? Trahern told me what he did to your hands.'

Connor inclined his head. 'He claims I defiled his daughter, and the *brehons* believed her.'

'Was evidence brought forth?'

'False witnesses. The fines nullified each other.'

'But you are not satisfied,' Patrick guessed.

'I want vengeance for what Ó Banníon's men did to me. I intend to fight him.'

Patrick shook his head and sighed. 'Did the *brehons* agree to it?'

'They did.'

'You should have accepted their first judgement.'

'I'll not pay for a woman's lies, brother.'

'I know it. But I also know you won't let Flynn Ó Banníon live.'

Connor's skin turned cold, but he met Patrick's gaze. 'He deserves death.'

'You're a fool,' Patrick said. 'Though I imagine I should do the same, were it me.' A look of understanding passed between them.

Connor sat upon one of the chairs, absently rubbing his right fingers. He'd need to splint them this night. Aileen had warned him that rain would often cause them to ache, and she'd been right.

Stop thinking of her. You did the right thing, leaving her. And yet, anger tightened in his chest.

He needed to defeat Ó Banníon and start his life anew. He could buy more land and compete to become a chieftain or a king. Perhaps marry a chieftain's daughter.

The thought evoked the image of Aileen in his bed, her warmth nestling close to his body. He shook it away.

'Draw your sword,' Patrick commanded, unsheathing his own blade. 'I would see your skills.'

Connor gripped the weapon with his left hand. His strength had returned, but he knew his reflexes were weak.

Patrick swung his sword toward Connor's head. With both hands, Connor blocked the blow. His brother showed no mercy as he lunged and sliced, testing for weaknesses. Connor defended each blow, but his wrists ached. Each strike rattled his arms, until it was only his training that kept him from dropping the sword.

Patrick swung the blade toward his middle, and Connor jerked out of the way.

'Have you lost all your skills, then?' his brother chided. 'Or do you remember anything of your training?'

Connor's blade struck Patrick's. 'I remember that you're not as quick as I am.'

He became the aggressor, swinging his blade overhead to strike down upon Patrick. Blow after blow, circling and dodging, they sparred.

Then Patrick struck him unawares and Connor's blade clattered to the wooden floor. He had not anticipated it, and the simple disarming shamed him.

'You are not ready to face Flynn Ó Banníon.'

'Not yet,' Connor acceded. 'But I will be.'

His brother's assessing stare brooked no argument. 'We've much to do. Lift your blade, and we'll begin again.'

'I won't come with you,' Rhiannon argued, as Aileen slowed the horse's pace. 'I want to stay with Lianna and Tómas.'

Rhiannon's reaction was not one she had anticipated. She had thought her daughter would enjoy the prospect of a journey, particularly one so far away.

They had stayed with her brother Cillian for a few days, and he'd journeyed with her to the border of the MacEgan lands. Though she had insisted she was fine, she doubted if Cillian had truly gone. Likely he was watching them until they were inside the gates.

Rhiannon had moped and pouted each day about having to leave her foster family. More than once, she'd threatened to run away.

'Connor MacEgan is your father,' Aileen said. She had told her daughter the truth before arriving at Laochre, for she knew it would take time for Rhiannon to accept it. 'And we are going so that you may become better acquainted with him.'

Over a sennight had passed since Connor's departure. Her heart beat faster at the thought of seeing him again. Each night had been lonely without him. But would he want her there? Or would he turn her away?

'Eachan was my true father,' Rhiannon argued.

'Eachan was my husband, not your father.'

A sullen expression tightened Rhiannon's mouth into a line. 'You can't make me stay here.'

But then the fortress of Laochre appeared upon the horizon. Aileen's fear turned into panic. She had not sent word that she was coming. She could not read or write, and to send a messenger cost more than she could afford. No, there had been no choice but to come and pray that King Patrick would grant them hospitality.

Rhiannon's chattering tongue stilled at the sight of the immense stronghold. Even at this distance, Aileen could see the numerous soldiers patrolling the battlements. Her stomach grew queasy with nerves.

At last they reached the gates. She lifted Rhiannon from the horse, and they walked to the entrance.

'We wish to see Connor MacEgan,' she said with false courage to one of the guards. 'Tell him Aileen Ó Duinne and his daughter Rhiannon are here to see him.'

The soldier bade her wait beside him while he sent a servant to inform Connor. With each passing minute, Aileen felt more and more frightened. Had she lost her wits, bringing her daughter across the countryside for a man who might turn them away? And what if the King refused them entrance? Her mind turned over all the problems while she waited.

A familiar face appeared, the young lad called Ewan MacEgan. Tall and skinny, he strode toward them with the arrogance of a boy who thought he was a man.

'Connor is training,' Ewan informed them. His gaze fell

upon Rhiannon, and surprise flushed his cheeks. 'Isabel asked me to make you welcome. She is preparing food and drink for you.'

'Does Connor know I am here?'

Ewan shook his head. 'I'll tell him when he and Patrick are finished. Isabel is waiting.'

He led them up a stone staircase into the Great Chamber. Colourful tapestries lined the walls, and sweet rushes covered the floor. Aileen wished that her *léine* were clean, that she had chosen a brighter colour than the soft green. She glimpsed ladies in fine silk gowns, with golden balls tied into their hair. Gold and silver bracelets gleamed upon their wrists.

She swallowed hard when a beautiful woman with long golden hair entered the Chamber. Dressed in a violet over-dress and *léine*, her stomach swollen with child, she held out her hands in greeting.

'I am glad you have come, Aileen Ó Duinne. I am Isabel MacEgan. Patrick is my husband.'

Aileen noticed the Queen's informal greeting, and she felt awkward at the woman's kiss of welcome. 'I apologise for not sending word of my arrival. I was unable—'

'Do not worry.' Isabel waved her hand. 'Trahern and Ewan spoke of you. I had hoped you might come.' She beckoned to servants to bring forward basins of water. 'Please sit and they will bathe your feet.'

Then she turned to Rhiannon. 'And this is your daughter?'

'Yes.' Taking a deep breath for courage, she added, 'She is also Connor's daughter.' Unbidden, tears sprang to her eyes. She tried to suppress the sudden rush of emotion, but the exhaustion of the journey and her fears made it impossible.

'Does he know?' Isabel asked, her voice hardening in defence.

Aileen nodded. 'But he will not expect to see us. I wanted him to grow better acquainted with Rhiannon.'

The Queen's expression softened. 'Would you like to bathe and partake of food and drink before he sees you?'

'I would be most grateful.' Aileen turned to Rhiannon, whose face was tight with rebellion.

Beneath her breath, Rhiannon muttered, 'I am not staying here. I want to go home.'

'Do as you are told, *a iníon*,' Aileen cautioned. 'I expect good manners from you.'

'And what of him?' Rhiannon sent a glare toward Ewan. 'He isn't showing good manners. He keeps staring at me.'

'Perhaps it is because you are fair of face.'

'But he is a boy, Mother!' Rhiannon's reaction of horror made Aileen want to laugh.

'He is also your uncle,' Aileen added. Rhiannon did not look reassured.

She scowled. 'He won't be telling me what to do.'

Aileen did not comment. After the servants took away the basins and they donned their sandals, she followed Isabel above stairs. Rhiannon trailed behind them, studying the stone fortress with interest.

Outside one of the rooms, she heard the clanging of swords. Aileen sent a questioning look toward Isabel, who nodded.

'My husband and Connor are inside. Would you like to wait for them?'

Aileen shook her head. 'Take Rhiannon, if you wouldn't mind. I will join you in a moment.'

The vicious clanging of swords sounded from inside. Connor could not possibly handle such brutal abuse against his hands. Aileen opened the door quietly, her mind reeling with ways to mend the swelling and pain.

The sword fight moved with deadly force. Connor blocked each strike of his brother's blade, but Aileen gripped her hands as if she were the one fighting. This was more than a practice sparring.

Patrick MacEgan moved with an uncanny swiftness. Their feet glided, swords meeting one another until they circled near her. Connor's attention lapsed for a brief second, and his brother exploded with rage.

'I could have killed you! Keep your mind centred and away from distractions.'

Aileen drew back against the wall, both men staring at her with anger. 'I am sorry. I should not have interrupted.'

'What are you doing here?' Connor demanded. Sweat beaded his face, his fair hair tied back. His grey eyes raked over her, and her cheeks grew hot.

The fierce anger in his expression made her want to retreat. The knots in her stomach twisted with the pain of seeing him again.

'I brought Rhiannon,' she said. Her tongue stumbled over the words. 'I thought—'

'We'll continue this conversation in private,' Connor said, opening the door and giving his brother a go-away stare. 'I shall see you later, Patrick.'

'Who is she?' the King demanded. He sheathed his sword but did not hide his displeasure.

'I am Aileen Ó Duinne,' she answered. 'The woman who healed your brother.' She raised her knee in a gesture of courtesy and tried to keep her posture straight. Even so, her mind was a mess of torn feelings.

'You caused him to lose his focus,' Patrick accused. 'He needs no distraction from his training.'

Aileen fisted her hands, her throat closing up with unshed tears. He was right. Though her daughter deserved to be here, she did not.

Connor gestured for his brother to leave. 'I will deal with Aileen, Patrick.'

When the door closed, Connor drew the heavy wooden bolt across it. 'Why did you come?'

Aileen stood before him, her heart trembling with dread. She lifted her face to meet his eyes. Beneath the rigid cast to his jaw was the man who had made love to her and the father of her child. Though she understood that he despised her, she wanted his forgiveness.

'There were things left unsaid.' She took a step forward, her body fully aware of his strength. Connor didn't move, but she saw the flash of interest in his darkened gaze. He hadn't forgotten the way it had been between them.

Before she could lose her courage, she raised her palms to his chest. It was meant as a plea, but his heartbeat quickened beneath her touch. She saw him fighting against his desires, in the way his mouth tightened. He looked as though he might push her away at any moment.

'What was left unsaid?'

Years seemed to slip by in that single moment. Every word she wanted to say died upon her lips when his hands covered hers. The man before her was consumed by vengeance. He didn't want her here.

But without warning, his mouth descended upon hers,

urgent and warm. His scent filled her, his strong arms holding her close. The kiss sent waves of longing through her body, his touch awakening her. Her breasts tightened, her womb aching to feel him inside.

She kissed him back, her hands wrapping around his neck. With eyes closed, she could almost imagine that he cared for her.

Then he broke the kiss as if she'd burned him. 'You know better than to pursue this, Aileen. We aren't meant to be.'

The resolution in his tone was a razor against her heart. She let her hands fall to her sides. 'And what of your daughter? Will you turn her away, too?'

'You told her about me.'

'She deserved to know the truth.'

'Then why did you not tell her the truth, years ago?'

She expelled a ragged breath. 'I was afraid. And Eachan loved her so.'

'You were right to let her believe the illusion.'

Her spirits plummeted. When had he changed his mind? 'You don't want her?' She could not believe he would turn his own child away.

His gaze remained firm. 'Don't give her false hope, Aileen. Until Samhain, it is best if you both keep your distance.'

She doubted if that were true. Even if he did survive the battle against Flynn Ó Banníon, something had changed between them. No longer sheltered from the rest of the world, here in his brother's domain Connor had transformed into the Irish warrior she'd idolised as a girl. Stoic and fierce, she could see no forgiveness within him.

This man was as unreachable as the stars. 'You want me to leave,' she whispered.

'That would be for the best.' He opened the door, and as Aileen stepped through it, she cursed herself for opening her heart to him.

Chapter 18

Connor groaned inwardly. He never should have kissed her. As soon as he'd touched Aileen, his body remembered the sensation of loving her. He wanted her in his bed, craved her with an insatiable hunger.

If she didn't leave, it would kill him. He'd lied when he said he didn't want her here. By the gods above, he wanted her.

She'd brought Rhiannon to him. He didn't know what to think about her gesture. He wanted to know his daughter, but not like this. Though the daily training with his brother had helped immensely, their healer bound his hands each night. He often drank painkilling brews, pushing his body to its limits.

He refused to accept himself as less than a whole man. And he could never assume the role of father or husband until he regained his strength.

He opened the door to his chamber and was startled to see Rhiannon sitting there. The girl raised a finger to her lips. 'They're looking for me.'

'You should not be in here.'

She crossed her arms and sent him a resentful look. 'You are not my father. No matter what she says, it isn't true. Eachan Ó Duinne was my father.'

'He was,' Connor agreed. 'In every way that I could not be.' Behind the angry words, he saw the girl's pain. Her world had come apart with Aileen's confession.

'I won't be your daughter.' She lifted her chin with stubbornness. 'You cannot make me.'

It was like watching his mother scold him once more. Her stance, the way she glared at him—every inch of her was a MacEgan.

'Your mother will be worried about you,' he cautioned. 'Perhaps you should go and find her.'

She seemed relieved that he did not argue with her. 'On the morrow, we will return home.'

'If that is your wish.' He said nothing about Aileen's banishment but poured water into a basin and wiped the sweat from his face. Rhiannon waited and handed him a drying cloth.

'Your hands are still bent.'

'They are, yes.'

Before he could stop her, she took his hand in hers to study the fingers. Something reached inside his heart and pulled at it. With her small hand in his, he wondered what it would be like if she were to accept him as her father.

Her face brightened. 'She did well, my mother. Other healers would have chopped your hand off.'

'It's glad I am that she did not.'

'Do you drink willow bark?' Rhiannon asked. 'It is said to be good for pain.'

Connor hid his amusement. Like a small bird, Rhiannon spouted off healing advice. 'Are you going to be a healer like your mother?'

The dark head bobbed forward. 'She is teaching me.'

Rhiannon glimpsed the wooden splints and bandages upon the table. 'Do you want me to bind your hands?'

'That would be most helpful.'

She gathered the materials, and he sat down. Her small fingers worked deftly, arranging each of his fingers and tying the bandages off. Though he would have to adjust the tightness later, he allowed her to work upon his hands.

'You're a good *cailín*,' he commented. 'Your mother would be proud.'

A smile played at her lips. 'Wear them each night,' she warned. 'They will help your hands to grow straight again.'

She left moments later, and Connor studied her handiwork. Though the bandages were not tied tightly enough, she had done her best.

Connor loosened the ties of his tunic and slipped off the garment. He stretched, his muscles sore from the exertion of the fight. Another day or two, he decided. They could stay a little longer. He would speak to Isabel and ask his brother's wife to find an excuse.

'And just where do you think you're going?' Aileen asked a guilty-faced Rhiannon. Her daughter had slipped behind one of the stone walls, eyeing the gate as if to escape.

'Nowhere.'

'I should hope not. You wouldn't think of trying to run away, now would you?'

Rhiannon shook her head, but she refused to meet her

gaze. Aileen caught a look from one of the guards, who offered a reassuring smile. She did not take comfort from it. Her daughter was quite capable of slipping away.

'Why don't you go to the stables? Ewan could show you the horses,' Aileen suggested.

Rhiannon shook her head. 'I want to go home. I don't like it here.'

'Has anyone been unkind to you?'

'No. But no one speaks to me, and I've nothing to do.'

Aileen took Rhiannon's hand. 'Let us go and see Isabel. She may find something for you. Perhaps you can help their healer by gathering plants and such.'

Rhiannon brightened. 'Do you suppose there are any wounded men?'

'In a fortress of this size, there will always be wounded men.'

As they moved toward the Great Chamber, they passed by a group of men training in the courtyard. Aileen stopped to watch. The men wore leather armour, several groups sparring with the lightweight *colc* swords. In the heat of the afternoon, their bodies gleamed with sweat. Had Connor trained like this once, his body moving in the exercises of these same soldiers? She imagined his muscles flexing, his intense concentration upon his foe.

'Did you wish to learn how to fight, then?' one of the soldiers asked. With an easy smile and black hair, his blue eyes captured hers in a teasing gaze.

Aileen shook her head. 'No. I was looking for Queen Isabel and stopped to watch.'

'You'll be finding her in her garden,' the soldier advised. 'But if you should like to fight, my name is Senan.' His eyes showed interest, but Aileen paid it no heed. Her gaze centred upon a line of blood flowing from his arm.

'You're hurt,' she said, moving closer to examine the wound.

'Only a scratch. A nick from a blade when I didn't move quick enough.'

'My mother is a healer,' Rhiannon offered.

'Is she?' Senan held out his arm. 'Will I lose it, do you think?' he jested.

Aileen shook her head. 'Bandage it, and it'll be good enough on the morrow. You're right. It is only a small cut.'

'You could tend it for me,' Senan suggested, his voice offering seductive promises. Aileen wanted to laugh, but truly, it did feel nice to have a man notice her.

'She has better things to do,' a male voice cut in.

Connor's searing glower did little to wrinkle Senan's mood. The soldier merely winked at Aileen as he rejoined the fighting.

'And what better things do I have to do?' Aileen asked, raising an eyebrow.

'Walk with me, and I'll tell you.'

She looked over at Rhiannon, who inched closer to the fighting. 'Would you like to come with us?'

Her daughter shook her head. 'I don't like him.'

'Rhiannon Ó Duinne! How could you say such a terrible thing?'

Connor did not seem surprised by Rhiannon's remark. 'She need not come along. If she wishes to stay and watch the men train, she may.' He directed his attention to the girl. 'Or, if you go into the weaver's huts, you'll find my brother's daughter Brianna. She arrived this morning and is about your age.'

Rhiannon brightened at the prospect of another girl. 'May I, please?'

Aileen hesitated, torn between Rhiannon's thoughtless comment and curiosity about what Connor wished to say to her. 'We will speak later about this,' she warned her daughter.

Connor led her outside the gate. The lush hills beckoned before them, stretching all the way to the glittering sapphire sea. He continued onward, bringing her to a small grove of rowan trees. The rich, loamy scent of earth and leaves surrounded them.

The sun warmed her face, and she should have felt content to walk beside him. Instead, she grew wary. He didn't want her here, nor Rhiannon.

'What did you wish to say to me?'

'You were looking at Senan. Don't.' He captured her chin as though chiding a young child.

She gave him a firm shove backwards. 'You cannot seem to make up your mind, can you? One minute you tell me I should not have come, the next you behave like a jealous lover? I do not belong to you. You've made that quite clear from your actions.'

'You're not going to stay here, Aileen.'

She didn't deny it, not when he'd treated her this way. Already she believed this had been a mistake. But she could not leave until Rhiannon's fosterage was settled. 'What of your daughter? Do you want me to take her away, too?'

'Rhiannon may stay.' His expression softened, and he glanced at his hands. Aileen noticed the splints, tied with the awkwardness of a child. 'She tells me she wants to be a healer like you.'

'Ever since she could talk, she has spoken of wanting to heal others.'

Connor sat down upon a moss-covered stone, leaning back against one of the trees. 'Tell me about her.' His tone remained neutral, but beneath it she sensed a greater need.

She sat apart from him, drawing her knees up. 'Rhiannon was born on a snowy morn after the Feast of Saint Agatha. It was not an easy birth. I laboured for two days and nearly died. I was afraid I'd never hold her in my arms.'

Connor's silence made her uncomfortable. Was she simply blathering on without his interest?

'You let Eachan believe he was her father.' His eyes were cool, his expression distant.

'No.' She picked up a small stone, tracing the sharp edges with her thumb. 'Eachan offered to wed me. He knew I was with child. And he knew the child was yours.

'I wanted her,' she said softly. 'Even though you were gone, I thanked God every day for the gift of her.'

Connor stood and knelt down beside her. Though she had hoped for forgiveness, she saw only anger in his face. 'You should have sent word to me.'

'I was only sixteen, Connor. I cannot undo the past. All I can do is try to heal it.'

'Some wounds cannot be healed.'

Her glance turned toward his deformed hands. 'No. Not all wounds.'

He caught her wrists, holding them still. 'Tell me one thing, Aileen. Why did you take Lianna's place? And do not say it was for the harvest. No girl would sacrifice her virginity to a stranger for such.'

'You were never a stranger to me,' she whispered. 'You

were my dream. A dream I couldn't have.' She knelt, tracing the roughened planes of his face with her palm.

But he didn't kiss her. His warm skin might well have been made of iron instead of flesh, so remote he was.

'Why is this fight so important to you?' She dropped her hand away, angry at herself for reaching out to him. 'Flynn will hurt you. Worse than he did the last time.'

'I need to be the man I was before.'

'And what if I want the man you are now?' She bared her heart before him, even knowing he would hurt her.

'Would you want a man without honour?' he asked in return. 'Do not ask me to stand aside like a coward.'

She lowered her head, realising that he would not be swayed. 'I want you to live,' she whispered. 'For me and for our daughter. And if you insist upon sacrificing yourself for honour, then there is nothing left.'

His face held a thousand regrets. Cupping her cheek in his gnarled palm, he leaned forward. His lips met hers in a soft, unexpected kiss.

'It's better this way, *a chroí*.'

Chapter 19

⸙

When the grey sky of dawn broke forth, Connor and his four brothers rode through the fields of Laochre. He took strength from his brothers' presence, though he had already warned them not to cross over into Flynn Ó Banníon's territory. This was his battle, not theirs.

Three days remained before the Feast of Samhain. Connor forced his right hand around the hilt of his brother's sword. The cool metal warmed beneath his palm, a mixture of steel inlaid with ivory. All throughout the ride, he focused his mind on the forthcoming battle. And still his thoughts dwelled upon Aileen.

She had wanted him to turn from the fight, like a coward. Why could she not see that his honour was all he had? In the past few days, she'd avoided him. He didn't like to admit that he'd noticed it. He'd grown accustomed to sharing conversations with her.

And the taste of her hung upon his memory, the sweetness she'd offered.

What if I want the man you are now? she'd asked. He

didn't believe her. No woman wanted a malformed man who could not protect his family. Until he proved his strength, he had no right to stand in as Rhiannon's true father.

In the past, he'd lived as a hired sword, travelling from one tribe to the next. The only hope of having a permanent home and family was by winning a position as a chieftain.

He glanced at his brother Patrick. Patrick had fought for the right to be king when their eldest brother Liam had fallen in battle. It was right for him to lead the tribe; he'd earned it. Even his brother Bevan had gained his own property by wedding a Norman lady.

Connor swallowed back the envy. Why could he not be content? Trahern and Ewan did not possess the same ambitions. He wished he could force his desires to be silent.

'Are you ready for this fight?' his brother Ewan asked when they stopped late in the afternoon to make camp. Worry furrowed the lad's face. 'I have not seen you training among the men.'

'I oversaw his training,' Patrick replied. 'He is ready.'

Connor caught his gaze, sending silent thanks for Patrick's confidence. Bevan, on the other hand, appeared doubtful.

'Flynn Ó Banníon will not be an easy warrior to defeat. He knows your weaknesses.'

'And I know his.' The clipped response ended the discussion. Connor had trained as best he was able. Now he could only wait for his opportunity.

They tethered the horses, choosing a spot not far from a nearby stream. A running waterfall cascaded into a small pool. Not far, they found an earthen trench lined with wood. The cooking site meant that other hunters had camped here before. The trench held rainwater, and Ewan emptied his water skin into the cooking pit. He returned with more water from the pool until it was full.

When they had a fire ready, Trahern dropped several stones in the flames to grow hot for cooking. He passed Connor a horn of ale, his eyes wicked. 'I'd like to be knowing more about your woman Aileen. And the girl who looks like our mother.'

'She is my daughter,' Connor admitted. 'I only learned about Rhiannon a short time ago.'

Rhiannon. The name of his daughter filled him with apprehension and humility. He wanted to know her better, to ease the resentment the girl felt toward him.

Patrick's gaze narrowed. 'Aileen should have told you about her long before this.'

'It was as much my own fault as hers,' Connor said. He took a drink from the horn, passing it to Bevan.

'Do you intend to wed Aileen?' Trahern asked.

The question caught him unprepared. 'I do not know.'

He hadn't allowed himself to envision a future. His attentions were tightly locked upon the outcome of this fight. Blinded, he was, to anything past it. He didn't dare imagine his prospects afterward.

Patrick and Bevan sent each other a silent look, one which Connor ignored. He could live without their speculations. It was none of their affair.

Trahern removed the hot stones from the fire and used a heavy cloth to drop them into the water-filled trench. Steam hissed and in time the water boiled. Patrick handed a haunch of venison to Trahern, who wrapped the meat in straw and tied it up. Trahern placed the meat inside the boiling water to cook, and later entertained them with stories while they relaxed in front of the fire.

As the afternoon drifted into evening, Connor studied each of his brother's faces. They had come to offer their support to him, refusing to let him take this journey alone. He was grateful for it. And he prayed that this would not be the last time he saw them. He didn't want to die, but a part of him was aware of his limitations. This battle would stretch every fibre of his strength, pushing him until he had nothing left to give.

A rustling noise made the men draw their swords. A single rider emerged in the darkness, and he saw Aileen dismount.

Her dark hair had come loose from its braid, long tendrils framing her face. She had ridden quickly, breathing hard at the pace.

Connor caught the mare's reins and helped her down. 'What is it? Is something amiss?'

Shadows of exhaustion lined her face when she stood before him. 'Yes, something is amiss. You left us behind without saying goodbye.'

Her hands reached up to his shoulders. In her eyes he saw apprehension and pain. She lowered her voice to a whisper. 'If you want me to go, I'll leave. But I wanted to see you before the fight.' Her hand moved to his hair, and a raw need reached inside him, taking apart all his reasons for denying her.

'Don't go,' he said. His thumb caressed her temple, and he pulled her body close to his. The scent of crushed sage flooded his senses. Though he believed there was no future for them, it felt right to have her here.

Aileen cast a look toward his brothers. 'Is there some place private where we may speak?'

Connor took her hand and walked with her into a grove of trees. Soft ferns carpeted the ground, fading sunlight glowing through the trees. When they reached a rocky area, the sound of a small waterfall greeted them.

Aileen sat down, releasing his hand. Her heart pounded furiously, her mind unable to think clearly. When she'd learned of his departure, it was as though someone had squeezed the very breath from her body. She couldn't allow him to leave, not without telling him how she felt.

But now, her tongue could not form the words she wanted. She couldn't let him go to Flynn Ó Banníon without being with him. Even if she had to watch him die, she could not remain at home. Waiting was the worst form of torment.

'Why have you come?' He knelt down beside her, hunkered upon one knee. In the dim evening light, his dark gold hair gleamed. She reached out to bring his face close to hers.

'Because I made a mistake seven years ago.' She leaned in so her forehead touched his own. 'And I need your forgiveness.'

Connor pulled back. His thumb caressed the curve of her jaw, and she shivered at the dark look in his eyes. 'Please.'

He lowered her onto the grass, his mouth hungry against her own. She tasted desire and desperation, mixed with a need so great it stole her senses.

When he ended the kiss, she unlaced his tunic and raised it over his head. Her breath shook when she saw the expanse of muscle and skin. He had indeed been training. Not a trace of excess flesh broke the firm planes. She traced every ridge, possessing him with her touch.

'I love you, Connor. And I need to be with you. Even if you die.'

'You still believe I will lose.'

Beneath his austere tone, she sensed his own fear.

'I don't know,' she answered honestly. 'But though I may not understand your desire to fight, I will stand by you.'

She could not read his response. He made no move to caress her skin, to love her the way she wanted him to. He was deeply aroused, she could feel it through the soft fabric of his trews. And yet, he held himself back.

'And afterwards?' he asked. 'What do you want from me, Aileen?' He rolled to his side to regard her. 'Do you think I'll become a farmer?'

'I don't know. But you could try—'

'That isn't what I want. I want what my brothers have. I want to be a leader, with my own people to protect.' He moved a strand of hair from her cheek, the subtle gesture burning her with need.

He dreamed of the impossible. How could he want so much? 'Is there something wrong with living in a simple manner?'

'It's not enough for me.'

The seriousness in his voice caught her heart. He meant it. If he somehow managed to defeat Flynn Ó Banníon, he would not be content to live with her. With a shattering clarity, she understood that their differences were greater than she had imagined. Once again, she felt like the young maiden reaching out for the warrior far beyond her reach.

'What will you do?' she managed to ask, though she feared his answer.

'It depends upon the outcome of this battle. If I win, then I will compete to become chieftain of a tribe. I have relatives in the west who could help me.'

Grief balled up in her throat, for she knew with a sense of finality that this was the end for them. 'There is another way,' she offered. 'You could marry.'

His hand moved down her body to the curve of her waist. The tender gesture startled her. 'I could,' he acknowledged. 'But few of the nobles would allow a younger son to wed their daughters.'

Aileen hid the sinking feeling in her stomach. He hadn't denied the possibility of marrying someone else. She already knew he would never surrender his dreams of defeating Ó Banníon.

It left her with this one night to be with him. She covered his hand with her own, lacing her fingers in his.

'I don't intend to marry,' he said. 'If I cannot gain what I want by my own strength, then I won't use a woman to get it.'

In a surprise motion, she rolled him to his back. Straddling his waist, she pinned him to the ground. He let her hold him captive, staring at her in disbelief.

'It seems I've gained what I want, with my own strength.' She wound her arms around his neck. 'Be with me this night. I need you.'

Connor reached up and lowered her gown from her shoulders, exposing her skin to the cool night air. His palms reached up to cup her breasts. Her nipples tightened with the roughness of his skin against hers. He sat up, keeping her straddled against him. The arousing feel of his erection rocking against her womanhood brought a rush of wetness.

His mouth moved to the curve of her neck, his hands slipping off the rest of her gown. She lay naked, exposed to the darkening sky and the man she loved. By the gods, she wanted to curl up and weep. But this might be her last night to ever see him. Tomorrow they would arrive at Flynn Ó Banníon's fortress, and preparations for the fight would begin.

'I am thirsty,' Connor said suddenly. Aileen pushed him back and rose. Her bare skin rose with goose bumps as she moved toward the stream.

No, she was not a woman whom he could wed. But for this night, she would take him into her arms, as before. She thirsted for him as well, to take him inside her and to feel the rush of pleasure burning in her womb.

Cupping water between her palms, she brought it to him. He drank from her fingertips, some of the water spilling upon her body. Connor removed the rest of his clothing and laid her next to the stream. He dipped another handful of the water and let it pour over her skin.

'It's cold!' she gasped, but her words broke off when he began to drink from her. His hot mouth tasted a path to her breasts. He took the nipple into his mouth, running his tongue over the cockled tip. Heat blazed within her, and he kissed a path lower, sipping water from the hollow of her stomach.

Lower still, to her hips. He spread her legs apart, and Aileen's breath choked in her throat. 'There's no water there,' she said.

'There isn't?' His gaze turned knowing. 'I'll have to look

and see.' He bent between her thighs, his tongue moving to her womanhood. Aileen gasped when he tasted her deeply, running his tongue to the most sensitive part of her. He sucked hard, and vicious pleasure rocked through her. She clutched his hair, her body shaking with desire. Coils of need wound tighter as he tormented her.

Then abruptly he moved atop her. She cried out in shock and ecstasy as he filled her, again and again.

'I love you,' she whispered. *Even though he would not stay*.

He covered her mouth with his own, pushing her over the edge until she trembled with release. It would never be like this again, not with any other man.

Holding him against her, she closed her eyes. He grasped the corner of her *brat* and rolled the long shawl to cover them. Their bodies nestled together, and Aileen closed her eyes.

When she was certain he was asleep, she whispered, 'God be with you, Connor.'

To their credit, Connor's brothers did not remark upon their absence that night. Ewan's face turned crimson when Aileen greeted him. She tried to behave as if nothing were wrong, but Connor's self-satisfied expression proclaimed exactly what they had been doing.

After another full day of riding, they reached Flynn Ó Banníon's stronghold. High wooden towers rose above an enormous *rath*. Though not as large as Laochre, the fortress had implemented several Norman building techniques. The outer curtain wall was over twelve feet high, and Aileen craned her neck to see the remainder of the dwelling.

Fierce and craggy, the fortress resembled its owner well. Flynn Ó Banníon was not known for being merciful to his enemies. Ropes of foreboding constricted within her.

Connor wheeled his horse to a stop. 'You are not going inside,' he told Aileen. 'Trahern will accompany me.' To Patrick, Ewan and Bevan, he added, 'That goes for the lot of you.'

Patrick only laughed. 'Do you really believe we will let you go in alone?'

'He betrayed me once,' Connor said softly. 'I would not put it past him to harm those close to me.' His gaze fell upon Aileen, and she warmed to it.

'In a few days more, I'll be home,' he promised. He pulled Aileen into his embrace. She laid her cheek upon his chest, inhaling the clean scent of him. He stroked her hair.

'I want to be with you,' she whispered.

'Wait for me,' he urged. 'Remain with my brothers.'

She drew back, drinking in the sight of him. On the morrow, the fight would begin. And she might lose him.

The icy fist of fear strangled her. Never could she remain behind, not while his life hung in the balance. But she feigned acceptance, his mouth kissing hers one last time.

After he said farewell to his brothers, Aileen watched as he and Trahern began their solitary walk toward the fortress. She turned to Patrick. 'I can't remain here. I can't stay idle while he faces his enemy.'

Patrick stilled her with a hand. 'All of us will be there for him. We MacEgans stand by one another in times of need.'

'How?'

'There are ways. Leave it to me.' His expression softened to gentleness. 'He loves you.'

She shook her head. 'If he did, he'd abandon this fight.'

'Connor may be many things, but he is not a coward.'

'Were you telling the truth when you said he could win?'

Patrick's eyes turned heavy, and she saw the doubt within them. 'A man can create miracles, when he has something to fight for,' he hedged.

Or someone, Aileen thought. Inspiration struck, and she turned to Bevan. 'I've a favour to ask of you. Can you help me?'

When he listened to her proposition, Bevan frowned. 'I do not know if this is a wise idea.'

'Trust me,' Aileen insisted.

Bevan sent a silent look toward Patrick, who nodded. 'Do it.'

Within moments, Bevan had mounted his horse, riding swiftly back to Laochre. When he had gone, Aileen asked, 'Is there aught else we can do for Connor?'

Patrick squeezed her shoulder. 'Pray.'

Flynn Ó Banníon handed Connor a goblet of mead. Connor accepted it, his eyes locked upon the man he intended to kill.

'Circumstances have changed since you last joined us for a meal,' Flynn began. A trace of irony lined his eyes. 'I look forward to the fight tomorrow.'

'As do I.'

The food tasted dry in his mouth, the familiar surroundings taunting him. Once, he had called this Great Chamber home. The soldiers had been like brothers to him. Since his arrival, none save Niall had greeted him. Their silence damned them, for they had given their loyalty to Ó Banníon.

He had shed blood alongside them, fighting against the

Norman armies, but it meant nothing. The word of their overlord meant more than his.

'You were like a son to me,' Flynn mused idly. 'The best fighter of all. And I wanted to kill you that day.'

'You believed her lies.'

Flynn's face darkened. 'My daughter has never lied. You were not there the morning when she came to me, weeping. You stole her virtue, and nothing can replace that. No man will have a woman who has lost her purity.'

Connor doubted if Deirdre was a virgin. The scheming *cailín* wanted one thing only—himself as a husband. But he'd refused.

'I was glad that you asked for this fight.' Flynn's eyes glittered with hatred. 'A simple fine is not enough to repay me for her loss. Your life will meet the price.'

'Or yours,' Connor said.

At the far end of the Great Chamber, a woman approached. Dressed in an emerald overdress and a saffron *léine*, Deirdre Ó Banníon walked gracefully toward their table, past the rows of soldiers and shields. With golden hair and green eyes to match her gown, she appeared like an exquisite being, one of the *sibh*. And a more treacherous woman he'd never met.

'Father.' She greeted him with a kiss upon the cheek. Her face flushed at the sight of Connor. 'So you intend to fight one another still?'

She sat beside Flynn, her eyes wide with mock-innocence. Connor looked away. He could hardly stand to look at her.

'On the morrow,' Flynn replied. 'At dusk.'

Deirdre's hand moved to her heart. She clutched at Flynn's palm, begging, 'Father, do not do this. The matter is finished.'

'It is far from finished,' Connor said. He rose to his feet, ignoring the breach of manners. 'Until tomorrow.'

He turned his back on the chieftain and moved past the line of soldiers.

'Wait!' Deirdre's voice called. Connor stilled, but did not face her. 'We have a chamber prepared for you. A servant will take you there.'

A manservant inclined his head, and Connor followed. Courtesy dictated that he thank them for their hospitality, but he could not bring himself to do it. Instead, the servant led him above stairs to a small chamber.

He declined the offer of a bath, and sank into a chair across from the fire. When he'd seen Deirdre, all the rage had returned without warning. Were she a man, he'd have killed her for her lies.

Instead, her father would die. He tried to gain comfort from it, but revenge would not fill the emptiness gathering inside him. He thought of Aileen, of loving her beside the stream last eve. Of her unwillingness to leave him.

Belenus, he'd fallen in love with her. He wanted to wake beside her, to grant her more children. He wanted to watch Rhiannon grow into womanhood and choose a strong husband for her.

His heart grew hollow. Everything rested on this fight.

Chapter 20

'Tell Flynn Ó Banníon that King Patrick of Laochre has come to bear witness to today's battle,' Patrick said to the guards at the fortress gate. 'We are the brothers of Connor MacEgan. Do not deny us entrance.'

The guards did not look surprised to see them.

'My orders are to bring you to the Great Chamber,' one said, lowering his battle axe. 'Our chieftain is expecting you.'

He bade them enter, and Aileen stood behind the brothers, her eyes studying the bailey. It was not as clean as Laochre. Odours permeated the courtyard, the scent of rotting decay mingling with unwashed bodies. She sensed illness, and her gaze snapped towards a man coughing.

They entered the Great Chamber, where trestle tables had been pushed back to reveal a fighting circle. Benches lined the area, and servants removed the rushes from the earthen floor. It was hours yet before twilight. Aileen's stomach twisted with foreboding.

Flynn Ó Banníon strode in from a corridor, his expression masked. 'King Patrick.' He lightly raised a knee in deference to his rank. 'I am honoured that you grace us with your presence.'

Patrick stared at Flynn Ó Banníon, his gaze threatening. 'I am here to ensure that this is a fair fight.'

'The fight was your brother's doing.'

'So it was,' Patrick acknowledged, 'and we will not interfere.'

Flynn's gaze turned toward Aileen. 'And why has the healer of Banslieve come? A dead man has no need of one to tend his wounds.'

'Why must there be death?' Aileen asked. Though her voice remained soft, she let the chieftain see her discontent. 'Blood will satisfy honour.'

Flynn Ó Banníon laughed. 'Spoken like a woman.' With an eye toward the MacEgans, he added, 'Connor will not stop until one of us is dead. And I do not intend for it to be me.'

Aileen caught sight of a woman staring at her. Dressed in a silken overdress of sapphire, the golden-haired maiden shot her a look of malevolence. It was the woman she'd seen kissing Connor at the *aenach*. Deirdre Ó Banníon, she guessed.

As Deirdre glided toward Aileen, men watched her with longing. Aileen shook her head in disgust. Could they not see the woman for what she truly was? Or did they see her as the chieftain's daughter, a woman who might advance their own stature?

When Deirdre reached them, she offered a sugary smile to her father. 'Father, I did not know we had more visitors.'

'The MacEgans have come to witness the fight this eve.'

Deirdre extended her hands to Patrick. 'I welcome you

to our home.' Signalling a servant, she added, 'Would you care for a cup of mead or some refreshments?'

Patrick glanced at his brothers, as if making a silent decision. Then, 'We accept your offer of hospitality.'

The brilliant smile across Deirdre's face was genuine. 'Please sit down and I will see to it.' Then she turned to Aileen. 'My ladies are above stairs. If you would like to rest and join us after the meal, you may.'

Aileen's suspicions rose. Still, she might learn more from Deirdre than from remaining with the men. 'Thank you.'

Servants brought a light repast of roasted mutton, bread, cheese and salmon. Ewan stuffed himself, attacking the food as though he had not eaten in a fortnight.

'Slow down, lad,' Trahern advised. 'The food won't be running away from you.'

'I remember when I could eat as he does,' Patrick remarked. 'Let him be, Trahern. He needs more muscle if he's to be one of our warriors.' Ewan's ears turned pink at the praise, and Aileen could see the young man's pride at the words.

Although she could not fault the food or drink, Aileen only picked at the bread. Her insides clenched with fear, and it hurt knowing that she could not see Connor. Even so, he had asked her not to come. Her presence was a distraction and not a welcome one.

'Come,' Deirdre bade her, beckoning toward a narrow staircase.

Aileen tried to behave as though nothing were amiss, but it was difficult to forget she was among the enemy. Were it not for Deirdre, none of this would have happened. Her anger rose higher, indignant that a woman's lies could bring forth a man's death.

When they reached the chamber, Deirdre dismissed her ladies. Aileen crossed her arms, unsure of Deirdre's purpose.

'Please, sit down. I have seen you before, but we've not met.'

'I am Aileen Ó Duinne, once the healer of our tribe.'

'And I am Deirdre Ó Banníon, daughter of Flynn Ó Banníon.' Though the words were a mere greeting, Aileen felt as though each had drawn a verbal sword.

She chose a chair carefully, all instincts alerted. What did Deirdre want from her?

She folded her hands and sat across from Aileen. Her pale face revealed a great deal of pain, all pretense of hospitality gone.

'I don't want him to die,' she said gently. 'That was not what I intended at all.'

'Your lies caused him to suffer.' Aileen refused to offer any mercy or pity. 'If you confess the truth, we could both stop this battle.'

'Neither of us can, and you know it. Both of them are too proud.'

'If there is naught either of us can do, why did you wish to speak to me?'

Deirdre smoothed her skirts, her gaze stopping upon Aileen's travel-stained gown. Aileen grew conscious of her own worn appearance. She should have brought another *léine*, but at the time her only thoughts were of Connor.

'You are his woman, aren't you?'

'I am.'

At the admission, Deirdre's eyes hardened. 'I can see that you are in love with him. What I wish to know is, if you could save his life by giving him up, would you do it?'

'What do you mean?'

'My father listens to me. I can bargain with him on Connor's behalf.'

'You said that neither of us could stop the fight.'

'And that is true. But when Connor loses, I can beg for his life. My father will grant that to me.'

'You seem overly confident that Flynn Ó Banníon will win.' Aileen bristled. She leaned forward. 'What is it you want from Connor?'

'I want him to be my husband. If he weds me, he may one day take my father's place as the chieftain.'

Her stomach sank, for this was what Connor had dreamed of. A fortress of his own, people of his own. Given the chance to possess it, would he not seize the opportunity?

But then, she knew he hated Deirdre. Aileen shook her head. 'It will never happen. If your father defeats him, the men will not respect him.'

Deirdre shrugged. 'They will see it as though his wounds have not healed. He fought among them, and they know his prowess in battle.' A smile laced with desire passed over Deirdre's face. 'He will make a good leader.'

'He would. But not of your tribe.'

Deirdre shrugged. 'I will ask my father, and we shall see if Connor chooses to wed me.' With her head held high, Deirdre swept from the room.

Aileen sat down in a chair, her spirits sinking. Right now, she wished she had her daughter to hold, to feel the slender arms around her waist. She missed Rhiannon and regretted that she hadn't told her about Connor sooner. Tonight her father might die, before she'd ever known him.

After the servant had left, she buried her face in her

hands. Deidre's suggestion burned within her mind. Could she give Connor up if it meant saving his life?

No. Deirdre had planted these seeds of doubt, hoping to win Connor for herself. But never would she hold Connor's heart. Aileen took a deep breath and folded her hands. She didn't know if Connor loved her, but she was confident that he would not want Deirdre as his bride.

The only way to stop the fight and save Connor was to force Deirdre to admit the truth.

'You weren't supposed to come,' Connor warned his brothers.

'And when would we start listening to your bidding?' Patrick retorted. His expression changed to one of brotherly support. 'We would not abandon you during the time when you need us most.'

'This is my battle to fight.'

'So it is. But Ó Banníon is not a man who fights fairly. We will be there to ensure it goes well.'

'And if he kills me?' He did not mince words, knowing that death was a real possibility.

'That, we will not allow. If you wish to keep your honour, brother, you must win. Else we will interfere.'

'Don't. This is why I did not want you here.' A sudden unease gripped him. 'Where is Aileen?'

'She is with Deirdre, among the women.'

His rage exploded. 'Have you lost your wits? The woman is not to be trusted. And you let Aileen go with her?'

'I should be more worried about Deirdre, were I you,' Patrick said. 'Aileen can hold her own.' His eyes saw through him. 'You have feelings for her.'

Connor gave the barest nod of acknowledgment. Little good it did him. He could offer Aileen nothing, not even the strength of his family name. He didn't deserve happiness with her, not unless he succeeded in defeating his enemy.

'What will you do?' Trahern asked.

'I have to win this fight.' Connor suppressed his own doubts of the outcome. 'She deserves a man who can keep her safe. If I prove myself today, I'll be worthy of her.' The smallest part of him believed that there was a chance of it. He knew Flynn, knew the way the warrior moved and fought. In his visions, he pictured the man falling beneath his sword.

'It is time to arm yourself,' Trahern reminded him. Connor extended his hands and his brothers helped him don a leather corselet. The light armour would protect him from minor slashes, but not fatal wounds. Around his shins he bound leather greaves to protect his lower legs.

Trahern handed him the round wooden shield, and Patrick unsheathed a sword. Connor recognised it as his own weapon, the sword stolen from him by the Ó Banníon.

'Where did you get this?'

'I ordered Flynn to return it to you. A man should have his own sword in a battle such as this.' Patrick plucked a hair from his head and the blade severed it. 'Is it sharp enough for you?'

Connor's mouth moved as if to smile, but a deeper emotion caught him. He would shed his life's blood for these men, his brothers. Sheathing the sword, he gripped his eldest brother's arms. 'My thanks.'

Patrick embraced him, thumping his back. Trahern and Ewan also gripped him. Tears shone in Ewan's eyes, but he valiantly held them in check.

'Where is Bevan?' He had not seen his older brother since they had broken camp.

'He went to retrieve something you left behind,' Patrick commented, but would not offer anything further.

When at last he was ready for the fight, his brothers left him alone with his thoughts. He centred his focus, forcing himself to imagine ways of bringing Flynn Ó Banníon down. His honour, his dreams rested on this fight.

And he meant to win.

The door opened, and Connor's hand reached for his sword hilt. Deirdre Ó Banníon entered.

'Stay away from me, Deirdre,' Connor warned.

'I came to apologise,' she said. 'For everything.' She trembled, her eyes misting prettily.

He rather thought she resembled a viper, winding her way toward him.

'I've no wish to hear any more lies from your lips.'

'You used to like my lips.'

He tightened his hold upon his temper. 'If I kissed you once, it meant nothing.'

'That wasn't what it seemed like to me.'

She placed her palms upon his corselet, tracing the leather. 'Forgive me, Connor.'

Her hands moved to his, and she raised his right hand, staring at the malformed fingers. 'I tried to stop him.'

'You stood by and watched them crush my hands.'

'No! I begged him not to do it. But he would not see reason.'

Connor jerked his hands away. 'I want nothing to do with you, Deirdre. Be gone from me.'

Her face flushed scarlet. 'You don't know what you're doing, Connor.' Eyes blazing, she smirked. 'Even if you win, you've lost. Our men will kill you where you stand. And your brothers.'

He strode across the room, grasping her arm.

'You're bruising me.'

Throwing the door open, he pushed her into the corridor. 'You never did listen well.'

She rubbed her arm. 'And you never understood how much I could give you. All of this land, this tribe, would be yours.' The glint of anger transformed her pretty face into ugliness. 'Wouldn't it be a shame if an accident were to happen during the fight?'

'Don't threaten me.' He started to close the door, but her next words stopped him.

'I could never threaten you,' she said. 'But if you were to wed me, this battle would end. And nothing would happen to Aileen Ó Duinne.'

'What have you done to her?' he demanded, shoving her against the wall. 'If you've laid a hand on her, I'll—'

'You'll kill me? Do it, and my father will slaughter her and your brothers. You may watch it happen before he kills you.' She laughed, a shrill sound that infuriated him. 'Release me.'

He did, and she rubbed her shoulder. 'I admire your strength, Connor. But you would be wise not to touch me again. Not until I ask you to.'

'Don't touch Aileen,' he warned. Every fibre of him raged at the thought of any harm coming to her. 'And you should go and say farewell to your father. Today is the last day you'll be seeing him alive.'

Chapter 21

Torches flickered, casting death shadows upon the walls of the Great Chamber. The Hall was filled with all members of the Ó Banníon tribe, soldiers whom he'd once called friends. He suspected most of the men knew of Deirdre's treachery, but as her father was blind to it, they could do nothing but watch the fight.

Sweat beaded Connor's forehead, his body feeling overly warm. He drew his sword with his left hand, circling Flynn. The older warrior had not suffered from age; rather, it had toughened him. Though his hair was nearly white, Flynn moved like a much younger man.

Connor gripped his sword, his stance relaxed. He awaited Flynn's swift attack, knowing that his enemy preferred to strike immediately.

Steel flashed and he blocked the first blow from instinct. He poured every year of training, every ounce of knowledge he held, into the fight.

Flynn struck hard and with a steady hand, Connor held

fast. 'I never touched her, you know,' he said. He wanted Flynn to know the truth, to undermine his confidence.

'You touched nearly every woman in my fortress,' Flynn retorted. His blade moved again, slicing toward Connor's middle.

Connor dodged the sword and circled from the opposite side.

'I enjoyed the company of a maid or two, but I did not dishonour them.'

For a time, it seemed that Flynn toyed with him, as if drawing out the fight. Then without warning, his blade struck with an arm-numbing blow. Connor's wrists ached with pain, but he held steady. Flynn saw his reaction and grunted with satisfaction.

Though Connor tried to take the offensive, his efforts focused on defending himself from Flynn's force. Each hammering blow intensified the pain.

'You were always a good fighter,' Flynn said, his gaze penetrating.

'I was trained by the best.' Connor swung his blade, metal biting against metal.

'You've healed better than I thought you would.'

Connor circled his opponent, judging Flynn. They were equally matched. He was glad of it. When he brought his enemy down, all would know he had regained his full strength.

The fight continued, each testing the other for weaknesses. Then abruptly, Flynn twisted his blade to the flat side and struck a savage blow to Connor's wrists. Pain lanced from the impact, his right hand crumpling. Struggling to grasp the hilt, Connor barely defended another harsh jolt from Flynn's sword. The chieftain seized his advantage. He moved in, and with another violent blow, Flynn disarmed him.

Connor dove across the floor, reaching for his sword. Flynn slashed downward, the edge biting into Connor's upper arm. But his hand found the hilt, and he lifted his blade in time to defend another strike.

'You cannot win,' Flynn said softly. 'But my daughter begged for your life. I may grant her wish, so that you may be shamed before our people.'

Blood streamed down Connor's arm, but he felt none of the pain. Behind Flynn, in front of the others, he saw Aileen. Clad in a green overdress and *léine*, she wore a simple green ribbon in her hair. He remembered the night he'd given it to her.

In her face, he saw the stark fear. Like everyone else, she doubted his abilities and believed he was going to die. Her lack of faith cut him to the bone as surely as any sword.

He had intended this fight to prove himself to her. But she saw, as the others did, that he was losing. Though he remained on his feet, the continuous twisting movements strained his wrists. His grasp slipped upon the hilt.

Seeing her sadness drained him of strength. He twisted to dodge another blow, his muscles burning.

Then she turned her back on him and left.

She would stop this fight, no matter what the cost. Aileen pushed her way through the crowd until she found Patrick. Reaching toward his waist, her hand closed over his dagger.

He gripped her wrist. 'What do you want that for?'

'I need it. This fight has gone on long enough.'

'Do you intend to fight Ó Banníon yourself?' A warning gaze filled Patrick's eyes. 'Do not be foolish.'

'Not Ó Banníon. His daughter.'

Patrick released her, amusement darkening his eyes. Aileen strode back toward the dais, rage brimming within her veins. Unless she acted, Connor was going to die.

She moved toward Deirdre Ó Banníon, while the crowd jeered. From the corner of her eyes, she saw Connor on the ground, with Flynn moving in.

Stealth guided Aileen behind Deirdre. None seemed to notice the motion, for all eyes were locked upon the battle between Connor and Flynn.

In one swift motion, she seized Deirdre's golden locks and sliced one of them off. Then her blade moved to Deirdre's throat.

'I think it's time that you confessed to your father, don't you?'

Deirdre shrieked, but Aileen kept her blade across the deceitful woman's throat.

'How dare you touch me? Father!' she screamed.

Flynn's blade halted, and Aileen suddenly realised that dozens of soldiers were ready to overpower her. Silence flooded the Great Chamber.

'Deirdre has something she wishes to confess,' Aileen said.

A soldier rushed forward, but Aileen pressed her blade until a thin line of blood welled from Deirdre's throat. 'Don't move.'

An archer drew his bow, the arrow aimed at her. By Danu, this no longer seemed like a wise move. She'd meant to force Deirdre to confess her lies. Instead, by threatening the chieftain's daughter, she had only endangered herself.

A man grasped her forearm from behind, and the blade clattered to the wooden floor. Aileen inhaled sharply at the pain, but the soldier wrenched her away from Deirdre.

To her shock, she saw it was Trahern.

'We swore to keep this a fair fight,' he said, 'and we MacEgans keep our word.'

Before Aileen could speak, Trahern dragged her away from the dais. 'Do not speak or else they'll take you. Do you want to spend this eventide wearing manacles about your wrists?'

She shook her head, realising that Trahern had likely saved her life.

In the fighting circle, Connor grasped his left wrist. Torches flickered against the wooden walls, the members of the tribe encircling the pair.

Blood poured from his forearm, and he struggled to stand. Aileen clenched her hands so tightly, her nails dug into her own skin. It was like watching herself dying. She couldn't bear it.

When Flynn advanced with his blade, Connor's movements were sluggish. His left hand slipped, but he managed to correct the grip.

The chieftain sidestepped, and all could see Connor's impending defeat. Trahern's palms tightened over her shoulders, warning her not to interfere.

But how could they stand there and watch him die? Never had she felt so helpless. Flynn glanced at her, his expression merciless.

Then he raised his sword and struck a final blow.

Connor knew it was coming, but he remained motionless as the steel came down. It was as though time were frozen, the blade lowering with infinite slowness. His brother Patrick reached for his sword hilt, and Aileen buried her face in her hands.

He understood what she'd tried to do by threatening

Deirdre. Thank the gods, his brother had stopped her. He did not like to think of Flynn's punishment, had Aileen succeeded in harming Deirdre.

His gaze moved over the faceless crowd, to his shock, he saw a haunting vision of a young boy. The ethereal face of Whelon stared back, the boy's eyes studying him. A heartbeat later, the child stood well and whole upon two legs.

Connor closed his eyes, trying to will the image away. Whelon was dead. Connor had watched him die with his own eyes.

Did that mean he was dead?

Whelon shook his head, as if in answer to the unspoken question. Connor's hand suddenly jerked as if pulled by an invisible force. Flynn's sword struck him, and his left hand lost its grip. A strange heat warmed his right hand.

Dimly he was aware of the blade cutting into muscle and skin, but his attention remained on Whelon. The boy moved through the sea of people until he stood beside a young girl.

A girl with his own eyes. Rhiannon.

The sight of his daughter infused him with despair and love. He didn't want her to see him like this. She deserved a father who could give her a handsome dowry. He'd threaten any lad who dared to look at her with anything but respect.

And then his eyes met Flynn's. Was the chieftain so very different from himself? If any man dared to touch his daughter, he'd kill him.

'Wait—' a woman's voice choked. Aileen stepped forward from the crowd, tears streaming down her face. 'Please stop. Deirdre wants to wed him.'

Flynn's eyes narrowed in disbelief until another voice called, 'She speaks the truth, Father.'

Deirdre rose from her chair upon the dais. 'I think all of us have seen enough. Connor has been well punished for his dishonour. But I want him still.'

The arrogance from Deirdre's voice infuriated Connor. How could she even think he would consider wedding her?

But Aileen's words reached deep inside him and pressed their thorns into his heart. 'Cease this battle, and let them wed.' To Deirdre she added, 'I won't stand in your way.'

'Is this what you want?' Connor asked in disbelief. Was she so convinced of his loss that she would walk away from him?

'I want you to live,' she whispered. 'And that will be enough.'

He wanted to go to her, to wipe the tears from her cheeks. Instead, his right hand tightened upon the hilt of his sword. Though his left hand was now useless, it was as though a strange power filled him.

'It isn't enough for me,' he said, and swung his sword toward Flynn.

By God, if it took the last bit of his strength, he would win this battle. His daughter and Aileen were looking on, and he would honour them.

From deep within, he pulled the last of his strength. He ignored the slashes Flynn struck, but focused upon disarming the man who had once been his sword master.

His feet moved forward, never retreating, pushing toward the victory he could taste. With a bone-shattering blow, he lunged forward and Flynn's sword went flying. The blade struck the earthen floor with a dull thud.

It lay out of Flynn's reach. Connor lowered the point of his sword to Flynn's throat.

'Don't—' Deirdre cried out. She tried to run toward them, but Trahern restrained her. 'Let go of me, son of a cur!'

Resignation lined Flynn's face. He stared at Connor with death's promise in his eyes. 'Do it quickly.'

Connor had dreamed of this moment, of sinking his sword into Flynn's heart. But then Rhiannon's terrified cry jerked him away from revenge. The young girl's face was frozen with fear.

He stared back at his enemy. Flynn deserved to die, for turning his men against him, for betraying him.

For believing his daughter's words.

Connor raised his glance to Deirdre. Horrified, she shook her head. 'No.'

'Do you want him to die without knowing the truth?' he asked, pressing the blade into Flynn's throat.

Scarlet rage transformed Deirdre's face. 'No, I don't want him to die,' she snapped. 'You are nothing but an ignorant barbarian. I don't know why I ever thought I wanted to wed you.'

'So be it,' Connor said, lifting his sword as if to strike a killing blow.

'Stop!' Deirdre begged. She closed her eyes, fully aware that Connor held the power to end her father's life. In a broken voice, she admitted, 'Connor never touched me. I wanted him to, but he clung to his foolish honour.'

Regret and sadness clouded Flynn's face. He lifted his gaze to Connor. 'It seems I owe you an apology.' The shame of his daughter's admission weakened his voice.

Connor lowered his blade and opened his arms to Rhiannon. She stepped forward, hesitant, but went to his side. He put his good arm around her shoulder, sending up a silent prayer of thanks.

'A man will go to great lengths for his daughter.' Weariness moved over him, his body aching. He cleaned his blade and sheathed it. 'I would ask for peace between us.'

Connor offered his hand to Flynn. The chieftain rose to his feet, gripping his arm for support. The motion sent another wave of pain through him, and he grew aware Aileen needed to tend his wounds.

'I have another proposition for you, MacEgan,' Flynn said.

'And what is that?'

'I owe you the full *eraic*, a body price for injuries done to you. But instead of silver, would you not prefer a *rath* of your own?'

The offer filled him with such hope, he wondered if he had misheard Flynn. 'I would, yes.'

He dimly heard Ó Banníon's terms, his vision swimming. Sounds mingled, and the pain of his injuries intensified.

Then he saw nothing more.

Chapter 22

Aileen raced to Connor's side. Blood seeped from his arms, but what concerned her most was the brutal heat of his skin. A film of perspiration lined his brow, and she understood suddenly that he was fighting another battle with the invisible demons of illness.

She cradled his head in her lap. 'I need to tend his wounds. Help me bring him to a chamber.'

'I'll send for our healer Illona,' Flynn offered. He gave the orders, and Aileen fought back the fear rising inside. She did not know if she had the proper herbs with her.

As the men carried Connor's body, she followed. To Rhiannon, she said, 'I need your help, *a iníon*. Can you bring me elder flowers, marigold roots and some clean linen?'

'Is it the pox?' Rhiannon asked, her face mirroring Aileen's fear.

By the blessed saints, she had not thought of that. Mentally she counted the days. A black terror invaded her senses. Sweet Belisama, it was possible. The harsh fever was identical to Whelon's.

'Go and fetch what I need,' Aileen ordered her daughter. 'Make haste!'

Her hands shook. She berated herself for not noticing the flush on his skin, the way he moved as if in a daze. The memory of death undermined her confidence. She hadn't saved Whelon or Padraig. Their deaths suffused her with guilt. What if she could not save Connor? Even the thought threatened to tear her heart asunder. She needed him. He was the missing part of her, the man she'd always dreamed of.

She could not let him die. He had fought his battle against insurmountable odds and won. Now she had to do the same.

As they laid him down upon the pallet, Aileen unlaced his tunic and drew it over his head. Her hands moved across his fevered skin, searching for all wounds. Minor cuts, bruises, a rib that might be broken. She memorised every injury, searching his skin for any sign of the pox.

For now, there was no sign of a rash. But she could not breathe easily until he had healed. The pox often did not appear for several days. She could only watch and pray.

Then she noticed the swelling upon his right wrist. Just as before, the angry skin rose with a purple tinge. *The pain he must have suffered.* She would need splints for the broken wrist.

How had he managed to finish the battle? No man could have won this sword fight, not with a damaged right hand. But somehow he had.

Aileen leaned forward. 'I know you cannot hear me,' she whispered, 'but I won't let you die. Not now, after everything else. And when you awaken, we'll heal your wrist, just as we did before.' She smoothed his hair, wishing for some sign that he had heard her. But there was nothing.

When Rhiannon arrived with the linen, Aileen washed Connor's skin, treating the cuts upon his shoulder and arms. One slash was deeper than she'd thought, and Aileen sent her daughter to fetch a needle and thread along with the splints.

Though her fingers moved through his skin with the detached air of experience, Aileen felt each stab of the needle. He had not regained consciousness, his body so still. Sweat lined his brow, his muscles were stiff.

She was aware of so many people watching, perhaps even their own healer Illona. But she didn't care what they thought of her skills. All that mattered was Connor. She touched a hand to his cheek.

During the battle, she'd offered to give him up if it meant letting him live. Even the thought of Deirdre touching him made her hair stand on end.

But he'd said no. He had turned Deirdre away, his eyes locked upon Aileen. In that fragile moment, she sensed that she meant something to him. Even though he'd never said the words, she wanted so much to believe that he loved her.

By the gods, she would not give him up now.

'Do you want the splints now?' Rhiannon interrupted.

She nodded, and started to wrap his wrist.

'I can help,' Rhiannon offered. 'I've done it before.' At her daughter's fervent plea, Aileen resisted the urge to refuse.

'Go on, then. I'll watch you.' Though she still felt the desire to take over and do it herself, Aileen forced her hands to remain at her sides.

Rhiannon held the splints in place, wrapping them firmly with the bandages. Watching her with her father sent a gathering of tears in Aileen's throat. She choked back the feelings. 'You did well.'

The small smile on Rhiannon's face at the words of praise bound them together. They would fight off the demons of illness together. Of a sudden, Aileen rose to her feet and turned to the folk watching. 'Where is your healer Illona?'

'Here I am.' The older woman stepped forward. They stood eye to eye, each judging the other.

Aileen took a breath to steady herself. 'Will you help me?'

A warm smile tipped at the healer's mouth. Illona held out a bundle of dried elder flowers. 'You may have need of these.'

It was as though the burden of responsibility slipped from her, to be shared with another person. In the past, she'd tried to shoulder every illness alone. Pride had kept her from seeking help.

But now, she watched while Illona prepared the brew, grateful to have another pair of hands. After tying off the stitches, she covered the slash on his forearm with a linen bandage.

Illona handed her a cup of cooled elder flower tea. Aileen lifted Connor's head to drink. The liquid dribbled down the side of his mouth, and she struggled to get him to swallow.

When a second effort proved fruitless, she tried another tack. She took the liquid into her own mouth and pressed her mouth against his. Slowly, in the most intimate way, she forced him to drink it.

The touch of his lips beneath hers reminded her of the night she'd spent in his arms. Like a man who did not want to be kissed, his mouth did not respond to hers. Though she continued to help him drink, her fears intensified.

'We can only wait now,' the healer advised. 'You have done all you can.'

This was the part Aileen dreaded, surrendering control to

fate. She did not let him lie alone upon the pallet, but instead she rested Connor's head in her lap, her back supported against the wall.

Outside the window, the sky had turned black. No stars dotted the midnight sky, and Aileen wondered how long she'd been with him. It seemed like only moments, and yet Rhiannon's eyelids drooped.

'Go to sleep, *a iníon*,' she urged. 'I'll stay awake with him.' At the questioning look in the healer's eyes, Aileen added, 'I would like to be alone with him for a time.'

'I will be just beyond the door,' Illona replied, leaving them.

'He fought bravely,' Rhiannon said. 'Even with his broken hands.'

'He did. You should be proud to have him as your father.'

A worried expression wrinkled across Rhiannon's mouth. 'I still think of Eachan as my father.'

'He was, sweeting. In every way, save blood.' She offered a tender smile. 'Not every girl is blessed to have more than one father.'

Rhiannon sat beside her, and took Connor's malformed right hand in hers. 'He is a stranger to me.'

'But you gave him strength. Did you not see how much you helped him? It did him good to see you there.' Aileen was grateful to Bevan for fetching her, though she had worried about Rhiannon's safety.

Aileen covered Rhiannon's hand with her own, the two of them seated with Connor in the middle. A sense of rightness encircled her heart, being here with those she loved most.

Hours passed and her throat grew dry. Rhiannon curled up beside Connor and slept. Aileen held Connor, her back aching and limbs sore from the position. But she could not let him face this struggle alone.

Perspiration beaded across his forehead, pain etched in the lines across his mouth. Aileen kept wiping his brow, speaking to him in low tones.

Then when the darkness faded into the deep grey of morning, Connor began to tremble. With great effort, his eyes opened.

'I'm here,' she whispered to him. Though she tried to cool his burning skin with her hands, inwardly she knew it could do nothing for him.

'Am I dead?' he asked. When she shook her head, his mouth tried to curve upward. 'This was not what I intended when I dreamed of waking in your arms.'

She helped lift him up until she could face him. His eyes held the sheen of fever, his body struggling to regain its control. 'My arm hurts.'

Aileen lifted the bandage, but there was no sign of swelling. The wound was clean, neatly stitched closed. But if he was in pain, perhaps she should treat it again.

'I'll make a wash for it,' she said, easing him back on to the pallet. The marigold roots or perhaps iris. Her mind raced with every cure she could think of, or perhaps Illona Ó Banníon knew more. She would ask.

'Don't go,' he said, reaching for her. 'If I'm to die, this is where I'd like to be.' He tilted his head. 'Of course, the best death would be to die with you naked beneath me.'

Aileen's cheeks flamed and she glanced at her daughter sleeping. 'You aren't going to die.'

'I might,' he said. 'Perhaps you should take me somewhere that I could have my last wish. I'm afraid you would have to be on top, as I am in a delicate condition right now.'

His voice was a combination of the teasing rogue she knew so well and a slight hint of seriousness.

'You are in no condition for that,' she retorted, though her body warmed at the image of him grasping her hips, filling her.

'We cannot be sure. I think you should ask Rhiannon to leave. If you tend me without wearing your clothes, I might get better.'

The warmth in his eyes filled her with hope. He was not as hurt as she'd believed. Were it the pox, he could not be so light-hearted. Relief rushed through her, along with exhaustion.

She leaned close to him, until her nose touched his. 'I promise you that I'll wear nothing at all, as soon as you've healed. So perhaps you'd best get started.'

His hand cupped her cheek, and he turned serious. 'I love you, Aileen.'

She couldn't stop the tears then, the joy that he was finally hers. He stroked her hair, and she kissed him softly. 'I love you, too.'

The ring fort was not as large as she'd hoped for, but Connor seemed well pleased with its location. Resting on the crown of a hill, the land stretched to the river boundary. A stone wall surrounded the *rath*, with four small huts inside.

'It's not the fortress you dreamed of,' Aileen said, afraid of his disappointment. Flynn Ó Banníon had kept his word, granting them the land as payment for Connor's injuries. 'It would not be large enough for a tribe of your own.'

'I don't need a tribe of my own,' he said, taking her hand.

'Flynn has asked me to train his new soldiers. We will live here, and the lads will learn to wield a sword under my instruction. You can tend their wounds, for there will be many of them.' He lifted his gnarled hand, smiling, though Aileen did not miss the flash of regret on his face. 'I may not be the warrior I once was, but I still have the knowledge. And it's enough for me to pass it on.'

He drew her to him, caressing the curve of her cheek. Aileen touched her forehead to his, almost afraid to believe that at last he loved her.

'One day I'll teach our sons,' he said.

She wanted to believe it so badly. 'What if I cannot give them to you?'

He kissed her, love passing between them in the soft embrace. 'Even if Rhiannon is our only child, I would call myself blessed. But I plan to try often to give you more children.' Wickedness flashed in his eyes, coaxing a smile to her lips.

'I am sorry I did not tell you about our daughter sooner,' Aileen said.

He nodded acceptance, and in his eyes she saw forgiveness. 'One day she will know me as her father.'

Aileen squeezed his hand, staring out at the verdant meadows rising to meet the edge of the grey sky. 'She will.'

As if he sensed the sadness lingering within her, he asked, 'Do you miss Banslieve?'

'I do.' She braved a smile. 'But I belong with you, at your side. I'll join Illona as another healer for the people.' Though it still hurt to think of her banishment, it was time for both of them to begin anew.

Connor led her inside the ring fort, startling her when

he stopped in front of a granite standing stone. The mega-lith stood at Connor's height with a fist-sized hole drilled through the centre. Her heart pounded, for she knew what he was about to do.

He reached inside the rock, joining their hands in the ancient marriage rite. '*Gráim tú*,' he murmured, caressing her fingers with his own. The worn stone surrounded their hands, and Aileen could almost imagine the thousands of men and women who had joined their lives together over the centuries in this way.

A tear of joy spilled down her cheek. 'As I love you,' she answered.

'Can you accept a broken man as your husband?' he asked.

Aileen smiled through her tears. 'You are whole in my eyes,' she whispered. 'And you're the only man I've ever wanted.'

* * * * *

Look out for Patrick MacEgan's story coming soon from HARLEQUIN HISTORICAL
THE MacEGAN *BROTHERS*
Fierce Warriors—Passionate Hearts!

For a sneak preview of Marie Ferrarella's
DOCTOR IN THE HOUSE,
coming to NEXT in September,
please turn the page.

He didn't look like an unholy terror.

But maybe that reputation was exaggerated, Bailey DelMonico thought as she turned in her chair to look toward the doorway.

The man didn't seem scary at all.

Dr. Munro, or Ivan the Terrible, was tall, with an athletic build and wide shoulders. The cheekbones beneath what she estimated to be day-old stubble were prominent. His hair was light brown and just this side of unruly. Munro's hair looked as if he used his fingers for a comb and didn't care who knew it.

The eyes were brown, almost black as they were aimed at her. There was no other word for it. Aimed. As if he was debating whether or not to fire at point-blank range.

Somewhere in the back of her mind, a line from a B movie, "Be afraid—be very afraid…" whispered along the perimeter of her brain. Warning her. Almost against her will, it caused her to brace her shoulders. Bailey had to remind herself to breathe in and out like a normal person.

The chief of staff, Dr. Bennett, had tried his level best to put her at ease and had almost succeeded. But an air of tension had entered with Munro. She wondered if Dr. Bennett was bracing himself as well, bracing for some kind of disaster or explosion.

"Ah, here he is now," Harold Bennett announced needlessly. The smile on his lips was slightly forced, and the look in his gray, kindly eyes held a warning as he looked at his chief neurosurgeon. "We were just talking about you, Dr. Munro."

"Can't imagine why," Ivan replied dryly.

Harold cleared his throat, as if that would cover the less than friendly tone of voice Ivan had just displayed. "Dr. Munro, this is the young woman I was telling you about yesterday."

Now his eyes dissected her. Bailey felt as if she was undergoing a scalpel-less autopsy right then and there. "Ah yes, the Stanford Special."

He made her sound like something that was listed at the top of a third-rate diner menu. There was enough contempt in his voice to offend an entire delegation from the UN.

Summoning the bravado that her parents always claimed had been infused in her since the moment she first drew breath, Bailey put out her hand. "Hello. I'm Dr. Bailey DelMonico."

Ivan made no effort to take the hand offered to him. Instead, he slid his long, lanky form bonelessly into the chair beside her. He proceeded to move the chair ever so slightly so that there was even more space between them. Ivan faced the chief of staff, but the words he spoke were addressed to her.

"You're a doctor, DelMonico, when I say you're a doctor," he informed her coldly, sparing her only one frosty glance to punctuate the end of his statement.

Harold stifled a sigh. "Dr. Munro is going to take over your education. Dr. Munro—" he fixed Ivan with a steely gaze that had been known to send lesser doctors running for their antacids, but, as always, seemed to have no effect on the chief neurosurgeon "—I want you to award her every consideration. From now on, Dr. DelMonico is to be your shadow, your sponge and your assistant." He emphasized the last word as his eyes locked with Ivan's. "Do I make myself clear?"

For his part, Ivan seemed completely unfazed. He merely nodded, his eyes and expression unreadable. "Perfectly."

His hand was on the doorknob. Bailey sprang to her feet. Her chair made a scraping noise as she moved it back and then quickly joined the neurosurgeon before he could leave the office.

Closing the door behind him, Ivan leaned over and whispered into her ear, "Just so you know, I'm going to be your worst nightmare."

Bailey DelMonico has finally
gotten her life on track, and is
passionate about her recent career
change. Nothing will stand in the way
of her becoming a doctor...that is,
until she's paired with the sharp-tongued
Dr. Ivan Munro.

Watch the sparks fly in

Doctor in
the House

by *USA TODAY* Bestselling Author

Marie Ferrarella

Available September 2007

Intrigued? Read more at
TheNextNovel.com

HARLEQUIN®

HN88141

HARLEQUIN Romance.

New York Times bestselling author

DIANA PALMER

Handsome, eligible ranch owner Stuart York knew
Ivy Conley was too young for him, so he closed his heart
to her and sent her away—despite the fireworks between
them. Now, years later, Ivy is determined not to be
treated like a little girl anymore…but for some reason,
Stuart is always fighting her battles for her. And safe in
Stuart's arms makes Ivy feel like a woman…his woman.

Winter Roses

Available November.

HRIBC03985

REQUEST YOUR FREE BOOKS!

Harlequin® Historical
Historical Romantic Adventure!

2 FREE NOVELS PLUS 2 FREE GIFTS!

YES! Please send me 2 FREE Harlequin® Historical novels and my 2 FREE gifts. After receiving them, if I don't wish to receive any more books, I can return the shipping statement marked "cancel." If I don't cancel, I will receive 6 brand-new novels every month and be billed just $4.69 per book in the U.S., or $5.24 per book in Canada, plus 25¢ shipping and handling per book and applicable taxes, if any*. That's a savings of close to 15% off the cover price! I understand that accepting the 2 free books and gifts places me under no obligation to buy anything. I can always return a shipment and cancel at any time. Even if I never buy another book from Harlequin, the two free books and gifts are mine to keep forever.

246 HDN EEWW   349 HDN EEW9

Name	(PLEASE PRINT)	
Address		Apt. #
City	State/Prov.	Zip/Postal Code

Signature (if under 18, a parent or guardian must sign)

Mail to the Harlequin Reader Service®:
IN U.S.A.: P.O. Box 1867, Buffalo, NY 14240-1867
IN CANADA: P.O. Box 609, Fort Erie, Ontario L2A 5X3

Not valid to current Harlequin Historical subscribers.

Want to try two free books from another line?
Call 1-800-873-8635 or visit www.morefreebooks.com.

* Terms and prices subject to change without notice. NY residents add applicable sales tax. Canadian residents will be charged applicable provincial taxes and GST. This offer is limited to one order per household. All orders subject to approval. Credit or debit balances in a customer's account(s) may be offset by any other outstanding balance owed by or to the customer. Please allow 4 to 6 weeks for delivery.

Your Privacy: Harlequin is committed to protecting your privacy. Our Privacy Policy is available online at www.eHarlequin.com or upon request from the Reader Service. From time to time we make our lists of customers available to reputable firms who may have a product or service of interest to you. If you would prefer we not share your name and address, please check here. ☐

Harlequin® Historical
Historical Romantic Adventure!

A WESTERN WINTER WONDERLAND

with three fantastic stories
by
Cheryl St.John,
Jenna Kernan
and ## Pam Crooks

Don't miss these three
unforgettable stories about
the struggles of the Wild West
and the strong women who
find love and happiness
on Christmas Day.

Look for
A WESTERN WINTER
WONDERLAND

*Available October
wherever you buy books.*

COMING NEXT MONTH FROM

HARLEQUIN®
HISTORICAL

- **CHRISTMAS WEDDING BELLES**
  by **Nicola Cornick, Margaret McPhee and Miranda Jarrett**
  (Regency)
  Enjoy all the fun of the Regency festive season as three Society
  brides tame their dashingly handsome rakes!

- **BODINE'S BOUNTY**
  by **Charlene Sands**
  (Western)
  He's a hard-bitten bounty hunter with no time for love. But when
  Bodine meets the woman he's sworn to guard, she might just
  change his life....

- **WICKED PLEASURES**
  by **Helen Dickson**
  (Victorian)
  Betrothed against her will, Adeline had been resigned to a loveless
  marriage. Can Christmas work its magic and lead to pleasures
  Adeline thought impossible?

- **BEDDED BY HER LORD**
  by **Denise Lynn**
  (Medieval)
  Guy of Hartford has returned from the dead—to claim his wife!
  Now Elizabeth must welcome an almost-stranger back into her
  life...and her bed!